Murder Has a Price

a Price

A Jason Hunter Thriller

Natasha Orme

*Thanks so much for
your support*

First edition 2024

ISBN 978-1-7394505-3-3 (paperback)

ISBN 978-1-7394505-2-6 (ebook)

PRAISE FOR MURDER IN THE FAST LANE

To Lauren, for being my biggest fan.

And because I know you're desperate to see what happens next.

THE GUNMAN

SOMEWHERE IN LONDON

Sunday 3rd October

He knew the moment he pulled the trigger he would have a limited amount of time to find what he was looking for. And if he didn't find it, there would be big problems.

He took a deep breath, and followed his target through the lens of his scope. The large, heavyset man walked from one room of the apartment to the next. He waved a hand in the air as he paced, talking animatedly into the mobile phone he held with the other. Maybe he could sense the sniper in the building next door. Probably not. But something had clearly put the man on edge.

Mentally, he calculated the route he would need to take in a matter of moments. As soon as the bullet left his L115A3 sniper rifle, he'd have approximately 17 and a half minutes, maybe more, but most likely less. He needed to be quick.

He closed his finger over the trigger, pressing it in slightly as he prepared to fire. He inhaled slowly and watched his target talking on his mobile phone. He needed to wait for the call to end.

He exhaled.

He'd lost track of how long he'd been sitting here. How long he'd been waiting. The window in front of him was open just wide enough for the barrel of his rifle to poke through; he needed to minimise the amount of evidence he left behind.

He knew an alarm would sound in the target's apartment when the glass shattered. His reconnaissance as a repair man the week before had confirmed as much. But that was fine. He was prepared for it.

The target stopped pacing and he watched him end the call. Now was his chance. He took a final steadying breath in and adjusted his grip on the rifle. He couldn't afford to miss.

As he exhaled, he pulled the trigger all the way and tensed against the sharp recoil of the weapon.

His target's head shot up and looked in his direction. *Why wasn't he dead?* A spiderweb of cracks appeared across the window. *Shit. Bulletproof glass.* Why hadn't he thought of that? Why hadn't he considered the possibility that the windows were reinforced? This guy was smart. There were a lot of powerful people who wanted him dead, and he knew it.

Mickey dove for cover.

Without pausing, he pulled the trigger over and over until the window shattered. He pulled the trigger again and watched as his target dropped to the floor. *Was he dead?* It was messy. And he didn't like messy. But he didn't have time to sit around and make sure.

In under a minute he'd disassembled his rifle and packed it away. He slung the custom-made rucksack over his shoulder and calmly left the apartment.

He walked past the bank of elevators and headed to the stairs. Once in the stairwell, he took them two at a time. There was a lot of ground to cover and the clock was already ticking.

He emerged into the lobby, breathing heavily through his nose but keeping his calm mask in place as he casually strolled out the front door. It had been 3 and a half minutes since he first pulled the trigger.

Crossing the street, he held a hand up in apology to the car that had to break hard to avoid slamming into him. Inwardly, he cringed. It was a mistake that could cost him, but the reinforced windows had rattled him and his careful plan.

He entered the building, headed straight for the stairs and started to climb up. He'd practised for this, timing himself over and over again to ensure maximum efficiency. As he climbed, the exertion helped him refocus. No more slip ups.

Exiting the stairs at the very top, he crossed the space to the front door of the penthouse in three strides. He pulled his lock picking kit out of his rucksack as he went, slipping out the tool he needed as he approached.

He could already hear the alarm ringing on the other side of the door.

On one knee, he slid the tension wrench in first, closely followed by the pick. 9 minutes down.

The satisfying click of the lock sounded and he opened the door. Pulling a Glock 17 from his waistband, he cautiously entered the apartment. He keyed the code into the pad by the door and the alarm stopped abruptly.

It was deathly silent.

He inched forward, carefully, quietly. The large open space left few places to hide. He knew where his target was meant to be, but was unsurprised to see the shattered glass on the floor, the blood splatter, and no body.

A trail of blood smeared across the floor showed him where to look.

In the kitchen, Mickey Bianchi lay in a pool of his own blood. His eyes locked on the intruder and watched as he raised the Glock.

The gunman fired one final shot.

12 minutes had passed and he was running out of time.

In the home office, he keyed in the code for the wall safe but when the door swung open it was empty.

Shit. Shit. Shit. This was bad. Very bad. Where the hell was it?

Chapter 1

JASON HUNTER

HYDE PARK

Sunday 3rd October

"Jason, there's a dead body."

My mouth went dry.

"Who?" I asked, my voice barely above a whisper.

"It's Mickey. Adrianna's fine," replied Hayley. "I'm at the scene now. She's with an officer in the lobby. I had to remove her from the apartment." There was a pause. "You need to get over here. Now."

The command was surprising as it was welcome. As a personal security specialist, I had no right to be at a crime scene. And Hayley had made that more than clear when she'd reluctantly accepted my help last year when Stacey's life had been in danger.

I glanced over at Stacey playing with Max and Lily on the swings. "I'll be there as quickly as I can." I hung up. There was no need for pleasantries with Detective Inspector Hayley Irons, we'd been through too much in the last fifteen months.

Stacey looked up, caught sight of my face and frowned. She gently excused herself from their game and came over.

"Everything okay?" she asked, tucking her long, blonde hair behind an ear.

"I need to go and see Adrianna."

"Okay? Jason, what's happened?"

"Someone's died."

Stacey's brown eyes went wide. "Who?"

"Mickey."

The shock on her face mirrored how I felt. "I need to go."

"Of course. I'll take the kids home."

I nodded my gratitude, unable to say anything else. Before I turned to leave, I pressed a quick kiss to her lips and she squeezed my hand.

"Sorry, munchkins," I said, raising my voice so Max and Lily could hear. "I've had a call from work. I've got to pop into the office." Max groaned. "I know, buddy. Can't be helped, I'm afraid." I forced a smile, trying to keep my voice light. "Stacey's gonna take you home and I'll be back in time for dinner." Max rolled his eyes and I couldn't blame him. It's a line he'd heard many times over the years. Sometimes it rang true and other times it didn't. One of the many reasons why Adrianna was my *ex*-wife.

I gave them both a quick hug and then headed for the park exit. As soon as I was out of sight, I broke into a jog. Now, the question was whether I headed home for my car or simply went straight there on the tube. I opted for the car.

Nearly an hour later I was pulling up outside the familiar apartment complex in Holland Park where Adrianna lived with her husband, Mickey, and the kids in the penthouse. Police cars were parked along the street and I spotted a couple of vans I assumed belonged to SOCO, the scenes of crime officers responsible for gathering forensic evidence.

The lobby was swarming with police. I spotted Adrianna huddled in a leather armchair, a policewoman crouching in front of her and patting her hand reassuringly. Her platinum blonde hair was a tangled mess and there were mascara tracks down both cheeks.

"Hey," I said as I approached.

Adrianna looked up and relief flooded her face. "Oh my God, Jason," she whispered before launching herself into my arms. I caught her and held tight.

"Hey now, it'll be okay."

"It's Mickey," she wailed as she pulled away from me. "He's dead!" Her words caught on a sob, and she buried her face against my chest, her usual glamorous appearance long gone. I always thought her dramatics were over the top, but this felt genuine.

I looked at the police officer who seemed relieved I was there.

"White male. That's all I know," she shrugged. "I was asked to keep her company and keep her calm. She was a bit distressed," she added.

I knew exactly what she meant.

"Are you okay to just stay with her a bit longer?" I asked, gently pushing Adrianna away from me. "DI Irons wanted me to go up."

"Sure."

Adrianna collapsed back into the armchair, tears carving a path through the already smudged makeup on her cheeks, and the police-woman held her hand again.

I headed to the elevators and made my way up to the penthouse, unsure of what I'd find.

Chapter 2

JASON HUNTER

ADRIANNA'S PENTHOUSE

Sunday 3rd October

The top floor of the apartment building made the lobby look deserted. Cops strode back and forth across the plush carpet, or stood in groups, talking earnestly. The moment I stepped out of the elevator, a large black hand pushed against my chest. I looked up into the unsmiling face of a policeman in uniform.

"Authorised personnel only," he said in a deep voice.

"I'm here with—" I began, fishing my wallet from my back pocket.

"No can do," he replied, not giving me a chance to explain myself.

"Tony, he's with me," a female voice called from the doorway of the apartment. Tony didn't look over his shoulder but simply shrugged and stepped aside.

Hayley stood at the other end of the corridor, talking with someone who looked to be the building manager. Dressed in her signature plaid shirt and jeans, she seemed to dominate the space despite her 5 foot 4 frame being dwarfed by almost every other person crowding the hallway. Her brown hair was cropped shorter than I remember it and I realised how long it had been since I last saw her.

"That would be great, thank you," she said to the manager and then turned to me as I approached. Her mouth was set in a grim line.

"Can I—?" I gestured to the apartment.

"Not just yet. I can't let you in there while the body is still here."

"What's the situation then?"

"Sniper."

I blinked. Did I hear her correctly?

"Did you just say 'sniper'?"

"Can you see why I need you here?"

"Ah fuck," I said, running a hand through my hair. "The same one?"

"I can't be sure. Gemma was killed in a public place. The setup was meticulously planned, abroad and in broad daylight right under the noses of the Hungarian police. This one is different. We think he shot from the building next door. He shattered a window. But that's not the worst part."

My stomach dropped. I wasn't going to like this.

"It looked like the shooter came into the apartment and put a bullet in Mickey's head."

I looked at her in disbelief. "You're joking, right?"

She shook her head.

"So, this sniper shoots from across the street, and then what? Comes over to finish the job?"

"Something like that."

I let out a breath. *This was bad. Bad. Bad. Bad.*

"I think they were looking for something."

"Looking for what?" I asked.

Hayley shrugged. "No idea. But I don't think they found it. The place has been ransacked."

"Who found him?"

"An alarm was triggered when the window smashed. We received a request from the alarm company. We must have only been about 20 minutes behind the killer. And when I say 'we', I mean the response unit."

"That's a tight window," I said.

"Tell me about it."

"Who's the alarm company?"

She looked down at her notepad. "KYS?"

"Ah, those guys. Yeah, we've worked with them in the past. They're pretty good."

"Anything I should know?"

"Not really," I shrugged. "Adam didn't like the profit margin. They're in what we'd call the elite category for security systems. Hence why your response team was able to get on the scene so fast."

"I see," she said. I was sure she knew what I was hinting at. If Mickey was paying KYS, he was paying *a lot*. "We're going to need to go through this in more detail." Hayley glanced over her shoulder and then indicated we should move to one side. A gurney appeared, a zipped body bag stretched across it, and was being steered by two men, who I guessed were from the coroner's office. A third man followed it out, lifting his chin in Hayley's direction as he went.

"I'll call you as soon as I have something, Detective Inspector," he said.

"Thanks." She turned back to me. "Do not make me regret this," she said, her voice turning stern.

I put my hands up, taken aback.

"It's likely I'll get it in the neck for letting you in, so don't cock this up."

"I won't touch a thing."

She gave me a long hard look before giving me a single nod.

"Webb, have we got some spare coveralls for Mr Hunter here?"

A young police officer in uniform dashed forward, almost tripping over himself in his haste. "Yes, Detective Inspector," he said breathlessly.

"I've told you before, you can call me Hayley." She let out a small sigh.

"Of... of course. Hayley. It just doesn't feel right. Ma'am."

Hayley rolled her eyes and I hid my smile as I bent down to slip the covers over my shoes.

Straightening, I looked from Hayley to Webb and back again.

"Shall we?" she asked, gesturing to the apartment.

I cautiously stepped over the threshold I'd crossed so many times before. This time I could feel the lead ball in the pit of my stomach. My mouth went dry and I fought to keep my breathing steady and even.

Through the doorway, the apartment opened up into a bright and airy space. A set of spiral stairs occupied the corner to my right, next to the doorway that led into the kitchen. Large glass windows looked out over Holland Park. To my left, the space was filled with large, comfortable-looking white sofas, accented with navy and mustard yellow cushions. A throw was casually draped over the back of one. Potted plants created pockets of dark green that stood out against the simple colour scheme. Apart from the sofa cushions, almost everything else was a simplistic and stylish white, making the green pop.

At first glance, everything looked to be as it was the last time I'd been here. Although that had been a while ago, now I thought about it. Worse, I couldn't see any evidence that two small children lived here. And that made me sad.

It was only then that I noticed the smashed window. Shards of glass lay sprinkled across one of the sideboards and trailed across a fluffy white rug.

Following a potential trajectory, I looked past the cosy living room setup towards the hallway where Mickey had his office. I took a deep breath and followed Hayley further into the apartment.

Before we even reached the hallway, I saw the smear of bright red blood on the floor. It had seeped into a pale yellow rug and started to congeal.

I swallowed and tried not to think about it too much. I followed the trail into the kitchen and stopped before I stepped in the sticky red pool in front of the sink.

A noise made me glance over my shoulder and I saw a pale Webb dash towards the door.

"He's new," muttered Hayley.

I half smiled, appreciating the distraction.

"Go easy on him," I said.

Hayley ignored me and – in typical Hayley fashion – got straight down to business. "As you can see, the victim was found here. Bullet to the head. But there was a second bullet in his shoulder and based on the shattered glass, and this blood—" she pointed to the trail of blood across the floor "—I'm guessing he was shot over by the window first, then the killer came in to finish the job, here." She pointed again to the pool of blood in front of us.

I looked back at the trail of red spots leading from the window. My line of sight had been obstructed by the sofa which was why I hadn't seen them before. I was trying to get my head around the brutality of it.

"Have you considered two people? One for the initial shot and a second who entered the apartment. Would explain the tight window of opportunity."

Hayley nodded. "Certainly not ruling it out at this stage."

"I thought you said the place had been ransacked? This looks pretty clean to me."

She gestured for me to follow. We stepped around the pool of blood and headed down the corridor. The closer we got to Mickey's office, the more evident it was that someone else had been here. There were shards of broken bric-a-brac and the contents of emptied drawers littered across the floor.

Stepping into the office, I saw the destruction. Papers were strewn everywhere, a safe in the wall was hanging open, the leather armchairs had been torn apart, and it seemed anything that was easy to pick up had been smashed on the floor.

This guy had been pissed.

"Someone needs anger management classes," I stated dryly.

"You have got to be bloody kidding me," said a voice behind us. We both spun around to be confronted by a small, balding man in his early fifties.

"Haynes, you're here," said Hayley.

"What is *he* doing here?" he asked, jabbing a finger in my direction with a sneer.

"Consulting." Hayley's tone had gone cold.

Haynes scoffed. "Pull the other one, Detective Inspector."

"Jason, I'd like to introduce you to Bronson Haynes, head of our forensics team." Hayley waved in Haynes' direction. "Don't be put off by his rude manner, he's actually quite good at his job."

"Quite good?" His sneer turned into a sarcastic smile. "I'm the best in the country and you know it."

"So am I," she quipped. "So keep your disapproving comments to yourself."

Haynes opened his mouth to reply and then shut it again. He smiled, genuine this time. "Touché, Irons, touché." He chuckled. "Just keep him out of my way. I don't want a contaminated crime scene."

"Wouldn't dream of it," I said with a small smile.

Haynes stalked out of the room, muttering under his breath.

"Is he always that friendly?" I asked.

"Pretty much," sighed Hayley. "He's actually not that bad, but he definitely takes some getting used to."

"Sure."

We turned back to the room. I looked beyond the chaos, taking in the large mahogany desk that stood in the centre, commanding attention. A wide executive desk chair sat behind it, it's back to the floor to ceiling window.

I stepped around the mess, careful not to disturb anything, and looked out of the window. It overlooked a large garden that clearly wasn't used. Pretty hedges and neatly arranged flowers were dotted around a perfectly manicured lawn. The low autumn sun cast a warm glow across all of it, making it look a lot warmer than it actually was.

I turned to the desk. Its placement was clearly deliberate. Designed to command the room, to intimidate any visitors. But what visitors? Who was Mickey expecting in his home? Did he bring his work into the family home at the end of every day? The thought made me uncomfortable. My kids lived here. In this apartment. Most of the time anyway – they only came to visit me every other weekend.

So what kind of people had Mickey been bringing home? And did they have anything to do with this?

Looking back at Hayley, I opened my mouth to ask a question but she cut me off.

"I've already checked."

"You don't know what I was gonna say," I replied, stumped.

"Sure, I do. I worked with you enough on Stacey's stalker case to know exactly how your mind works." She dug her fingers into the front pockets of her jeans and gave me a smug smile.

I frowned. "Am I really that predictable?"

Hayley shrugged.

"What was I gonna ask then?"

"Have we got any footage of someone suspicious coming in or out of the building? Or something along those lines."

I folded my arms and continued to frown. She was good.

"Policing 101, of course I've checked," she tutted and rolled her eyes.

I looked back out the window, not sure what I was hoping to see.

"How is Stacey, by the way?" asked Hayley.

"She's good. Doing better. I think the therapy is really starting to pay off. Seems more like her old self." I moved away from the window and crossed to the other side of the desk where the safe door was hanging open on the wall, about five feet off the ground.

"Oh, good for her. That'll help keep her head in the game. I saw she's doing pretty well this season. Looks like she might have her mojo back."

I nodded. Being the only female driver in Formula One came with its own set of challenges. And after the events of last year, there was a time when I wondered if she'd ever race again. But the determination that had helped her face up against blatant discrimination resurfaced and she was back in top form.

"Yeah, although she's decided she's gonna go see Diane." I gave her a pinched look.

"Is that wise?" Hayley asked as she slipped on a pair of blue latex gloves. Hayley had been just as shocked as the rest of us when we'd found out Diane, Stacey's PA, had been blackmailed into laundering money for Alik Gromov, suspected crime boss.

"Doesn't matter what I think. I've told her I don't think it's a good idea, but her therapist seems to believe it could help." I shrugged and then looked around for something that would have hung on the wall to hide the safe.

"What about Bill Cooper? Have you heard from him?" Crouching down, she carefully began sifting through what was on the floor, careful not to cause too much disturbance.

The mention of Stacey's ex made me bristle. I hadn't relished working with Cooper when things had gotten intense last time, but leveraging his specialist set of skills for Alik Gromov's party had been important, both for Stacey's safety and for finally discovering that it had been Liam tormenting her.

I winced at the thought. My boss, Adam, was dead, Diane had suffered some kind of breakdown, threatened us all and was now in prison, and after all that, Liam had still managed to get away.

After months of terrorising Stacey, sending creepy messages and manipulating her security detail, the bastard had limped from the wreckage of a stolen Lamborghini, leaving Stacey to die. Thankfully I'd arrived in time, but saving Stacey had meant letting Liam go free. And I kicked myself about it almost every day.

Every time I saw her flinch when there was a loud noise. Every time she redirected an unknown caller through to her new PA, a young woman in her early twenties called Aliesha. Every time she woke with a start in the middle of the night covered in sweat, thinking I was still asleep and hadn't noticed. But I wouldn't have been able to do things differently. The leaking fuel line had caused the car wreck to explode just moments after I'd managed to pull her free. Going after Liam would have meant Stacey died.

"Is that a no?" asked Hayley, jarring me from my thoughts. She was looking up at me from her crouched position on the floor.

"Sorry," I mumbled. "No, I haven't heard from Cooper. And I'm not likely to either. I think he occasionally checks in on Stacey, but mostly when she's abroad."

"Of course he does," said Hayley, rolling her eyes. "He's too smart for his own good, that one."

"Tell me about it."

I hadn't been able to spot anything that was meant to hang on the wall, and now that I looked, there weren't any fixtures on the wall anyway. But looking closer, I spotted a rail at the bottom, just above the skirting board. I frowned and stepped back.

"What's the latest with Gromov?"

Hayley let out a small bark of laughter and straightened. "Absolutely nothing. We can't touch him. There's just no evidence."

I turned to look at her. "Even after the stuff the FSB sent you?"

"Absolutely nada. The guy has powerful friends. He's not new to this game so I wouldn't expect anything different, really. And in all honesty, it's a problem for another day."

"That's a bit complacent isn't it?"

"Not really. I've got my eye on him, but there's no point chasing him now. What would I gain? I'd just waste time while others get away with murder."

"I guess." Turning to face the safe again, I took another step back and looked up. There was another rail, about two feet above me. I took a few more steps back so I could see both of them more clearly, watching them disappear behind the bookcase to my left as I moved. "Hey, can I get a pair of those?" I asked, pointing to Hayley's hands.

She glanced over her shoulder and down the corridor to see if we were alone. "I can't let you go interfering with the crime scene," she said in warning as she pulled out a second pair of latex gloves.

"I know. But you also can't let me start leaving my DNA all over the place and contaminating any evidence."

"That's true," she said and handed me the gloves. I snapped them on and then walked a few paces to my left where the end of the bookcase was only a few centimetres away from the wall. With both hands on the side of the wood, I carefully tested my theory. It moved, ever so slightly. Hayley watched me. Using a bit more of my weight, I pulled on the bookcase and it slid smoothly to the right.

"Interesting," said Hayley.

"No point pushing it all the way across with the safe still open," I said.

"Agreed, but can't close the safe until we know we're done with it. Might never be able to get it open again."

"Adrianna might know the code."

"I'll check with her before we do anything. Meanwhile, let's get Haynes in here to dust that bookcase for prints."

Chapter 3

JASON HUNTER

HOME

Sunday 3ʳᵈ October

There wasn't much else I could do at Adrianna's apartment but I was glad that Hayley had brought me in so early on. Last time, I'd spent ages trying to convince her I could be useful. More importantly, I'd wanted an inside track on the investigation so I could keep Stacey safe. Our usual methods were proving to be ineffective, and when her body double, Gemma, had died on the podium, I knew we needed to change things up.

It looked like I'd proven my worth because this time Hayley wasn't messing around. And for that I was especially grateful. Mickey's death was far too close to home for comfort. I couldn't help thinking about what would have happened if the kids had been home. Or whether the killer had planned around that, and if so, how long had he been watching their routines, getting to know their schedules? The thought made the hairs stand up on the back of my neck.

I took a steadying breath and unlocked my front door.

The moment I stepped into the hallway, a small bundle came barrelling into me, almost knocking me over. I chuckled and stroked Lily's hair.

"Hey sugar puff," I said. "Everything okay?"

She nodded. I bent down and scooped her up into a big hug.

I need this right now, I thought as I gave her a squeeze.

It's true what they say about kids sensing more than they understand. A moment later, another pair of small arms wrapped themselves around both of us and I could smell Max's familiar scent.

Gently, I pulled back. Both my kids were looking at me, eyes wide. They were waiting for something. Did they know? Surely not.

"I wasn't gone that long," I laughed, trying to dispel the tension. Lily gave a small smile as she tucked her blonde hair behind an ear. "Come on, you two." I gestured to the living room and they both scampered ahead.

I followed. By the time I walked in, Max was slouched on the sofa playing on his iPhone and Lily was watching Shaun the Sheep on CBBC.

Stacey appeared in the doorway leading to the kitchen. "I thought some screen time wouldn't hurt," she said. "Figured they needed a distraction. Fancy a coffee?" She gestured over her shoulder. I nodded and followed her into the kitchen.

"How bad is it?" she whispered as she pulled a mug from the cupboard.

"Really bad," I groaned. I glanced over my shoulder to make sure the kids were both engrossed in their screens before turning back to Stacey. "Looks like a sniper job." I dropped onto the stool at one end of the kitchen island.

"Sniper?" hissed Stacey, the colour draining from her face.

I nodded.

"Shit." She put the mug under the spout of the coffee machine and loaded in a coffee pod.

"Yep."

"Hayley got any ideas yet?"

I shook my head. "She says hi though. It's been a while."

Stacey rolled her eyes and pressed the button. "So, what happened?"

I glanced over my shoulder again as the machine whirred to life. "Let's talk about this later. I don't want little ears hearing anything they shouldn't."

"Sure," she said as she handed me the coffee.

I took a tentative sip, just for something to do, ignoring the burning on my tongue.

"How's Adrianna doing?" asked Stacey, leaning back against the counter.

"Not great. She's given a statement and said she's going to stay with a friend for a few days. I did say that she could stay here, but she wasn't having any of it."

"I can't imagine what she must be going through. Is she the one who found him?"

I shook my head. "Automatic security system notified the police." I took another sip. "Adrianna arrived just after they did. Couldn't stop her from seeing his body on the floor."

Stacey shivered.

"Remind me," I said, deliberately changing the topic. "What time is your flight on Thursday?"

"Mid-morning. About 11, I think."

"Sam prepped to go with you?"

"Yes, although I think it's totally unnecessary."

A topic we regularly disagreed on. Although Liam had disappeared, and the threatening calls and manipulations with him, I knew he was still out there. And while that was the case, I wouldn't leave Stacey unprotected.

Sam was the best I had. My right hand man. The one I trusted the most. And that's why he was Stacey's detail. He'd been there when everything had gone south before so he knew what we were up against, knew what the signs were and what to look out for. More importantly, Stacey trusted him. I trusted him.

I thought back to my conversation with Hayley earlier in the day. She'd asked about Cooper and while I had told her the truth, I hadn't been completely honest. It was true, I hadn't heard from Cooper, and it was also true that I wasn't likely to either. The part I'd left out was that we did have a communication channel open, it just wasn't two-way.

As per his request, I reluctantly shared Stacey's schedule with him on the understanding that he would keep a watchful eye from a distance. Of course, I hadn't told Stacey. She'd completely fly off the handle and I really didn't want to be on the receiving end of that.

"Dad," called Max from the sofa.

"Yes, bud?" I turned around on the stool, coffee still in hand.

"I'm bored!"

Lily sent him a scolding look and I laughed.

"PlayStation?" I asked. Max looked up from his phone, his face eager.

"Only if Stacey plays too."

Now it was Stacey's turn to laugh. "Go for it. You could do with the practice."

"I'm so close to beating you."

"You wish."

"What about something all four of us can play?" I suggested.

Max groaned. "Fine."

Chapter 4

JASON HUNTER

HOME

Sunday 3rd October

Once the kids were in bed and I was settled on the sofa with a beer in hand, Stacey didn't waste any time.

"How did he die?" she asked, looking far too enthusiastic for my liking.

"This isn't a crime drama on TV," I chastised. "Mickey is actually dead. Adrianna's lost her husband and the kids have lost their step-dad."

"I know," she said, deflating. "I'm just trying not to think about that side of things because it makes me panic."

"I know what you mean," I said, pulling her close.

"It just reminds me of everything that happened last year and then all of a sudden I can't breathe again."

"I thought the therapy was working?" I asked gently.

"Yeah, it is," she replied dismissively. "I mean, it is what it is. She says we're making progress but it just doesn't feel like it. It makes me so angry. The whole world thinks I'm some fierce racing driver while inside I'm absolutely petrified. It just makes me feel so small."

"I think you forget that you are fierce. You're a badass," I said and kissed her gently on the lips. "Who else could possibly have gone through what you have, survived a car wreck like you did, and then come back to race the next season?" I kissed her again, this time my lips lingering on her skin. "Very badass," I whispered.

She laughed. It was a real laugh, and I smiled. I felt like I'd seen less of Stacey laughing recently.

"Stop changing the subject," she said suddenly and slapped me on the chest.

"Sorry." I shifted on the sofa so we were facing each other more. "Someone shot Mickey through the window."

"Through the window?" She frowned. I could already see her trying to connect the dots, trying to work out if there was any connection between this shooter and the one that killed Gemma.

"Through the window." I confirmed. "But it wasn't enough. Looks like it got him in the shoulder first. It was reinforced glass so it would have taken a few rounds to get through." I paused, unsure how she'd react to the next bit. "Then he came into the apartment to finish the job."

"Sorry, what? He came *into* the apartment?"

I nodded and took a swig of my beer. It sounded even worse out loud.

"Where did he shoot from?"

"Don't know yet."

"Hang on, let me get this right. Shooter goes for Mickey through the window. Mickey drops like a sack of potatoes and matey thinks 'job done'. Then sees Mickey moving or getting up or whatever, so decides to physically go into the apartment to finish him off?" said Stacey, stunned.

"Something like that. From what I could see, Mickey dragged himself out of view so the killer had no choice but to be in close proximity in order to finish the job. But that's not why I think he was in the apartment."

"Enlighten me."

"His office had been torn apart. Everything was shredded, destroyed or tossed across the floor."

"So, he was looking for something?"

"Most likely. At least, that's the theory we're going with so far."

"Hmmm." Stacey looked thoughtful. "Any idea what he was looking for?"

I shrugged and took another swig of beer.

We fell silent, and I could see the wheels turning in her brain. She would never admit it, but she was relishing the puzzle. It had been great to see her back behind the wheel, and the leaderboard spoke for itself, but this was a true spark. The old Stacey was coming back.

Chapter 5

JASON HUNTER

THE OFFICE

Monday 4th October

Like most Mondays, I'd been stuck in meetings all morning. Things had been hectic since I'd taken over, since Adam had been shot dead by Liam in Gromov's home office. Not only had Adam been skimming from the accounts, but helping Gromov with weapons trafficking had been a whole new low.

It had been tough claiming the business after Adam's death. As expected, there had been a lengthy and detailed investigation into how corrupt the business was. Was it just Adam or were we all involved? Was the business itself tangled up in these affairs or was it separate? Thankfully for all of us, it was the latter. It seemed Adam hadn't wanted to mix his 9-5 business with his more shady goings on. Maybe that was an insurance policy in case he needed to pull out. Either way, I'd been left to clean up his mess.

It had taken everything I had to buy Adam's main stake, but I believed in the business. We had a strong client base, a good reputation and the best people in the business. At least we used to. Things had taken a serious nosedive since word of Adam's extracurricular activities had become public knowledge.

It felt like I was sailing a sinking ship.

Over a year later and we were still fighting for some semblance of normal. Our clients had been understandably shaken, and it had been hard to keep them on board. I'd resorted to discounted rates and special favours – anything to keep the business going.

And now it finally felt like we could see the light at the end of the tunnel.

A knock at my door brought me out of my reverie. I glanced through the glass to see Sam and waved him in.

"You wanted to see me, Boss?" Sam's huge frame filled my office. Dressed in his usual dark suit, Sam had more muscle than I thought was humanly possible and was an intimidating figure because of it. Which is what made him such a good deterrent when it came to protection.

"Stacey's not too thrilled about you going with her on Thursday," I said, gesturing to the chair opposite my desk.

"She never is," he chuckled.

"Do you think it's still necessary?"

Sam paused a moment before replying, always careful with his choice of words.

"Knowing what Liam did, and that he's still out there, I think a bodyguard as a precaution is reasonable."

I nodded. That was all I needed to hear. I knew that if I was being insane, Sam would say something. He wasn't one to beat about the bush.

"Do you think we need any extras because it's Istanbul?"

"Not sure. Richard will know."

I rolled my eyes. Yes, Richard would. Richard was our Operations Manager but my god did I not like the guy. Granted, he was good at his job. The issue was he was just so damn annoying, and always flip-flopped between being a know-it-all or a brown-noser. Anything I could do to avoid talking to him was a plus.

"I'll ask Lucy to track him down. Thanks Sam."

He gave me a single nod and then left.

I rang through to Lucy's desk to request what I needed.

"No problem," she said. "There are two new client appointments in your diary this week as well."

"Good news. I'll take a look."

"Let me know if there's anything else you need."

"Thanks Lucy."

I hung up the phone and logged onto the calendar on my computer. Opening the appointment for Wednesday, I read the notes. It was a meeting with Iris Mccleary's manager. She would be touring the country at the end of the year and needed a protection team to accompany her. After a few incidents of rowdy fans at her concerts from a past tour, her manager wanted to take a few extra precautions. Starting with a protection detail for when she appeared in public. There was an additional note at the very bottom. I read it and rolled my eyes. It appeared Iris Mccleary's manager had some concerns about 'the recent scandal'.

How long was this scandal going to follow us around? It was frustrating. And it felt like no matter what I did, we would forever be stuck in its shadow. I knew what Mccleary's manager was after, the same thing almost all our long-standing clients were after; a discount.

I closed the appointment in my calendar and then opened the one booked for Thursday. This one seemed pretty straightforward. An agency was looking for a security training specialist to step in and train their new recruits on an on-going basis. They wanted to run quarterly SIA licensing for new starters and those already on the payroll. Easy.

Something Roman, our Head of Training, would be able to pick up once I'd negotiated the contract.

My diary was a lot less cluttered with client meetings these days. Being the big boss meant I had more important things to think about. Like how we were going to expand the business. We had enough clients on the books at the moment to keep us going. But we couldn't keep ticking along as we were; we needed something fresh and interesting, something that would expand our horizons, bring in new custom and help revitalise the company name.

I was toying with the idea of port security. There were some big ports in the country, all of which needed contracted security. It would be a big job but would provide a regular stream of income if I could pull it off.

I closed the appointment and switched back to my inbox. At the very top was an email from our Head of HR about our latest recruitment campaign. She wanted a sign off on the strategy and confirmation of the available budget, plus a written confirmation on the number of positions I wanted to hire for.

All of it brought back memories of Gemma. It had been over a year since she'd been shot on the Hungarian podium, but I still thought about her often. Her death felt like my responsibility and her killer was still out there.

She'd been a new recruit, not long out of university, and she'd been so keen to be part of Stacey's security team. Her life was taken from her way too soon.

I desperately hoped we'd never repeat that mistake.

The door to my office swung open and Lucy appeared, somewhat ruffled.

"Sorry, Jason. I tried to stop him—" she said before a hulking man with a cane pushed past her and strode confidently into the middle of my office.

"It's okay, Lucy," I said, holding up a hand to placate her.

She opened her mouth to say something, then closed it, and left, shutting the door behind her.

"Please," I said, gesturing to the chairs on the other side of my desk. "Take a seat, Mr Gromov."

Alik Gromov did as invited, lowering his wide frame into the chair on the left. He made himself comfortable, propping his cane against the spare chair and casually leaned back, surveying the room.

"This is a nice office," he said, looking around at the framed certificates on the wall, the few personal items on my desk and then out of the window.

"What can I do for you, Mr Gromov?" I asked calmly.

"I need a residential team," he said.

I let out a short laugh. "You know I can't do that."

"Sure, you can."

"No. I can't," I said more seriously. "And even if I could, I wouldn't want to."

Gromov watched my face.

"I'll pay you double," he said.

I knew he'd try to pull something, it was totally his style. And I was sort of prepared for it.

I plastered my pleasant-to-horrible-clients smile onto my face and said, "Unfortunately, Mr Gromov, no amount of money will be able to change my mind. We are unable to work for those involved in criminal activities."

He scoffed.

We definitely did work with a fair number of individuals involved in criminal activities. However, the difference was we didn't actually *know* they were involved in criminal activities, only suspected they were. And if we ever received confirmation, that client's contract would be instantly terminated.

Gromov levered himself out of his chair, using his cane as a support, and walked over to the window.

"How is the lovely Stacey?" he asked, turning around with a sly smile on his face.

"Recovered and doing well, thank you. How is Dima fairing this season?" I replied. *Two can play at this game.* I watched his expression sour. While Stacey had managed to recover from a rocky start to the season, Gromov's protégé was struggling to keep up.

"It's not been his best season, I'll admit."

I couldn't help but feel a little smug.

"I really wish you'd reconsider offering me a residential team," he added.

"As I've already explained, it's simply not possible," I said, getting to my feet. "Now, if you'll excuse me, I'm quite busy."

"It's a shame we can't continue our professional relationship," he said. "Perhaps we'll see each other trackside."

"Perhaps," I replied, gesturing toward the door. The hairs on the back of my neck prickled. This felt too easy. I followed Gromov out into the open plan office and as there was nothing left to say, I simply watched him walk to the bank of elevators on the other side of the room and disappear from view.

"What did he want?" asked Lucy the moment the elevator doors closed.

"A new contract," I said, still unsettled that he'd left so quickly.

"You're joking?" she asked incredulously, looking up at me from where she sat behind her desk.

"Nope." I turned to my PA. "Can you chase Richard for his end of month report please? It should have been in last week and I'm still waiting."

"Of course." She gave me a smile and turned back to her computer, nails already clacking on the keyboard.

I stalked back into my office.

Chapter 6

JASON HUNTER

THE OFFICE

Monday 4th October

No sooner had I sat down than my mobile started ringing. One look at the caller ID and I answered.

"Hayley, that was fast. What have you got?"

"Not a lot, I'm afraid," she said.

"That doesn't sound good. And annoyingly familiar."

"Tell me about it," she said. "We have managed to identify where we think the first shot came from. I'm currently standing in an apartment across the street. Another penthouse, with perfect views of Adrianna's place."

"But you're not sure?"

"It's more of an educated guess; I don't actually have any evidence to suggest he was here."

I wasn't really sure how to reply. Had Hayley really phoned me to tell me they didn't have any evidence? She wasn't usually this forthcoming with details. Which instantly made me suspicious.

"What do you need from me?" I asked.

"What do you mean?"

"You know exactly what I mean. You've phoned me up to tell me you've made almost no progress? That's not like you."

Hayley sighed. "Okay, you got me. I need to ask a favour."

"Could you not have started with that?"

"I promise I will in the future."

"Go on, then," I said, pulling a pen and notepad toward me. "What do you need?"

"When did you last speak to Adrianna?"

"Yesterday." I frowned, sure that Hayley already knew this.

"Are you planning to see her today?"

"Yeah, I was gonna swing by after work." I looked down at my watch to see it was already 3pm. I had planned on finishing a bit earlier so I could go and see Adrianna and still get home in time for dinner without feeling rushed. I figured a couple of hours would be enough time.

"I don't think she's telling me the whole story."

"What do you mean?"

"She gave her statement and that was all fine. I believe her when she says she wasn't in the apartment when it happened. And I believe her when she says she doesn't know who did it. I don't believe her when she says she doesn't have any ideas *why* somebody would want to hurt her husband. Something just didn't sit right with me. I definitely think she's hiding something."

"And you want me to fish it out of her?"

"I figured she's more likely to open up to you than she is to me."

"That's an accurate assumption. I'll see what I can do."

"Thanks, Jason. I'll let you know if we find anything here."

We ended the call and I let out a breath. It had been quite an eventful day. Gromov turning up out of the blue had definitely been a surprise. I hadn't heard from him in over a year, not since that night at his mansion. One that would be etched into my brain forever. Not only had Stacey nearly died after Liam had kidnapped her at gunpoint, but he'd also murdered my boss and some American business partner. I'd never stopped to find out exactly who he was. I figured the less I knew about Gromov's shady weapons trafficking business, the better. But here he was, asking for protection again. The last time I hadn't been able to get the protection in place quickly enough and he'd suffered a bullet wound to the shoulder.

I wondered if his need for protection was related to Mickey's death. It seemed like too much of a coincidence for him to turn up the day after.

Briefly checking through my emails to make sure all the important stuff had been taken care of, I powered down my computer and left, letting Lucy know I was available on my mobile for anything urgent.

Adrianna had told me she was going to stay with her friend, Imani. While I was happy she had a friend she could lean on, Imani wasn't my biggest fan, especially not after the divorce.

I knew where the townhouse was, having been invited to a number of awkward and uncomfortable dinner parties where half of us would impatiently clock watch while the other half got drunk. The memories made me grimace as I climbed into my old BMW.

Turning left out of the company car park, I headed towards Kensington and Chelsea. Imani was nothing if not pure class, and she had the lifestyle to prove it.

Almost an hour later, I parked in Lennox Gardens, a quiet residential street in the heart of Knightsbridge. The house was stunning, and I always had to brace myself before entering. Imani's husband, Najib, owned a law franchise and had made a considerable amount of money during his career. These days he acted more as a silent partner, reaping the rewards of working hard for so many years.

Picking up the flowers I'd bought en-route, I made my way up to the front door and rang the doorbell, only to be greeted by Imani herself. She was stunning, her black skin standing out against the yellow silk dress she wore, her afro braided into an elegant updo. I don't know why I was so surprised; she always took meticulous care with her appearance and an autumnal Monday afternoon at home would be no different.

"I wondered how long it would be until you showed up," she sniped, a hint of her American accent coming through.

I held the flowers up, feeling as lame as I must look. "I came to see how she's doing."

"How do you think she's doing? The poor woman is a widower." Her tone was harsh but I knew it wasn't aimed at me. "Come in then." She stood aside to let me pass.

"Thanks," I mumbled and entered the minimalist white hallway. The parquet floor gave it a softer, more homely feel, as did the deep blue drapes and matching blue chairs arranged to one side. The kind of chairs you really wanted to collapse into, but were obviously just for show.

I followed her down the hallway, her heels clicking with every step. It was hard to believe she'd had two kids and this place had once housed two rowdy teenagers. Everything was pristine and untouchable.

She took me downstairs and along another well-lit hallway to their home cinema. She gestured for me to go in and then disappeared into the adjacent room. I entered the dimly lit room to see Adrianna curled up on the sofa watching Cool Runnings, the volume turned down low. The bright light from the huge TV screen that spanned the entire length of the room lit up her face. It was scrubbed clear of makeup, her eyes were red-rimmed and slightly puffy, and her hair was piled up on top of her head with a scrunchie. She was dressed in an oversized hoodie, mindlessly chewing the end of one of the hood drawstrings – I guessed it belonged to Mickey – while her legs were tucked in tight to her chest. For someone who was always larger than life, it was heartbreaking to see her taking up so little space.

She looked up at me as I entered and gave a small smile.

"How're you doing?" I asked, taking a seat next to her.

"Numb," she said as she leaned against me.

"Yeah, I bet." I put an arm around her. "I know they won't help, but I brought you these." I handed her the flowers. She took them from me and buried her nose in the petals.

"I love peonies," she said with a small smile.

"I know you do." I gave her shoulder a small squeeze as Imani reappeared, carrying a bottle of wine in one hand and three glasses in the other.

"You arrived just in time," she said to me. "I'd just opened a bottle of red." She held up the bottle in question and waved it slightly in the air.

"Perfect," I said with a smile.

Chapter 7

JASON HUNTER

IMANI'S HOME

Monday 4ᵗʰ October

I'd promised myself I'd only be at Imani's for a couple of hours because I wanted to get home in time for dinner with the kids. With everything going on in their lives, they really needed someone they could rely on. I wanted them both to know that I was there for them, even if it felt like their mum wasn't right now. I didn't want Adrianna worrying about the kids; I just wanted her to have the space and time to grieve properly.

Despite this, the two hours I sat with Adrianna and Imani went by with alarming speed. It wasn't that I was enjoying myself, but I wasn't watching the seconds tick by, waiting for an appropriate time to leave.

I'd forgotten how charming Imani could be. She was always an excellent host, so I shouldn't really have been surprised.

As I glanced down at my watch and saw how late it was, I made my excuses to leave.

"I'll walk you out," said Adrianna.

On the front steps to Imani's immaculate, high-end townhouse, I wondered how to breach the subject.

"I'm not stupid, Jason," she said.

I frowned. "I know that."

"So why are you really here?" Before I could answer, Adrianna held up a hand. "And don't give me the same bullshit you gave Imani. There's more to this visit than checking in with me – as nice as that may be."

I opened my mouth to say something, and then closed it again. She had me rumbled. "Honestly, I wanted to make sure you were okay..."

"But...?"

"No, no buts. I got a phone call from Detective Inspector Irons. Is there more to this than you're letting on?"

"Is that what she said?" asked Adrianna, her feathers well and truly ruffled.

"No, but she's not stupid either, and she knows when a person of interest isn't telling her the whole story."

"Person of interest?" I could hear the indignation in her voice. "Am I a suspect?"

"Of course not, but there's more going on here, isn't there?"

Adrianna sighed.

"I don't even know if it has anything to do with this," she said, waving a hand around.

"After what happened with Stacey, I can tell you that most things are related in some way or another."

Adrianna mumbled under her breath and wrapped her arms tightly around her middle. Suddenly, she wouldn't meet my eye.

"Was Mickey caught up in something shady?" I asked, the thought suddenly occurring to me. I'd obviously done my due diligence when the man had come into Lily and Max's lives, and there was nothing that had been an obvious red flag. He owned a few clubs – high-end clubs – which was where he made most of his money and how he was able to keep Adrianna in the lifestyle she wanted. Something I'd never been able to keep up with.

"I don't know," said Adrianna, barely above a whisper. "And that's God's honest truth."

I frowned. "So what is it?"

"I don't know. I just don't know. Something was going on. His business partner had been calling him more than usual. Mickey seemed on edge and grumpier than usual. There was something going on, Jason, but I just don't know what."

"When you say grumpier, what do you mean exactly?"

"He would snap at me, at the kids." I bristled at the mention of another man being short with my kids. Even if he was their stepdad, it didn't give him the right to be aggressive towards them. "He... he was spending more time in his office. Screening more calls—"

"What do you mean?" I interrupted.

"Just that his phone was constantly ringing but he never answered it. Or would only answer it occasionally. Only when Cameron would call. That's his business partner."

"Okay, I'll look into it."

"Jason, don't do anything stupid. You did enough of that with Stacey. I don't want you tempting fate twice."

"I promise," I said. "I'll just ask a few questions and then I'll pass on what I find to Hayley."

"Hayley?"

"DI Irons."

"Right." She chewed her bottom lip, her brow furrowing in the middle. "Be careful. Whatever Mickey was up to, it got him murdered in my living room." She let out a half sob and clapped a hand over mouth. "I don't know how I'm going to get past this."

"Hey," I said and reached out a hand to take hold of her upper arm. "No-one should ever go through what you're going through. It's gonna take time to feel any kind of normal again. Just concentrate on yourself. The kids can stay with me as long as they need to," I added, knowing full well that was a lie. Stacey was due to fly out to Türkiye on Thursday, which would leave me high and dry. I felt bad for using her as a glorified babysitter, but I think she was enjoying the distraction.

"What have you told them?" she asked quietly.

"The kids?"

Adrianna nodded.

"Nothing yet. I didn't know if you wanted to be the one to tell them."

Another small sob escaped Adrianna's lips.

"Don't worry, I can do it," I said.

She nodded wordlessly again.

"Alright, you just let me know when you want them back."

She nodded again.

"Thank you, Jason."

I pulled her into a hug. Our divorce had been the right thing to do. We'd never been right for each other and I think deep down I'd always known it. The separation had been amicable enough, and the kids hadn't got caught in the crossfire like they often do in these situations, but for the first time in a long time, I felt like we could be friends.

Chapter 8

JASON HUNTER

HOME

Monday 4th October

The kids were asleep and I was nursing a beer on the sofa.

"So what did Adrianna have to say?" asked Stacey, dropping onto the sofa next to me.

I'd just about made it home in time for dinner, thank God. I didn't want to face the wrath of Stacey if I stood her up. I'd seen her nasty side when she was speaking to Diane, her old PA. More importantly, the kids had breathed a sigh of relief when I'd come through the door. I hadn't quite anticipated just how much they were relying on me being there for them, and the pressure of that weighed heavily on my shoulders.

After dinner we'd sat them down in the living room and told them Mickey had died. I'd spared them the gory details, of course. Not that it'd made a difference. I was taken aback by how upset they'd both been. Turns out Mickey had been a pretty good stepdad to them both; he'd taught Lily how to ride her bike and he'd taught Max how to swim. I tried to swallow the guilt and jealousy that threatened to take over; some could argue that he'd been more of a father to them than I had. What had I been doing these last few years?

After tears, hugs and watching *Despicable Me* for the hundredth time, the kids had gone to bed, exhausted from an emotional evening.

"Apparently Mickey had been on edge for the last few weeks," I replied.

"How so?" She picked up the remote and started flicking through the channels.

"I'm not sure. She reckons he was getting more calls than usual but was refusing to take any of them. Unless it was Cameron, his business partner."

"Business partner?"

"Yeah. Don't ask me what kind of business, because I have no idea."

"You have no idea what your ex-wife's husband did? The stepfather to your children? You. Who runs one of the most prestigious security firms in London?"

"Of course I know what he did," I said, bristling. "Who do you take me for?"

She gave me a smirk.

"And I'd say we've probably lost any kind of prestige we might have had once upon a time." I let out a long, slow sigh.

"What about a rebrand?" asked Stacey. She'd gotten bored of channel hopping and had now switched over to Netflix.

"Rebranding what?"

"The business."

I let the idea sink in a moment as I contemplated her suggestion. Rebranding could get rid of the bad press. It could relaunch us and emphasise the new management. Would it impact our credibility? Maybe. But maybe no more so than Adam's lingering shadow.

I'd need to speak to our marketing team, but a rebrand opened up new possibilities. A fresh start. A new name. A company that was entirely mine.

"I think you might be onto something," I said eventually. "How is it you're always so intuitive?" I asked.

Stacey shrugged. "I'm just good like that," she said. "Call it a woman's prerogative."

I laughed just as she settled on watching a new Arnold Schwarzenegger show. Something about him and his daughter working in the CIA. It looked entertaining enough, so I didn't mind. It wasn't like I was actually watching it. My mind was whirling a million miles an hour.

Stacey did always manage to see things in a clearer light than me. She was a lot more empathetic, that's for sure. I don't know what it was but she did seem to have a better perspective on things that I couldn't seem to get my head around. I often found myself asking for her opinion and she would always see something I'd missed.

Perhaps it was just her female perspective. There was a lot to be said about the different ways of thinking between men and women. I'd seen *Men Are from Mars, Women are from Venus* in all the bookshops back in the day. It wasn't anything new. And yet there was still a distinct lack of women in the security industry. Gemma, Stacey's original body-double in Hungary, had been a breath of fresh air on the team at the time. So why didn't I have more women on our payroll?

"What do you think about having some all-female security teams?" I asked Stacey.

"What a great idea!" she said, her reaction instantaneous. She looked at me, the Netflix show forgotten. "Don't you have female teams already?"

"No more so than in Formula One," I said with a small grimace.

Stacey's mouth set into a hard line. "Something needs to be done about that," she said.

"Well, between the two of us, we might be able to make some headway."

Stacey went back to her show and I went back to my thoughts. It suddenly felt like I had a lot to do.

Chapter 9

THE GUNMAN

SOMEWHERE IN LONDON

Monday 4ᵗʰ October

"I'm telling you, boss man. It wasn't there."

"I don't believe you. It had to have been there. Where else could it be?"

He shrugged, not liking Alik Gromov's tone.

"I did as you asked. I checked the apartment afterward. I followed your instructions. There was nothing there. No USB, no money, no documents. I don't know what you want me to say." He shrugged. This was not his problem. The job had been carried out. The fact that it hadn't had the desired outcome wasn't his problem.

He sat back on the plush sofa in Gromov's club office and draped an arm across the top. Lifting his left leg, he placed the ankle on top of his right knee and tried to feign nonchalance.

Alik Gromov looked incredibly unhappy. He wasn't used to not getting his way. He was too used to barking orders and having his every whim indulged and delivered to him on a silver platter. Gromov scowled and leaned back in his chair.

Everything in the room was a gaudy, over-the-top deep purple. Everything from the thick carpet to the velveteen walls. There were no windows, and golden low-light sconces cast an eerie glow around the room.

"I tell you what, Alik," he said. "You've been a client for a long time, and you're a loyal customer. I'll give you a ten percent discount just this once."

Gromov's eyes narrowed. The man was no fool.

"I need to make sure you won't go telling anyone. This is a one-time offer and it's not open to anyone else."

Clearly feeling like he'd managed to come out on top, Gromov grunted before reaching into his pocket and pulling out a box of matches. He reached into the mahogany box on his desk and pulled out a thinly rolled cigar. Placing the cigar between his lips, he struck a match and then lit it.

"Ten percent?" Alik asked.

He nodded. "I don't like to see you disappointed. It's the best I can do," he said and then raised a finger. "And don't go thinking I'll ever do it again. Like I said, a one time courtesy. In future, I suggest you vet your sources more accurately."

Gromov scowled. The man was unused to being chided.

"Sure," he eventually grunted. "Cigar?" Gromov waved a hand towards the box, a pointless gesture as he knew the gunman didn't smoke. He politely declined.

They sat in silence while Gromov took a few pulls on the cigar.

"I'm sorry it didn't work out the way you'd hoped, Alik," he said. "But I hope you'll still consider my services in the future."

"Of course," said Gromov and inclined his head. "This changes nothing."

"I appreciate that." He smiled and then stood up. He made his way out into the main part of the club, escorted by two of Gromov's hulking bodyguards, despite knowing the way. He left via the discreet

VIP entrance at the back, and once he was out on the street, a strange quiet enveloped him.

After a moment, he reached into his pocket and pulled out a small black rectangle. It's shiny exterior glinted slightly under the dim street lighting. Smiling to himself, he casually tossed it into the air and caught it, grinning to himself. Then, he tucked the USB stick back into his pocket.

Chapter 10

JASON HUNTER

THE OFFICE

Tuesday 5th October

Our Head of HR was looking at me suspiciously.

"Don't look at me like that."

"Is this a PR stunt?"

I laughed. "No. I think women would be more effective in some situations. But since Gemma, we haven't recruited any female operatives."

"Can you blame them?"

Divya was the best person I'd ever worked with in HR. She was no-nonsense and didn't sugar-coat anything. She could smell bullshit a mile away and would always call you on it. She sat opposite me, her back ramrod straight, her long brown hair draped over one shoulder, and her slender hands clasping the planner she took everywhere with her.

Stacey's enthusiasm about my idea had spurred me on and led to this sit-down meeting with Divya. I'd told her what I'd wanted, but in her usual style, she was making sure I wasn't being an ass.

"Imagine if I sent two females into the field instead of two guys. If you saw two guys sitting on a bench one evening, you'd likely avoid

them, right? You'd clock them and then instantly want to avoid them."
I said.

She nodded hesitantly.

"Now replace that scene with two women. I bet you'd even look up and smile at them."

She looked thoughtful for a moment and then nodded. "Probably."

"Exactly. If my next client is the prince of wherever, he's going to feel a lot more comfortable going to a gala event with a woman on his arm as opposed to some unit of a bloke trailing around after him. Would be a lot more subtle too. A team of female operatives would be invaluable."

Divya nodded again and then smiled.

"I'll see what I can come up with. It's not an industry known for its equal opportunities so we might need to get creative."

"Sure. Just let me know what you need from me."

"Of course." She smiled again, gathered up her papers and left my office.

I let out a sigh of relief. I was convinced this would work, I just needed Divya to pull it off. But I didn't have time to pause, the next item on my agenda was a meeting with the whole marketing team and I was pretty sure they weren't going to like what I was about to say.

Scooping my mobile off my desk, I glanced at the screen before shoving it into my front pocket, and then headed out to the board meeting.

I entered the boardroom to see the marketing executives already gathered. Their conversation died as I entered, something I was becoming increasingly used to now that I was the head of the company. Our Marketing Manager and Head of Marketing appeared moments later, both looking slightly flustered.

An awkwardness settled on the room as everyone waited expectantly to hear what I had to say.

I wasn't sure how this was going to go down, but I was pretty confident it wasn't going to be a popular decision.

I cleared my throat and shifted uncomfortably in my seat.

"Okay, so I'm just going to come out and say this." I took a breath. "I think we need a complete rebrand." There was a moment of silence, so I continued in a hurried explanation, "Things have been spiralling since Adam's – shall we say – activities became public knowledge. I have clients trying to negotiate lower fees, claiming our impacted reputation is tainting theirs by association, and others are cancelling longstanding contracts. I need a way to turn this around, and fast. A rebrand would hopefully address this and allow us to have a fresh start."

I looked around the room to see Zack, our Head of Marketing, grinning at me. I smiled nervously back at him.

"I thought you'd never ask," he said.

I laughed, not expecting his response.

"In fact, I've been working on a rebrand strategy for a while now. I just wanted to finalise a few things before presenting it as a proposal."

"Really?" I asked, taken aback.

"Of course. You're completely right; things are shocking at the moment. Our reputation has taken a huge hit and the quickest way to turn that around would be to rebrand the company."

I watched the others furiously scribbling notes as Zack talked.

"Let's reconvene when I've got the plan finished and we can discuss the details. I'll make it a priority this week, so we should be able to put a meeting in the diary for next week." He looked around the room at his executives who all nodded in agreement.

"Sounds like a plan," I said, feeling a weight lift off my shoulders. Zack's preparedness made me feel like this was definitely the right choice and I left the meeting feeling more in control than I had in a long time.

Back in my office, I sat behind my desk. I'd kept my old office; I didn't feel comfortable moving into Adam's so I'd left that to Richard. The entitled prick had jumped at the chance to look even more privileged than the rest of us. I just left him to it. The thought of sitting in the same office that Adam had made my stomach churn. I hadn't enjoyed working for him. God knows why I'd stayed for so long. Although, thinking back to when I'd first started, it hadn't always been like that. Adam had recruited me for my experience in security, my specialist skills in dealing with negotiations, and being able to structure and deploy a high-stakes mission. My success rate had always spoken volumes. It was only later on that the animosity began to grow.

Lucy's head appeared around the edge of my office door.

"Coffee?" she asked.

"I'd love one," I replied.

She reappeared five minutes later with a freshly brewed coffee and a packet of biscuits.

"Stole these from the kitchen," she said with a sly smile. Her chin-length blonde hair fell forward as she leaned over my desk to place the coffee and biscuits within reach. I glanced at the packet; chocolate digestives. *Good choice.*

Standing back from my desk, she tucked one side of her hair behind her ear.

"Meetings go okay?" she asked.

"Yep. Zack will have a follow up in the next week or so. I suspect Divya will too."

Lucy scribbled something down on one of the pads of post-it notes on my desk and peeled it off the stack.

"Good to know. Buzz me if you need anything else."

"Thanks Lucy." She waved a hand over shoulder as she exited and I didn't hesitate in tearing open the biscuits.

It had already been a productive day. Divya's work on putting together an all-female team would work out brilliantly for my meeting with Iris Mccleary's manager in the morning, and Zack was already on board with the rebrand.

There was something else I was meant to do, but I couldn't remember what.

I picked up my coffee, took a sip and ate a biscuit.

Adrianna had text this morning to check in on the kids, and Stacey had called to say she was taking them out for the day.

Then I realised I hadn't heard from Hayley since yesterday. Since she'd asked me to speak to Adrianna. Which I'd done, I just needed to update her. But something from my conversation with Adrianna niggled at the back of my mind. Suddenly the penny dropped; Cameron.

Who the hell was this guy and did he have anything to do with Mickey's death?

I took another swig of coffee and opened up Google. So Mickey Bianchi owned a club – that had come up in the initial background check on him – and his business partner was Cameron – that hadn't.

I started with looking at the clubs Mickey owned. It didn't really tell me much, other than Tuesday was Student night, Thursday was Ladies' Night and Friday was 2-4-1. Their flagship club, the one that had high profile clientele, had three dance floors over two different storeys, private rooms, VIP booths and daily entertainment. Not quite what I was looking for.

Changing tactics, I opened up Companies House to see if I could track down the registered owners. Unsurprisingly, the club was owned by a Horizon Co, the most generic of generic company names. Mickey's name didn't appear anywhere. Of course it wouldn't be that easy. I was looking at a shell company, one that wanted to cover its tracks. So my next question was; why? What were they hiding?

And with no mention of Mickey, there was no mention of Cameron. So how were they connected? And how did I get in touch with this Cameron guy?

I drank another mouthful of coffee when my thoughts were interrupted by Lucy popping her head around my door again to tell me Richard had emailed through the data on Istanbul that I'd requested.

"Thank you," I said.

Switching from my internet browser to my emails, I opened up Richard's attachment.

The report started by outlining the current political stability in Türkiye, including a list of all public demonstrations in Istanbul and how the police had responded to each incident, often using tear gas and water cannons.It then went on to list the most popular crimes, including street robbery and pickpocketing, sexual assault, and drink and food spiking, before detailing how the Turkish police detained suspected criminals, and what the process was for negotiating release, avoiding sentencing, or serving time.

I was impressed with the level of detail Richard had included. It gave a clear picture of what we'd be dealing with should something go wrong.

The final section was what I was most interested in and it outlined Türkiye's terrorism threat. Ranking 18 on the Global Terrorism Index meant that the impact of terrorism was high, as was the likelihood of an attack occurring. I wasn't overly surprised but it did have me concerned. We would need to have an extraction plan in place.

Satisfied I'd read enough, I closed the report. Stacey would be having a security detail whether she liked it or not.

Getting up from my desk, I closed the door to my office. Through the glass I could see it was quiet in the main open-plan area. I leaned down and opened the bottom drawer on the left-hand side of my desk. In one fluid movement, I flipped up the false bottom and pulled out the disposable mobile phone. Turning my chair so my back was to the glass walls, I typed out a quick message.

Thursday arrival. One man team.

I hit send and replaced the phone in its hiding place.

Chapter 11

JASON HUNTER

THE OFICE

Tuesday 5th October

"And?"

"Oh, hi Hayley. It's great to hear from you. Yeah, I'm doing okay, thanks. You know, under the circumstances. Yeah, what a great idea; we *should* get together for a drink some time, so nice of you to ask."

I could hear Hayley grumbling on the end of the line before she came back to the phone and said in her sweetest voice, "Hi, Jason. How are you? How are the kids?"

I laughed. "It would just be nice not to be barked at down the phone. I know you like to get to the point but still, a hello would be enough."

"Sorry. It's been hell this end. I'll try to remember a hello in future."

There was a pause.

"So...?" she asked. "Adrianna?"

"She didn't really know much, I'm afraid. She did give me a name though; Cameron. Heard of him?"

"No. Who is he?"

"Adrianna said he was Mickey's business partner."

"What kind of business?"

"I'm not sure. She reckons Mickey was running this club, but I can't find anything on him. He's not listed as an owner on Companies House and he's not listed as an owner of the shell company either, just another shell. Looks like it's quite the cover up."

Hayley was silent for a moment.

"What are you thinking?" she asked. "That Mickey was into something shady?"

"I don't know." I shrugged, even though the gesture was lost on the phone. "I wouldn't be surprised."

"Adrianna have anything else to say?"

"Just that he'd been particularly on edge lately. He was being inundated with calls but would only ever answer if it was Cameron."

"Calls about what?"

"No idea. Adrianna got the impression he was paranoid about something. He was working longer hours than usual and just didn't seem himself."

Hayley didn't reply. I could almost hear her thinking down the phone.

"Okay, thanks. I'll look into this Cameron and see if I can get hold of Mickey's phone records."

"Sure. Let me know if there's anything else I can do."

"Will do, thanks Jason. Oh, and let's put that drink in the diary."

I smiled and hung up. Then realised Hayley hadn't told me if she'd made any progress on her end. My grin grew wider. Damn woman. She was sneaky. While she was happy to ask for my help, she was still reluctant to share with me. She'd been willing enough to have me at the crime scene, but it felt like she was once again keeping her cards close to her chest. Typical Hayley.

Chapter 12

JASON HUNTER

THE SAVOY

Wednesday 6th October

Iris Mccleary and her manager Vance Cherry sat opposite me in the plush elegance that was the Savoy's River Restaurant. A circular central bar took up a large portion of the room with dangling spherical lights that emitted a cosy and inviting glow. The seats, a combination of pale leather and deep mahogany, were soft and supple.

I leaned back into my chair as the waiter elegantly filled our glasses and then placed the bottle of Australian Pinot Noir on the table between us.

Cherry tried to smile but it was more of a leer. He was clearly unaccustomed to being nice; he looked like he was holding himself back. Part of me wished I'd brought Stacey along, mostly because Iris looked more uncomfortable at this table with two men who were invested in her safety than on stage in front of 30,000 fans screaming her name. Stacey would have known how to make her feel at ease.

Then I mentally chastised myself. *I* knew how to make her feel at ease. Hell, I'd been schmoozing clients for nearly ten years. I wasn't a newbie.

I leaned forward, placed an elbow on the table and carefully picked up my glass. I sniffed the wine before taking a tentative sip, and the flavour exploded on my tongue. It was delicious. Fruity yet earthy.

"So, Iris," I said. "Are you looking forward to your upcoming tour? Must be exciting to see everyone appreciating all your hard work?"

She smiled at me, a tentative smile, and some of the tension in her shoulders eased slightly.

"Oh yes. I love touring," she said, her voice soft and feminine. A singer's voice. "It's such a thrill."

"Tiring, though, I bet?"

"Exhausting." She laughed, a light tinkling sound. "Always on the road, always travelling from one destination to another. There's no rest. But I find that so much inspiration strikes when I'm on tour."

"That's good to hear. I bet the recent incidents have put a downer on things?"

I turned to look at Cherry who was frowning.

"It's certainly been a bit of a shock," said Iris.

"And we want to make sure nothing happens both on tour and afterwards," added Cherry. "If you're able to deliver, then we're willing to consider a long-term contract."

"Of course." I nodded my head and took another sip of wine. Cherry picked up his glass and did the same. "So, take me through exactly what's happened so far."

Cherry placed his glass back on the table and leaned forward.

"We've had a couple of fans who are particularly *keen* on Iris. Her apartment was broken into. Thankfully, she wasn't home."

"Did they take anything?" I asked quickly.

Iris shook her head. "Just some underwear," she said with a wrinkle of her nose.

Ah. We were dealing with those types of people. Unfortunately, it wouldn't be the first time.

"Right. What else?"

"Well, before the break-in, we'd started receiving some letters. At first, they weren't anything out of the ordinary. But they began to get a bit more earnest; declaring their undying love, stating that Iris was destined to be with them, that sort of thing. We've already reported it to the police and they have it all in hand. The individuals have been apprehended and there's a court order in place to keep them away. But for some peace of mind, I thought it best we employed some extra protection."

"Of course. I'm glad the police have been able to do something. It can often be frustrating when nothing happens."

"Like with Stacey, you mean?" asked Iris. Though gently spoken, her words made me freeze, and I felt like the whole restaurant had gone silent too.

"I was thinking more of past cases where we've helped celebrities in a similar situation, but yes, you could say like Stacey."

The waiter returned to our table and gently placed our three meals in front of us; beef wellington for Cherry, lobster for Iris, and a steak for me. I picked up my knife and fork as a way of buying myself more time.

"I'm glad you've brought that up, Iris," said Cherry, tucking into his wellington. "I am a little concerned about that whole... situation. While I don't doubt you did as much as possible, it obviously does lead me to question how suitable you are for this job."

I swallowed my first bite.

"And it's only right for you to be concerned. Your client's safety is at stake." *And your money*, I thought to myself.

Cherry smiled his leering smile at me and began tucking into his food.

"Let me put your mind at rest," I said. I was weighing up exactly how much I told them as I took another bite. "Stacey's situation was quite different. Yes, she had an overly enthusiastic fan, but this was an inside threat." Iris's eyes widened at my confession. I put a placating hand on the table. "I won't deny it was a shock. And it also highlighted some concerning gaps in our internal security program. Unfortunately, Liam was very skilled in covering his tracks and staying anonymous. We don't have that problem here; the culprit has already been identified, so we're an active deterrent more than anything else."

Iris nodded as she expertly twisted off the lobster tail and then cracked it open on the table.

"I take it you've fixed these gaps that you've mentioned," said Cherry, waving his fork around nonchalantly.

"Of course. It was the first thing I did. I carried out a full assessment of our current program, as well as a deeper dive into his background – with the help of the police – and a cross reference against the current system we use for conducting background checks. This is now more rigorous and we have access to additional databases as well as AI algorithms that help to identify concerning patterns in behaviour. All of our current staff have been reassessed against this new protocol to ensure there are no more loopholes."

Cherry nodded appreciatively but Iris continued to focus on de-shelling her lobster.

"Iris," I said gently. She looked up at me. "I know it's scary. But I promise your safety is my top priority. And I will do everything in my power to ensure that you're safe."

She smiled but didn't reply for a moment.

And I wasn't sure what to do next.

"I believe you have the job, Mr Hunter," she said gently.

"What?" spluttered Cherry.

I laughed. "Just like that?"

She nodded and took a bite of her food. "Your honesty is commendable. And I believe you'll do a great job."

"Iris," said Cherry, trying to intervene. "We need to discuss this before making any-"

"Vance," she cut in. "I know you're going to say. And despite Mr Hunter's unfortunate recent events, I do believe he would be the best man for the job. We've spoken to several firms now, and he is the one who's made me feel most comfortable."

Cherry opened his mouth to say something, but Iris didn't give him a chance.

"We all deserve a second chance, right? Isn't that what you said to me when I wanted to cancel my recording contract? And you were right."

I fought to hold back my smile.

"If you're sure," he said.

"I am."

As trumped up as Cherry was, it was clear he genuinely cared for Iris. There was still concern etched across his face, but he wasn't going to override his client's decision.

"I'll tell you what," I said, hoping to smooth things over. It was all very well and good getting Iris' support, but really, I needed Cherry to be on board too. "Call me Jason, and why don't we spend the rest of lunch going through the details of how we'll keep Iris safe?"

He turned his attention back to me. "Where do we start?"

In between bites of food, sips of wine and a few anecdotes, I outlined how we'd perform our checks, rotate the team, escort her from

A to B and be the muscle she needed to keep creepy fans at bay. Then I explained my plan to hire some all-female teams.

By the end of the meal, Cherry was on board, Iris was relaxed and telling me about the time a fan had managed to get into her dressing room, and things seemed to be on the up.

Chapter 13

STACEY JAMES

SOMEWHERE IN CHELSEA

Wednesday 6th October

Stacey pulled at the sleeve of her jumper. There was the tiniest thread unravelling at the seam and she couldn't help but pick at it. It was a favourite; an oversized, comfy grey thing she'd had for years. If the sleeve started to come apart, she'd be gutted. But for some reason she couldn't fight the compulsion to pull at that thread. Its imperfectness was almost too much.

She realised what she was doing and forced herself to stop. Bringing the sleeve to her nose, she inhaled its familiar, comforting smell. It smelled like home, like cosy evenings with Jason, like safety.

"And how do you feel about it now?" prompted Professor Irhaa Lindberg.

"I don't know," mumbled Stacey. She looked across the carefully decorated room at the woman sitting just a few feet away. Professor Lindberg was impeccably dressed, as always. Her sleek, ebony hair was carefully draped over one shoulder. She was dressed in a cream silk halterneck and cropped cream trousers, which contrasted beautifully against her olive skin. She sat back in her chair with one leg crossed over the top of the other and her notebook resting on top. On her feet she wore cream block heels that exposed her perfect French pedicure.

"I'm sure you do," said Professor Lindberg.

Stacey's gaze flickered to the other woman's face, finding those startling green eyes were watching her. Stacey sighed and stood up from her chair. *When did it get so hot in here?*

"I feel on edge," she said.

"Go on."

"Every time I feel myself starting to relax, I panic. It's like I *know* something bad is about to happen, I just don't know when." She paced over to the window and looked down at the quiet residential street.

"Considering what you've been through, I'd say that's a perfectly normal response."

"But how do I stop it?" asked Stacey, frustrated. She turned away from the window, marched back to her chair, and slumped into it.

"Have you started using those breathing exercises we discussed in your last session?"

"Yes. And they work when I'm caught up in the moment, but they don't help me prevent them in the first place."

"Unfortunately, that feeling may never go away. When we experience—"

"Trauma changes us forever," interrupted Stacey. "I know, I know." She let out a breath. "I just want to get past this stage of being on edge all the time. I want to regain the easy confidence I had before."

"And you will. You need to be kind to yourself, more than anything."

"I guess," she mumbled.

A silence filled the room. Not an uncomfortable one. Professor Lindberg made some notes in her notebook and allowed Stacey a moment to regain control.

Sitting up straighter, she began to fiddle with the thread on her sleeve again.

"Are you ready for your visit to see Diane?"

She shrugged. "As ready as I'll ever be."

They lapsed into silence again.

"When's your next race?" asked Lindberg.

"I leave tomorrow," replied Stacey.

"Feeling ready for that?"

"Yeah, I think so." She smiled, and her whole body seemed to suddenly relax.

"Is Jason going with you?"

Stacey flinched slightly at the question.

"No," she said. "He's busy with the business, and his kids. His ex-wife's husband has been murdered, so everything's a bit chaotic at the moment."

Professor Lindberg raised her eyebrows and Stacey inwardly felt smug that she'd managed to surprise the woman.

"That's a lot to process."

"Yeah, you're telling me," said Stacey.

"How's Jason taking it?"

"Surprisingly well. Although he was never that friendly with Mickey—"

"Mickey's dead?" Professor Lindberg's eyes widened in shock.

Stacey frowned. "Yes," she said slowly. "Do you know him?"

"I've seen him once or twice in the past. Community service," she added quickly. "Mickey's, not mine." She paused and she looked unsure. "Sorry, I interrupted you."

Stacey continued to frown. It was unlike Professor Lindberg to get flustered. In fact, Stacey had never seen the woman so much as ruffle a strand of hair. And yet in the space of thirty seconds, her cool exterior had slipped. And how the hell had she known who she was talking about anyway?

"I was just saying, he's spending a lot of time with Adrianna, helping with the kids, that sort of thing."

"Does it bother you?"

"Does what bother me?"

"Jason spending a lot of time with his ex-wife?"

Stacey laughed. "Not in the slightest. There's nothing there. It's nice to see they can be civil to each other, for the sake of the kids."

"Of course." Professor Lindberg made another note in her notebook and then glanced up at the clock that hung above the door. "It looks like our time has come to an end today."

Stacey got to her feet. "Same time next week?"

"I may have to postpone next week's session, but I'll let you know. Good luck with the race."

"Thanks." Stacey exited the room, headed down the stairs and out into the street. The cool October air hit her and she immediately felt lighter. It was a strange one; she never felt like her sessions with Professor Lindberg made much progress until she was outside.

She didn't notice the familiar figure watching her from the end of the street as she turned towards her car and headed home.

Chapter 14

JASON HUNTER

HOME

Wednesday 6th October

"Come on, you two. Bedtime."

Max let out a groan and Lily sighed. I tried hard not to laugh.

"You know the rules. It's a school night."

Max padded into the kitchen as Lily got to her feet. She scooped up her favourite soft toy, a dog named Patches, and approached Stacey who was still sitting on the sofa. She held out her arms and Stacey didn't hesitate in scooping up my little girl for a hug.

She gave Lily a good squeeze and said, "Goodnight, sweetheart."

Max reappeared in the doorway to the kitchen, a glass of water in hand, and said, "Half an hour, right?"

I nodded and got to my feet. "Reading or on your Switch. But I'll be up to check at lights out, okay?"

He nodded and disappeared from the room. "Night, Stacey," he said over his shoulder.

I rolled my eyes but Stacey just laughed.

"Come on, you," I said to Lily. She gave me a sleepy smile, took my hand and turned back to give a wave to Stacey, who blew her a kiss.

We headed upstairs to Lily's room and she immediately climbed into bed, pulling Patches in close to cuddle. He was a worn little thing, a gift for when Lily had been born and she'd taken to him instantly. I had a photo somewhere of her cuddling him when she was just a few days old. The two were inseparable. These days he was a lot more droopy, and incredibly dirty. No matter how often he went in the wash, he was always a grey off-white colour. His long floppy ears were still brown though, and there was a brown patch over one eye, hence the name.

I sat down on the bed next to her and picked up the book from her bedside table. We were reading *Dragons at Crumbling Castle and Other Stories* by Terry Pratchett and it was turning out to be one of her favourites. Each night we read a different story from the book, and tonight's was all about Father Christmas going to work at the zoo.

It didn't take long before she was giggling into her duvet.

Just as the story came to an end, she yawned.

"Alright, you," I said as I replaced the book on the nightstand. She wiggled under the duvet before settling down. I pulled the duvet right up to her chin and kissed her forehead as she closed her eyes. "Goodnight, sugar puff."

"Night Daddy," she mumbled.

I carefully closed the door behind me and headed downstairs.

Stacey wasn't in the living room when I returned, but I could hear her rummaging around in the kitchen. I followed the noise to find her pulling different cheeses out of the fridge. She looked over her shoulder at me as I entered.

"I know you had a big lunch with that new client so figured something lighter for dinner."

"Good idea."

"You can open that," she said, waving at a bottle of wine on the countertop. I did as she asked and poured it into the two wine glasses that stood waiting.

Satisfied she had what she needed, she began unwrapping the cheeses and laying them out on a chopping board. Then she opened a pack of cured meats and lay them alongside the cheese.

"Fancy," I said as I watched.

She flashed me a grin over her shoulder and then opened the fridge one last time to retrieve a tub of olives.

"You know me," she said, still smiling. Satisfied, she reached across me, lingering for just a moment so my nose filled with the scent of her shampoo, to reach for one of the wine glasses.

"You could have just asked," I said.

"Ah, but where would be the fun in that," she said with a smirk.

I picked up the second wine glass and moved the cheeseboard to the kitchen island where we both took a seat.

"So how was your day?" I asked.

"Yeah, pretty good," she said, taking a sip of wine. "I had my appointment with Professor Lindberg."

"And?"

"I like her. Feel like we actually got somewhere today, you know?"

"Well, that's good."

"It is. We talked about my panic attacks today. Well, not panic attacks, as such. I've had one of those before. But the sense of panic I get."

"I think you can still class that as a panic attack," I said and helped myself to a couple of olives.

"I guess. It's just not quite all consuming."

"I'd disagree." I'd seen one of these 'moments of panic' as she described them, and they were definitely panic attacks. It was actually horrible to witness; she would start shaking, go white as a sheet and struggle to control her breathing.

The last time it happened she was on her way to a red carpet event and the car had done three laps of the block before she was able to get it under control. Admittedly it had been a while since she'd had one that bad, but occasionally I'd come into a room to find her standing or sitting perfectly still. I'd even found her once with her coffee halfway to her mouth. It always took her a few moments to snap out of it and she'd be really disorientated afterwards.

"Actually, I'll tell you what did happen," she said, snapping me from my thoughts. "So I mentioned there was a lot going on at the moment, you know, with Mickey's death and all that, and she actually knew who he was."

I frowned.

"As in, knew from the news?"

"No, I don't think so."

"Ah shit," I said, glancing at the clock on the wall. "Hold that thought." I grabbed a slice of salami and popped it into my mouth as I headed upstairs to Max's room.

"All okay, buddy?" I asked as I put my head around his bedroom door. He looked up from his Nintendo Switch and nodded. "Manage any reading?"

"I read a chapter," he replied, switched the console off and placed it in the drawer of his nightstand.

"That's not too bad."

"It's just really boring."

"Oh, dear." I glance at the book next to his lamp. "Stuart Little?"

"Uh huh. I've seen the movie, and that was alright. But the book is just boring."

"Is this one from school?" I asked as he snuggled down.

"No, Nana bought me a box set of classics."

Ah. Adrianna's mother always had the best intentions, but they never quite landed right.

"You know you don't have to read it if you don't want to."

"Of course I do," he said and rolled his eyes.

I laughed. "What were you playing?" I asked, changing the subject. I didn't want to get caught out giving my opinion on Adrianna's mother. She'd never liked me, had flat out told me to my face that I wasn't good enough for her daughter on our wedding day. *On our wedding day.* Who does that?

"Lego Harry Potter."

"You're obsessed."

"It's really good!"

"I'm sure it is. You'll have to show me some time."

His face lit up and my heart gave a little squeeze.

"I'll see you in the morning," I said, kissing his forehead.

"Dad?"

"Yeah?"

"Stacey's racing this weekend, isn't she?"

"Yep, in Istanbul."

"Is Sam going with her?"

"He sure is. She'll be safe."

"Good," he mumbled as he closed his eyes. I brushed his hair back from his face and kissed him once more before leaving the room.

Chapter 15

JASON HUNTER

HOME

Wednesday 6th October

"Max is still worrying about you," I said as I re-entered the kitchen.

"About me racing?"

I nodded.

"He's a sweet kid. Lily too. I love them both as if they were my own."

"I know you do," I said and placed a kiss on her lips. "What were we talking about?" I helped myself to some of the cheese and crackers.

Stacey paused, taking a sip of wine. "Oh, Professor Lindberg," she said and placed her glass back on the counter top. "She knew who Mickey was."

"But not from the news?"

"No. I said Mickey's name, and she asked 'Mickey's dead?' as if she'd seen a ghost. And then when I said yes, she honestly looked a bit scared."

"And you're sure she didn't know about your connection to him before?"

"I don't think so. And even if she did, her reaction was strange. I've never seen her falter on anything before. Honestly, the woman is immaculate from head to toe. And it's not like I gave her his surname either, so no idea how she knew who Mickey was."

"That is strange." I frowned and drank some of my wine.

"I even called her out on it. Asked if she knew him. She just said something about community service," said Stacey, waving a hand dismissively.

"Community service?"

"She didn't elaborate. And was quite keen to move the conversation along. Plus, I'm paying her to give me therapy, not the other way around."

I chuckled. "Community service suggests he might have been to prison. And it's weird she'd react that way."

"Weird enough to tell Hayley?"

"Maybe. I'll mention it next time I speak to her."

"I was just about to ask if you've heard anything from her recently?"

"I spoke to her yesterday. Told her about Cameron but she didn't share anything with me."

Stacey smiled. "Typical Hayley."

"I know, right!"

"Doesn't bode well though, does it?"

"What do you mean?"

"Well," said Stacey. "It's now Wednesday. That's three days with no real progress. I mean, they never caught the guy who killed Gemma. Never even came close. And now it's looking like the same thing might be happening all over again."

"Let's not get carried away," I said. "It's not the same and we know it. The whole MO is different, so it's unlikely to be the same killer."

Stacey rolled her eyes. "The guy is a professional. Clearly. His MO is gonna change. He's not stupid."

"I personally wouldn't know. I've never been a gun for hire."

She gave me a wry smile. "Very funny," she said between bites. "I mean, where are we at? So far, all we know is that Mickey was acting strangely in the weeks leading up to his death. He would only talk to his business partner Cameron, of whom we know nothing. And his office was ransacked. Someone was clearly looking for something."

"True. What I want to know is whether the initial sniper shot was intended to kill or just maim."

"What do you mean?"

"Did the shooter need Mickey to tell him how to get into the safe before he killed him? Did he need him alive for information before finally shooting him in the head? Maybe the sniper shot was just a way of making him defenceless so they could get what they needed from him."

"That's cold."

"Doesn't make it untrue though," I said with a shrug.

"That's accurate."

We both ate in silence for a few moments.

"That's assuming there was only one shooter," I added.

Stacey looked at me, eyes wide. "You think there could be more than one?"

"Sure, why not? Let's look at it logically. Guy shoots through the window, triggers the security system. Now, someone with his experience and talent—"

"Let's not use that word," said Stacey, scrunching her face up.

"What word?"

"Talent. Let's not glorify that this guy is committing cold-blooded murder."

"Okay, maybe talent isn't the right word. Skill? I mean, it does take skill to shoot a rifle that accurately."

"Yeah, fine," she said, nose still scrunched.

"With his experience and *skill*, he's gonna know there's a security system in place. He'll have done his due diligence in selecting the right place to shoot from..." I trailed off.

"What?" asked Stacey, sitting upright.

"I wonder if Hayley found anything at his shooting location."

"Like in Budapest?"

"Yeah, although that didn't provide us with much to go on."

"No, but it did rule out Cooper. And told us more about the weapon."

That much was true. The bullet fragments had only been recovered once they'd been able to pinpoint the shooter's location and, in turn, that had told them it was a military grade hit. I just hoped this wasn't going to be a repeat.

"Sure," I mumbled. "Anyway," I said, trying to clear my head. There were so many thoughts running around, I was struggling to keep track of them. It was as if I had a hundred post-it notes fluttering about in there, all just out of reach. "So this guy would have known that he didn't have long to get from wherever he was to the apartment."

"How long are we talking?"

"Hayley said 15-20 minutes tops. Now it's not impossible, but it seems incredibly unlikely. Why do it all on your own, when a two-man team would be much more effective?"

"Because you don't trust anyone?"

"There's that," I said, nodding. "Hayley said she wasn't ruling out the possibility."

We both fell silent. I took another sip of wine and tried to see if any of the pieces of the puzzle would fit together yet.

"So what's next?"

"What do you mean?"

"Don't be coy with me, Mr Hunter. I know you can't help but get involved."

I laughed.

"I don't know," I said.

Stacey raised an eyebrow at me.

"Alright, alright," I said, raising a placating hand. "I need to speak to Hayley. See what she found at the shoot site, and whether she's got hold of any CCTV yet. Although I could potentially help with that."

"How?"

"Anyone can go into a store and ask to see footage from their cameras. It's up to the store to say no."

Stacey laughed. "How very bold of you."

I shrugged. "I want to track down this Cameron, though. Something tells me he's involved in all of this."

"Just promise me you'll be careful." She reached across the counter and placed a hand on mine.

"Of course," I said, turning my hand over so I could give hers a squeeze.

"Good. Can't have anyone messing up that pretty face of yours."

Chapter 16

HAYLEY IRONS

HAMMERSMITH POLICE STATION

Wednesday 6th October

Wednesday 6th October

Hayley sat in her office in the semi-darkness, wondering what the hell she should do next. It was late, the police station was almost empty, and in front of her sat the latest dead end.

Mickey Bianchi's fingerprint analysis results sat open on the desk. And it looked as though he didn't exist.

Haynes and his team had found a number of fingerprints in the apartment including Adrianna's, both the kids', the cook's, the cleaner's and three more that were unidentifiable. One, of course, belonged to Mickey Bianchi. They'd easily been able to match them to the body. The issue was that the fingerprints for Mickey Bianchi were drawing a blank. So who the hell was this guy?

Unease lay heavily in Hayley's stomach, making her feel sick. There was something much bigger at play here. Mickey had served time. But it was starting to look like someone might have tampered with his file.

And why would they do that?

Mickey Bianchi didn't exist in the Police National Computer. There was no record of him anywhere.

Two tattoos on the preliminary autopsy report stood out; a single dot between the forefinger and thumb on both hands. Mickey was covered in tattoos. Up and down both arms, his legs, his chest, back, shoulders. Almost every part of him was inked. But these two tattoos stood out specifically. Not just because they were the only ones visible when he was fully clothed, but because these had a universal meaning. One symbolised going into prison, and one symbolised time served.

If Mickey Bianchi had been in prison, his details would definitely be in the PNC.

So why weren't they?

Reading through the notes for the hundredth time, she paused on something that caught her eye. They'd found residue on two of his fingers. It was still unidentified, but thought to be an adhesive.

An adhesive? Why the hell would Mickey have adhesive on his fingers?

She glanced at her phone, noting how late it was. Too late to call Jason.

Did Adrianna know who her husband really was? Or was she just as in the dark as everyone else? She still wasn't sure if the woman had told them everything. And relying on Jason to get information out of her was unprofessional as well as risky. Not because she didn't trust him, but because she couldn't gauge the woman's reactions for herself. Jason's personal history with Adrianna might cloud his judgement, and that wasn't a risk she was willing to take.

Chapter 17

JASON HUNTER

THE OFFICE

Thursday 7th October

The door opened and I looked up to see Hayley walking in. Lucy hovered in the doorway but just shrugged before disappearing back to her desk, closing the door behind her.

"Good morning. How are you?" asked Hayley. She sat down in one of the chairs opposite my desk and looked at me expectantly.

I couldn't help but laugh. "Detective Inspector Irons, what a pleasant surprise," I replied.

"That doesn't really answer my question."

"Busy. To what do I owe this visit?"

She crossed her legs and looked out of the floor-to-ceiling windows at the London skyline. "I felt like we needed a catch up."

I followed her gaze out the window and watched the bustle of the city for a moment before asking, "How's the investigation going?"

"We're working on it. Wanted to ask you about Mickey."

"What about him?" I turned to look at her, but she was still resolutely looking out the window.

"How well did you know him?"

I frowned and she turned to look at me.

"I wasn't overly friendly with him, if that's what you mean? He was married to my ex-wife. And I can't say we divorced on the best of terms. So I wasn't all that pally with her new husband."

"But as the stepfather to your kids and considering he was living in the same apartment as them, surely you did your own digging? I know you well enough Jason to know that."

"Of course. We ran background checks on the guy. I needed to make sure he wasn't a psycho."

"And?"

"And what?"

"And, what did you find?"

"Not much," I shrugged. It was the truth. There hadn't been much on the guy. And although part of me had been a tiny bit disappointed – who doesn't want a one-up on the new guy? – I was also relieved. "But if recent events have told me anything, our processes weren't exactly up to scratch. How else would we have missed Liam?"

"Liam was sneaky. And you know there's nothing on his record. He was squeaky clean."

I didn't reply and she turned to look out the window again.

"Oh just spit it out, Hayley," I said, letting my frustration get the better of me. She'd clearly come here for a reason and she obviously had an agenda.

She turned to look at me, a strange expression on her face.

"I have a bit of an issue," she said eventually.

"About Mickey?"

I waited. A familiar dread crept into the pit of my stomach.

"Mickey Bianchi isn't a real person."

The room was silent as I processed what Hayley had said. I frowned, convinced I'd misheard her. What was she on about? Of course Mickey Bianchi was a real person. I'd met him. He'd married my ex-wife. He'd lived with my kids.

"I don't follow," I said, unsure how I was meant to respond.

"It's an alias. Mickey Bianchi doesn't exist. Fingerprint analysis came back and they don't match what we have on file."

"How's that even possible?"

Hayley shrugged. "Beats me."

"So who is he?"

"I was hoping you could tell me. Or better yet—"

"Do not say it." I held up a hand to stop Hayley in her tracks. It did the trick.

"Jason—"

"I'm not doing it. I've got enough on my plate as it is, and so has she. She's grieving, Hayley."

"I know, I know," she said, holding up a placating hand. "I wasn't actually going—"

"Sure."

We both fell silent. But I didn't apologise for snapping. Hayley had overstepped and she knew it. Adrianna was fragile. Her whole world had just been ripped apart.

"So go back to the bit where you said Mickey isn't actually Mickey."

"He has prison tattoos, so he should be in the system. But it looks like someone might have tampered with his file because the database is drawing a blank."

"How is that even possible?"

"I have no idea."

I dragged a hand over my face as I tried to process this new information. First, I wanted to know why Mickey had served time, and then I wanted to know why his identity had been wiped from the system. That sounded like some shady shit.

"So, how do we find out who he is then?"

She shrugged. "I'll need to speak to Adrianna. I still get a feeling that she knows more than she's letting on."

"I'm not so sure," I said.

"Well, I've got to ask anyway."

I nodded.

"And then we'll go from there."

She didn't say anything else and I let out a whoosh of breath.

"What a turn of events. I mean, I still can't quite believe it. How does someone create a whole fake identity?" I asked.

"It's surprisingly easy."

"What? And fake it for years? Get married? Raise kids? And no one's any wiser?"

"Who says no one's the wiser? What about his business partner? This Cameron guy? You reckon he doesn't know?"

"Good point. Any luck tracking him down?"

Hayley shook her head. "I haven't got round to it yet."

There was a light knock on the door and Lucy opened it.

"Everything okay?" I asked.

"Sorry to interrupt. I just wanted to let you know FixRecruitment has arrived."

I glanced at the clock, shocked to see that it was almost 11am.

"Ah shit," I muttered.

"No worries," said Hayley. "I'll get out of your hair. I'll call if I find out anything else."

"Thanks Hayley," I said, getting to my feet and gathering the files I would need.

"I'll see myself out." She gave me a quick smile and left.

Chapter 18

JASON HUNTER

THE OFFICE

Thursday 7ᵗʰ October

"They're in the boardroom," said Lucy once we were alone.

"Thanks. Richard and Roman?"

"Richard's already with them," she said with a wince. "Roman's running five minutes late."

"Ah, shit."

There was no denying that Richard was good at what he did. I wouldn't keep him around as an Operations Manager if he wasn't. But the guy irritated the shit out of me. He was nice enough, just annoying. And I wasn't the only one who thought so either.

I made my way down the corridor to the boardroom where I could hear muted chatter, followed by Richard's laugh. I fought back the eyeroll.

With my hand on the boardroom door, my phone vibrated in my pocket. I pulled it out to see a text from an unknown number.

Return what you've taken or pay the price.

My mouth went dry as I read the words on the screen.

What was I meant to have taken? It was a threat, clear as day, but I had no idea why. I read the words again, my brain scrambling to understand them. Part of me hoped it was just a case of mistaken identity, a mistyped number, but who'd ever heard of accidentally receiving a threat meant for someone else?

"Alright, boss?" said a voice, and I looked up to see Roman striding down the corridor towards me. A large, bald man, Roman always commanded the space. A great trait for our Head of Training who would often be in a room with a bunch of trainees. Even better when it came to demonstrating how to deal with rowdy club goers during an SIA training session.

"Yeah," I replied, plastering a smile on my face and tucking my phone back in my pocket. "Ready?"

He nodded and I opened the door.

The room was dominated by a large pine desk that could comfortably seat up to 12 people. We used it to brief larger teams, but we also hosted the majority of our client conversations in it. At one end of the desk sat Richard. Leaning back, with one ankle casually resting on his other knee, he was the picture of ease.

A few seats away sat a man and a woman, both dressed in stiff and uncomfortable-looking business attire. Most days I wore a shirt, but these two looked like they'd been starched to within an inch of their lives. They sat ramrod straight, not touching the table, and their eyes snapped to me and Roman as we entered.

"Sorry to keep you waiting. I was just finishing up another meeting," I said as I entered.

"Not a problem," said the woman, giving me a tight and painful-looking smile. "We were a little early."

The atmosphere in the room felt odd. I couldn't tell if it was down to whatever Richard may or may not have said, or if it was something else entirely.

"Jason Hunter." I leaned across the table and offered a hand.

They both looked at it for half a second before the woman took it.

"Serina Walton," she said and shook my hand. "And this is my brother, Chay Walton."

Chay reached across the table and we also shook hands.

I sat down opposite them.

"You've already met my colleague, Richard," I said, gesturing in Richard's direction. "And this is our Head of Training, Roman West."

Roman leaned across to shake hands. "Great to meet you," he said.

"Yes," said Serina. I glanced at Chay, unsure why he wasn't saying anything.

"So," I said, playing for time. I opened my leather folder and pulled out my notes. "You're looking for security training. Tell me more." I leaned back and casually clasped my hands together, elbows resting on the arms of my chair.

"Yes," said Serina. "We own FixRecruitment. An agency that helps hire that hard-to-find talent. We've recently branched out into security. Mostly for retail establishments, night clubs, that sort of thing. One of the concerns our clients have brought to our attention is ongoing training."

I nodded. How did I feel working with someone who was essentially our competition? While placing ad hoc security guards into different locations wasn't exactly something we did often, it was definitely more of our remit then theirs. Training them to offer it would strip us of the opportunity for larger contracts, providing a complete security package for premises.

But right now, we couldn't afford to turn the work away.

"You're listed as an SIA training provider so I was hoping you would be able to provide our hires with the appropriate training to obtain their SIA licence if they don't already have it. And some of our clients have requested additional ongoing training."

While we were listed on the Security Industry Authority's website as a training provider, we hadn't provided that as a service to anyone outside of our own company. It was always internal training, but I didn't see any reason why we should turn down the request. After all, it would be a way to recoup some of our recent losses, especially as an ongoing contract.

"Of course, we'd be willing to pay the appropriate rate, as well as a percentage commission on every successful placement."

I raised an eyebrow at this. It was certainly unexpected, and made me think her appropriate rate would be very different to mine. But maybe we could meet in the middle somewhere and an additional commission on top would help improve cash flow.

"Do you have an estimate on how many new hires we'd be training on a monthly basis?" I asked.

"Somewhere in the region of 50 to 100. I'd estimate 20 to 50 applying for new licences and the remainder would be getting a refresher," said Chay.

So he could speak.

"That's a lot of people," said Roman, surprised.

"We're quite a big agency," said Serina. "With multiple branches across London, Surrey, Essex and Hertfordshire."

"Apologies. When you said you've only recently branched into security, I expected a smaller number," said Roman.

"50 to 100 a month is quite a commitment. Is this how many you're currently placing? Or is this a forecast?" I asked, trying to get a better handle on their thinking.

"It's a forecast," said Serina. "We're currently placing around 30 to 50 a month. This includes our temp contracts. But the interest from clients is growing fast. We want a security training program in place as soon as possible."

I nodded. "I don't see that being a problem." I looked across to Richard who had been surprisingly quiet so far.

"Sounds good to me," he said.

I turned to Roman. "In that case, it'll be down to you."

Roman nodded. "I'll need a list of your locations as these training sessions will need to be carried out in person. And I'll be able to pull together a preliminary training schedule."

"Of course." Serina nodded.

We ran through a few more details, including the terms of the contract, before Serina and Chay said their goodbyes and left. Richard escorted them to the elevators and then returned to the boardroom where me and Roman were discussing costs.

"Was it just me, or did they give off a weird vibe?" asked Richard.

"Very weird," I said.

Chapter 19

STACEY JAMES

IN THE SKY

Thursday 7ᵗʰ October

"You could have just paid for first class," said Sam, trying to read his book. Stacey's knee jiggling up and down was distracting him.

"I don't like drawing attention to myself," she replied.

"Because sitting at the back of economy wearing a baseball cap and sunglasses is much less conspicuous," he said, smirking.

She punched him in the arm.

"I just feel on edge," she said tensely.

"I'd never have guessed."

"I thought you were reading your book?" she asked, turning to face him.

"I am," he said, still smiling. She knew full well he hadn't read a single word for the entire flight so far. But she almost couldn't help the jitteriness she felt. What was wrong with her? She'd raced in hundreds of races. Travelled to countless countries. This was no different.

Mickey.

Of course, she didn't normally race just days after her boyfriend's ex-wife's husband was murdered.

She let out a whoosh of breath and forced her shoulders to relax.

"Excuse me," she said, leaning across Sam to catch the attention of a passing air steward.

"How can I help?" he asked with a smile, half bending so he could hear her better.

"Could I get a drink, please?" she asked in an almost-whisper.

"Of course. What can I get you?"

"Vodka Coke, please. A double."

"I'll just be a minute." The air steward straightened and disappeared behind the partition just behind their seats.

"Is that a good idea?" asked Sam.

"Oh yes, trust me."

"Whatever you say, boss."

Stacey caught the eye of the two guys in their mid-twenties in the seats opposite. They were whispering to each other and shooting furtive glances her way.

"Ah, shit," she muttered.

"Told you," mumbled Sam. "Also, being at the back of the plane means you're closer to the toilets and therefore you get more foot traffic going past."

"Well, I didn't know that, did I?" she grumbled.

Sam tried not to smile. "Of course not. Just something to remember for next time."

Stacey folded her arms and looked out the window.

The air steward returned a few minutes later with two miniature bottles of Smirnoff vodka, a can of Coke and a plastic cup.

"Thank you," she said, fumbling with the clasp of her tray.

Sam placed his book in the pouch hanging from the chair in front and took the proffered goods from the air steward. He stood the drinks up on Stacey's tray one by one and then held out the cup.

She twisted the lid off the first vodka and downed it in one.

"I thought you wanted it with a Coke," asked Sam, his eyebrows shooting up in surprise.

"I do." She opened the second vodka and downed that in one as well.

"Steady now," said Sam, concern lacing his voice.

Stacey exhaled a deep breath and opened the can of Coke, taking a sip before putting it down.

"Honestly, I'm fine," she said, taking another deep breath. The burn of the alcohol instantly made her feel better and she relaxed into her seat, closing her eyes.

The plane touched down an hour later and Stacey insisted they wait to be the last ones off.

"Is there something I need to know?" asked Sam.

"No. I just don't want any fanfare."

They said their goodbyes to the staff as they left the plane and made their way to passport control, and on to baggage claim.

Sam grabbed Stacey's bag from the carousel and they headed out into departures.

The moment they stepped foot into the arrivals hall, there was an eruption of noise. Stacey was bombarded by fans, cameras and journalists who all started shouting at once. The throng of bodies crushed closer and Stacey smiled. She removed the shades she'd been wearing since Gatwick and waved. Sam pushed through the crowd, carving a path for her to follow. She stopped for a few selfies and signed a few autographs, slowing their progress considerably.

Airport security, noticing the commotion, rushed forward and took control of the crowd, forcibly pushing them back when they wouldn't listen.

Eventually, they emerged on the other side and out into the warm evening air.

Sam hailed a taxi and they headed to the hotel.

Chapter 20

STACEY JAMES

SWISSÔTEL THE BOSPHORUS

Thursday 7th October

"Tell me you're joking," said Stacey. She walked from the bedroom into the sitting room where Sam sat on the single-seater sofa, his back to the floor-to-ceiling glass doors that led out onto the balcony.

He looked up from the book he was actually reading this time, his expression alert.

"Listen to this," she said and held the phone out, face up. "You're on speaker."

"Hi Sam," said Jason, his voice slightly tinny as it came through the iPhone speakers.

"Hi boss. What's up?" he asked as he got to his feet and stepped around the glass-topped walnut coffee table so he could better hear the reply.

There was a moment's pause.

"Mickey Bianchi isn't a real person."

Sam's eyes widened and he looked up at Stacey.

"What do you mean he isn't real?" asked Sam, a frown creasing his forehead.

"Don't breathe a word of this to Hayley or she'll skin me alive. But Mickey's fingerprints didn't come up with a match. So the system thinks he's a John Doe. Except the guy has prison tattoos so there should be a match."

"Has he changed his name or something?" asked Stacey.

"No idea. Hayley thinks someone's tampered with the records. As far as the systems go, Mickey Bianchi doesn't exist."

Sam rubbed the bottom half of his face. "Well, shit."

"Tell me about it."

"What do we do now?" asked Stacey.

"You need to race. Get your head in the right space and knock it out the park. Show them what you're made of," said Jason.

Stacey smiled.

"How was the flight?" he asked.

Sam opened his mouth to reply but Stacey silenced him with a glare. "All good," she said, sounding a lot more upbeat than she felt. "Give the kids a hug for me and I'll speak to you later."

"Will do."

She cut the call and pocketed her phone.

"Why'd you lie to him?" asked Sam.

"He has enough to worry about as it is. I don't want to add to that."

Sam nodded his understanding before bending down to retrieve his book.

"Do you want to get outta here?" she asked.

"And go where?"

She shrugged. "I don't know. I just feel like I need to de-stress."

"Sure," said Sam. "Why don't we go sightseeing?"

"I know you're not being serious."

It was Sam's turn to shrug. "Might as well. We could do one of those hop-on, hop-off buses," he said. "I'm pretty sure they're still running."

"It's 9 o'clock at night," she said, laughing.

"Maybe a boat ride then?"

She laughed harder. "You're a dark horse, you know that, right?"

"Women love a mysterious man," he said with a wink.

"If you say so," she said, still laughing as she grabbed her denim jacket.

Chapter 21

JASON HUNTER

THE OFFICE

Thursday 7ᵗʰ October

I knew she was lying. Her answer was far too quick and she'd ended the call too abruptly. I also knew she'd tell me if it was anything serious, so I just put it down to race nerves. She hadn't been the same since Liam and I felt truly guilty for that.

It wasn't like it was my fault *per se*. But I was at fault. I'd been unable to keep her safe. I'd been unable to sniff out the rat right under my nose. And that stung. No wonder our clients were giving us a wide berth. I couldn't blame them. I'd do the same if I was in their shoes.

She'd come so close to dying. Even after I'd dragged her from the wrecked Lamborghini, it wasn't a guarantee that she'd live. She'd spent a week in hospital, and for a while it felt like her racing career might be over.

And now, she was struggling to race because of it. The sassy, badass Stacey I knew was still in there but she was hiding inside this fragile shell of a person. She was almost unrecognisable sometimes.

I stood by the wall of windows facing out onto the London skyline. Below me the street bustled. The iconic red buses pulled up at the bus stop opposite, waited for their passengers to get on and off before pulling away from the curb.

And here I was again. Another murder. It didn't feel like the blood was on my hands this time, but I still felt useless. I'd meant to ask Hayley about the CCTV.

I was still struggling to get my head around the whole Mickey thing. No, I wasn't going to speak to Adrianna on Hayley's behalf. She was the cop, she could do that herself. But I did intend to speak to Adrianna about Mickey's real identity. I was sure she didn't know anything about it, but these days I never really felt sure about anything. Assumptions are what had caused everything to go so drastically wrong with Gemma and Stacey last year.

But there was something that kept cropping up: Cameron. A name that was almost meaningless, and yet, somehow tied everything together.

It seemed both Mickey and Cameron didn't exist. But they did. How were they both so allusive?

My thoughts drifted back to the text I'd received yesterday. The threat had been clear. But how was I meant to return what I didn't have?

Is that what this was all about? Had Mickey taken something he wasn't meant to? And whoever had been looking for it at the apartment now thought I had it? More importantly, were they watching me now?

I shuddered, turned away from the window and glanced at my watch. It was nearly 5 o'clock which meant the after school clubs would be over and the kids would be on their way home. I started tidying up and shut down my laptop when a knock at the door interrupted me.

I looked up to see Divya enter. "Sorry, am I interrupting?" she asked.

"I'm about to head home on Dad duty," I said. "But I can spare five, what's up?"

"Just thought I'd let you know that I'm making some headway with recruiting. We've had a surprising amount of interest so far."

"Good news."

"Did you want to sit in on the interviews?"

"If I can, that would be great."

"Of course. I'll start scheduling them for next week then."

"Brilliant," I said. "Good work on turning this around so quickly."

Divya gave me a smile before leaving.

One last glance across my desk confirmed I had everything I needed to work from home for the evening. Before leaving, I reached into my drawer and pulled out the hidden mobile. Turning it on, a message popped up on screen.

Safe.

It was the first time I'd ever had a reply and I wondered what that meant, if anything. I returned the phone to its secret location and exited my office. I said goodnight to Lucy and headed home.

Chapter 22

JASON HUNTER

HOME

Thursday 7th October

"Mummy!"

I poked my head into the hallway to see Lily throw herself at Adrianna, who currently stood in my doorway dressed in a pair of skintight jeans and a casual hoody, her usual glam look still absent.

Max came shooting out of the living room behind me to join in. I'd never seen the boy move so fast. It was clear the kids had missed her.

"Adrianna," I said, stepping into the hallway. "You should have said you were coming over. I could have made dinner."

"Oh no," she said. "I didn't want to make a fuss." She was talking to me but her eyes didn't leave the kids. She cupped a hand on Lily's cheek while her other arm was wrapped around Max. For a brief moment, she looked happy.

"Why don't you guys let your mum through the door, eh? The temperature in here is dropping by the second." I mock shivered and Lily giggled, over the moon that she'd been reunited with her mum. The three of them shuffled down the hallway and into the living room, still not letting go of each other.

"I'll close the door then," I mumbled under my breath. I shut the front door but not before glancing down the street, then joined them in the living room. Adrianna was sitting on the sofa, Lily curled up next to her and Max on the floor, reunited with his PlayStation controller.

Adrianna looked so much more relaxed than when I'd seen her last, but she still looked like she'd aged ten years. She was still free of makeup and jewellery. And it was weird seeing her without it; I was so used to the occasional blinding reflection when a ring or an earring caught the light. She'd laugh, turn her head and then suddenly a reflective glare would catch you off guard. But not today. Although she'd upgraded from the sweats, this was still the grieving Adrianna I'd seen on Monday.

The rest of the evening passed by contentedly. The kids soaked up every second of having their mum back, while Adrianna seemed to become more herself the longer she was here.

I let her put them to bed, guessing the normalcy was what she needed right now and slipped a couple of frozen pizzas into the oven.

She reappeared just as I was plating up the pizzas.

"What's this?" she asked.

"I'm hungry, and figured you could do with something to eat too. No pressure, it's a help-yourself situation, but it's there if you want it," I said, setting a couple of plates on the kitchen island. "Wine?" I asked.

She nodded, so I pulled a bottle from the rack under the island counter and twisted it open. Perching on one of the stools, she took a glass and swallowed a gulp of the rich, red liquid.

"Kids okay?"

She nodded. "If you don't mind having them tonight, they can come stay at Imani's with me tomorrow after school."

"Sure," I said. "Have they told you when you can go back into the apartment?"

She shook her head. "I think it'll be a while yet."

We fell silent.

"Adrianna," I said cautiously. "I need to ask you something." She paused with her wine glass halfway to her lips. Neither of us had touched the pizza yet. "I'm not sure how to ask it really."

She frowned at me, her eyes narrowing. "Spit it out, Jason."

"Who's Mickey?"

"What do you mean 'who's Mickey'?"

"Who is he? Cause Mickey Bianchi isn't real."

"Of course he is. I married him."

I held her gaze.

"Except that's not his real name, is it?"

"What are you talking about?" she asked, lowering the glass.

I could sense she was starting to get frustrated with me. My stomach sank.

"You knew."

"Knew what?" Now she was exasperated, and I knew I was right.

"Fucking hell, Adrianna. Did you think the cops wouldn't notice?"

"What are you talking about, Jason?"

"You know damn well what I'm talking about. Mickey Bianchi isn't a real person. He never was. It was a fake identity. My question is; did he tell you before or after you married him?" I paused to let her reply but she said nothing. "Well?" I prompted.

"I guess I am feeling peckish, after all," she said, helping herself to a slice of pizza and avoiding my question.

I let out a groan of frustration.

"Alright, alright," she said. "Yes, I knew."

"And you didn't think to tell me?"

"What was I supposed to say?" she shrugged.

"You've made me look like a fucking idiot," I said, straining to keep my voice under control. The last thing I needed was for the kids to hear us arguing.

"No, I haven't," she said, her own temper starting to flare.

And suddenly I remembered why we'd gotten divorced. We were just incompatible. I had too many memories of us arguing in the kitchen, in the living room, in the car. The woman drove me fucking mad. And not in a good way.

"I asked you outright what was going on. What you knew. And you flat-out lied to my face."

"What was I meant to do, Jason? Yes, by the way, my husband has been living under a fake identity for the last twenty years. That would have been a great bombshell to drop."

"It was going to come out sooner or later. Did you think the police just wouldn't notice?"

"I didn't know what to do. I'm scared, Jason. Absolutely terrified. My husband is dead. My kids need me to be strong for them but I'm literally drowning in grief. The last thing I needed was to open that can of worms. I was just hoping I could catch my breath before I had to get into it all."

I walked into the living room. I just needed to get away from her for a moment. To regain my composure and process this rationally. I dragged a hand down my face and forced myself to take a couple of deep breaths before re-entering the kitchen.

I downed the rest of my wine, reached into the cupboard under the kitchen island and pulled out a bottle of vodka. I found a couple of shot glasses in the back of the mug cupboard and poured us both a shot.

Adrianna took hers without speaking and downed it in one. I did the same, slamming the empty glass upside down on the countertop.

"Let's start again," I said as calmly as I could muster. "And from the beginning."

Adrianna gestured to the bottle of vodka and I gave her a refill. She downed the second shot and winced.

"No, I didn't know when we got married," she said. "I actually didn't know until fairly recently."

"How recently?"

"July? August, maybe. When he started acting weird. I confronted him. Told him I knew something was going on. He tried fobbing me off with some lame excuse, but I knew he was bullshitting. I called him out on it. And that's when he told me."

"So who is he?"

"His real name is Sonny Serrano."

I almost laughed. "Is he a wannabe gangster?"

"This isn't funny," said Adrianna with a scowl.

"Sorry." I held up a placating hand. "So why the name change?"

"He told me he changed it when he turned 18. He'd gotten into a bit of trouble as a teen. Got involved in gangs and the like. He wanted to get away from that life. Have a fresh start."

"Except, he wasn't exactly law-abiding nowadays either."

"What do you mean?"

"Well, why else would he be acting so shifty recently?"

"He said he had something that belonged to some really angry people. Angry and powerful people. They were chasing his original name but he knew it would only be a matter of time before they worked out who he was."

"So he knew someone was after him and yet he didn't think you and the kids should go somewhere safe?"

"He thought that would tip them off. He was worried they were watching him. Listening to his conversations. He didn't want them to think he had anything to hide. He told me to just act as though everything was normal."

"For Christ's sake, Adrianna. Do you not think you should have spoken to me? I work in security! I could have done something to help."

"Like how you helped Stacey?"

Her words felt like a slap across the face.

"I'm sorry, I didn't mean that," she said quickly.

"Yes, you did."

"No, Jason, I'm sorry. I—"

"Just tell me what else he told you," I said, resigned.

"He said if anything was to happen to him, then I was to call Cameron. Cameron would know what to do."

"So you have his number?"

"I do, but it doesn't work."

"What do you mean it doesn't work?"

"Whenever I try calling the number, it tells me it's not a valid number."

"Have you got the number on you?"

"It's in my bag." She climbed off the stool and disappeared into the living room. I hung my head in my hands. My mind was spinning. Just this morning Hayley was telling me that Mickey wasn't who he said he was, and it turns out Adrianna had known all along. Hayley had said she did. I made a mental note to never doubt her instincts again.

I ached to hold Stacey. It had been hard letting her get back to racing this season. We were almost inseparable when she was home. But with everything that was going on, I felt her absence more than usual.

"Here," said Adrianna, reappearing in the kitchen with a crumpled sticky note. She handed it to me and I read the number: 07790653770

"And when you dial it, it doesn't work?"

She shook her head. "It just says that it doesn't exist."

I frowned. "So why has he given you a dud number? I assume that wasn't his intention."

She shrugged. "Maybe he wrote it down wrong. Maybe I can't read his writing as well as I thought. I don't know, Jason," she said, sounding defeated. "I've asked myself the same thing over and over again. It feels like a cruel joke."

"I don't think that's the case. He clearly loved you."

"And what gives you that idea?"

"Whether he was feeling threatened or not, he wouldn't just tell anyone about his identity. And he clearly wanted you to be safe, or he wouldn't have given you Cameron's number."

She didn't answer, just looked down at the eleven digits.

"I really miss him, Jason."

"I know you do," I said, and pulled her into a hug. She sank into me and let out a small sob.

"Will it ever become bearable?"

"Of course it will," I said, stroking her hair. "You just need to give yourself time. It's only been a few days. You're only just getting over the shock of it."

She pulled away but kept her arms wrapped around me, our faces just inches apart.

"Thank you," she whispered. She leaned up on tiptoes just as I moved my face to the right. Her kiss landed on the stubble on my cheek.

"Hey now," I said, gently disentangling her from me. "None of that."

She turned away from me, a bright blush creeping up her neck and cheeks. "I'm sorry," she said, burying her face in her hands. "I don't know why I did that."

"I do. You're overwhelmed and confused, and you need comfort. Go home to Imani's and drink some wine."

She nodded and went into the living room to retrieve her bag.

"Can we please forget this ever happened?" she asked as she made her way to the front door.

"I don't know what you're talking about," I said with a smile.

She didn't look at me, just quickly left, closing the door behind her.

I let out a long sigh and walked back into the kitchen where the pizza was going cold next to the crumpled sticky note that had been pressed flat on the kitchen counter.

Chapter 23

JASON HUNTER

THE OFFICE

Friday 8th October

Zack sat back, looking pleased with himself.

"What do you think?" he asked after a beat. He glanced around at the other members of the marketing team, suddenly looking anxious about my answer.

I slowly nodded my head.

He'd given me a first look at the brand concept he was working with. It was a complete overhaul of our current brand which is exactly what we needed.

"I like it," I said. "It's fresh, different. It avoids the overly corporate feel most of our competitors go for but still retains our authority."

"Exactly," he said, animated. I'd clearly said the right thing.

"Good work," I said, getting to my feet. He was beaming as I left the boardroom. It seemed the business was finally turning a corner. And yet, my personal life felt like it was derailing, and fast.

I knew Adrianna would have instantly regretted trying to kiss me last night. Her head wasn't in the right space and she was just looking for comfort. I knew that. But it made me feel all sorts of complicated feelings. Made worse by Stacey's absence. God, I missed her.

I walked into my office and stopped. Pulling my phone from my pocket, I quickly sent her a text, wishing her luck for today's practice sessions. Then I turned around and headed for the door.

"I'll be back this afternoon," I said to Lucy as I went past her desk.

She looked up at me with raised eyebrows. "Do I need to hold calls? Or forward them?"

"Take a message for the moment, please."

She nodded and watched me leave.

I couldn't face sitting in my office any longer. The memories of the night before were circling around in my head, and I desperately needed a distraction. What's more, I really needed to feel like we were making progress with Mickey's murder. I'd yet to speak to Hayley about what I'd learned. I'd been meaning to call her all morning but things just kept getting in the way. But if I was being honest, I knew that I was putting it off.

Climbing into my old BMW, I started the engine and exited the car park that sat under our office block, ducking through traffic into Soho. Parking was a nightmare, but I finally managed to squeeze into a spot, grumbling in frustration.

I looked up and down the street to get my bearings and then headed north towards Oxford Circus. Dodging shoppers, I turned down a narrow side alley between Calvin Klein and Reiss. Emerging from the other end, I was thrust into the very heart of Soho. Boutique shops and eateries lined the narrow side street. It was quieter than the main shopping streets but still bustling. Turning left, I passed a traditional English pub where people milled about outside, enjoying the crisp autumn sunshine while it was still pleasant. On the corner was an up-scale cocktail bar, and I turned right.

I came to a stop outside an inconspicuous black door. It definitely didn't look like the right place but my map app told me this was it.

There was no signage, no indication of what I'd find inside, just a single large brass door knocker in the shape of a dolphin's head. Looking up, I saw a camera watching me, its little red eye blinking steadily.

Casting a quick glance up and down the street, I stepped forward and lifted the knocker. It thudded against the black wooden door and I waited. When nothing happened, I raised my hand to knock again just as the door opened. A tall security guard filled the doorway. He crossed his arms over his thick barrel chest and stared down at me.

"I'm here to see Cameron."

"Do you have an appointment?" he asked, an unmistakable Jamaican accent coming through.

"I have a number." I held up the sticky note Adrianna had left.

The guard eyed me for a moment before stepping aside and indicating I should enter. I stepped inside and the door closed behind me, plunging us into darkness. As my eyes adjusted to the dim lighting, the guard turned around and headed up a flight of stairs covered in thick red carpet. At the top, we emerged into a huge, cavernous room that must have been at least two storeys high, and much better lit than the stairway.

"Wait here," said the guard. "I'll see if Cameron is in."

I did as I was told and looked around. At the far end was an empty DJ booth, elevated on a platform between two floor-to-ceiling statues. The one on the right was a bearded man with cloth draped over one shoulder and wrapped around his waist, leaving his torso mostly exposed. His right hand was clutching the cloth at his hip while the other was raised above his head, holding a bolt of lightning.

The statue on the left was also a bearded man, with a cloth wrapped around his waist, leaving his torso completely free. From where I stood, one hand was partially hidden behind the rest of the statue while the other was holding a three-pronged trident. Billowing fabric hung from the ceiling in waves. Marble columns divided the room into different areas and smaller statues were placed on plinths around the edge.

It was an impressive space. I could only imagine how it felt when the lights went off, the music started and the space was filled with hundreds of bodies moving together on the dancefloor.

Glancing past the marble columns, I could see that the very edges of the room were taken up by small booths, each with its own archway entrance. The VIP areas, I guessed. More fabric hung from the arches, affording the club's VIPs with their necessary privacy.

The security guard reappeared on the other side of the dancefloor and strode towards me. I watched him approach, trying to gauge what would happen next.

"Cameron isn't in today," he said as soon as he was close.

"Do you know when he will be?" I asked. "It's urgent," I added.

The guard shrugged. "How am I supposed to know?"

I gave him a tight smile. "Good point." I turned around and started for the stairs. After a few paces, I stopped and dug around in the pocket of my coat. "Perhaps you could leave my business card on his desk or something?" I said to the guard, holding out the small bit of card with my details on it. I made a mental note to get Zack to print some more once we'd finalised the new branding.

The guard hesitated before taking the offered card and sliding it into his pocket.

I thanked him and left.

Chapter 24

JASON HUNTER

HAMMERSMITH POLICE STATION

Friday 8th October

"And you left without causing a scene? Who'd have thought," teased Hayley, who was leaning back in her chair, her feet propped up on the edge of her desk and crossed at the ankle.

I rolled my eyes. "I can be civilised," I said.

"Doesn't give us much to work with though, does it?" she said.

"No," I admitted.

She looked thoughtful and began chewing on the end of her pen. I weighed up whether I should tell her about Adrianna knowing Mickey's real name or not. It could be valuable information, but then it could also land Adrianna in the shit and that was something I really didn't want.

"Any progress on identifying Mickey?" I asked.

"Actually, yes," she said, her attention flicking back to me.

I raised an eyebrow, half dreading what would come next.

"I had a chat with your ex-wife this morning. She had a lot to tell me."

"Oh, really?"

"Don't pretend you don't know," she said, dropping her feet to the floor and sitting up straighter. "I know she told you."

I let out a breath, looking sheepish.

"I wasn't sure how to tell you."

Hayley rolled her eyes.

"No, seriously. I didn't want to get Adrianna into trouble. She's going through a lot at the moment." My thoughts flickered back to the attempted kiss.

"I'm not unsympathetic," she said, and it was my turn to raise an eyebrow. She swatted her hand in the air. "I'm not."

"I believe you," I said.

"Well, tell that to your face. Anyway, she told me about the mobile number. Said you had it?"

I nodded and pulled the crumpled sticky note from my pocket.

"I really wish you wouldn't handle evidence," she said as she pulled out an evidence bag and held it up so I could drop the note into it.

"I didn't think."

"Of course you didn't. Have you tried calling the number?" She sealed the bag, laid it flat on the table and took a photo of it.

I shook my head. "I figured heading to the club would be more likely to get me somewhere." Except it hadn't.

Hayley nodded her head, not looking at me.

"So, what now?"

She looked at me for a long time before answering. "There's a lot more to this murder than first meets the eye."

"Tell me you didn't?" I said, a smile pulling at the corner of my mouth. Hayley was nothing if not diligent, detailed and thorough. She liked to be able to see all the pieces of the puzzle in one place so her brain could do the hard work and piece it all together. And that meant she was heavily into mind maps. The kind that spanned three different corkboards and had endless bits of string connecting all the random moving parts.

She rolled her eyes at me again before getting to her feet. "Come on," she sighed, reluctance heavy in her voice.

I followed her out of the cramped office and down the corridor. The police station was alive with activity, and several officers nodded their hellos in Hayley's direction as she passed. We entered an open plan space filled with the sound of telephones ringing, voices talking, and the clacking of keyboards.

"Webb," Hayley yelled without slowing her steps. She continued past the open plan office and further down the corridor. I looked over my shoulder at the sound of scurrying steps to see the young cop from the murder scene following us. He gave me a small smile as a hello just as Hayley pulled open a door on our right and stepped in.

We stood in a boardroom. Memories of being cooped up in here with Hayley for hours on end, trawling through all of the information we had on Stacey's competitors, flooded my mind.

Hayley picked up the remote from the middle of the oversized table, pressing the button and waiting as the projector above my head whirred to life.

"What? No corkboard? Where's all the string and drawing pins?" I asked.

Hayley laughed and pulled the blinds so we had complete privacy.

"Welcome to the 21st century," she said as the computer screen loaded on the whiteboard at the other end of the room. "Take a seat," she said, gesturing to the chairs. I did as I was told while Webb hovered by the computer tucked into the corner of the room.

Hayley sat down next to me and Webb loaded an interactive spider diagram onto the screen in front of us. In the middle was Mickey Bianchi's face. There were branches everywhere linking to the toxicology report, fingerprints, murder weapon, motive, suspects, acquaintances, and evidence. Most of the branches ended at a question mark, but others branched out further. The evidence branch held the most detail, listing fibres, DNA, CCTV cameras (hotel and street), footprints, and more. But even most of these still had question marks next to them.

"Still got a lot to fill out then?" I said, noting how empty the screen looked.

One of the branches detailed identity, and 'Sony Serrano' had been added. Under the suspects branch, I noticed Adrianna's name. The only name.

"You can't—"

"No, I don't," said Hayley, before I could finish. "But she has to be listed there for the moment."

I nodded, understanding what she meant. While Hayley knew Adrianna hadn't done it, she couldn't be ruled out completely right now, especially not when she'd already lied to the police once.

I took a few more minutes to absorb everything on the board in front of me.

"Add 'Club Dionysus' next to Cameron, please," said Hayley. Webb's fingers flew over the keys. She pulled out her mobile, tapped the screen and a little notification popped up in the corner of the board in front of us. Webb opened it and dragged the image of the mobile number to sit under Cameron's name too.

"I've just remembered something," I said, suddenly remembering my conversation with Stacey.

"What?"

"Stacey said her therapist knew Mickey."

"Right..."

"Like she was surprised when Stacey mentioned he'd died. She seemed to know who he was and it kinda shocked her."

"The therapist or Stacey?"

"The therapist."

"Hmmm. What's the therapist's name?"

"Professor Lindberg."

Webb made a note and the name appeared on the screen under 'acquaintances'.

"Shouldn't there be a longer list of people there?" I asked, pointing up at the board.

"Yep," said Hayley. "When I say this guy kept a low profile, I mean it."

We sat in silence again.

"CCTV?" I asked, pointing over to the other side of the board.

Webb zoomed in and double clicked. A collection of photos exploded onto the screen.

"Uniforms have combed through everything from the building's surveillance as well as anything given up by local businesses or nearby homes with those fancy Ring doorbells. We've narrowed the window to a half hour slot, and focused on only those who came and went during that time frame—"

"Ruling out a two-man team?"

"Not completely, just focusing our efforts for the moment. This guy," she pointed to the board, "is seen both entering and exiting the apartment block during the timeframe. He's carrying a BattlePouch rucksack. Heard of them?"

I shook my head.

"They're American. They make rucksacks that carry hunting rifles. The target audience is mostly deer hunters in the US. But their bags are custom-made. They're made to the specs of the customer."

My eyes widened at what she was saying.

"So, you mean to say—"

"This guy would have made a specific request for this particular rucksack. Which means he might be identifiable. But it also tells us that it's likely he's carrying a rifle in it. Dismantled, of course."

"Of course," I muttered. I looked up at the grainy images of a tall guy, dressed all in black. "Have we been able to get spec on him?"

Hayley hesitated before she answered. "Specs match Budapest."

"Fuck," I whispered. "So this could be the same guy who killed Gemma?"

She nodded. "It's likely."

Chapter 25

STACEY JAMES

TURKISH GRAND PRIX

Sunday 10th October

The engine thrummed under her fingers. She could feel the vibration of the car beneath her. Her headset crackled as the team ran through final checks.

Her body was tense and ready. She gripped the steering wheel and let out a steadying breath. The noise of the crowd was a distant roar, drowned out by the growing hum of the engine as she gently pressed on the accelerator.

All weekend she'd felt this pent-up anxiety. It had fuelled her, allowed her to unleash a new kind of aggression on the track. One that gave her a competitive edge. It was as refreshing as it was exhausting. For the first time in a long time, she felt confident. Confident that she was going to win. Confident that first place would be hers. Those championship points were screaming her name.

A light drizzle began to fall, specks of it landing on her visor. She took another breath, the sound loud in her ears. Words of encouragement from her team manager crackled in the headset.

The lights began their countdown. The five-second warning lights lit up. Then the four-second lights. Then three. Two. One. All five went dark and everyone moved at once. It felt slow at first, like they were wading through treacle, but then the cars moved faster. She weaved left, then right, accelerating faster than the car in front. She didn't care to note who, it didn't matter.

She overtook one car, then another just before she rounded the first corner.

Every bump, every turn, every minute change to the road surface reverberated through the car and made her feel at one with the powerful machine at her fingertips. Her mind emptied of all the stress and worry that plagued her on a daily basis. Instead, all she could see was the tarmac, the upcoming turns in the track, and the car in front of her.

She relaxed into the race, embracing the skill it took to navigate around the competition and almost smiled. She overtook another driver and leaned into the next turn. Her heart was still pounding but it was a rhythm she was familiar with. An adrenaline rush she knew all too well.

She was a woman in a man's world. And she was born to race.

Chapter 26

JASON HUNTER

HOME

Sunday 10th October

Max was bouncing on the edge of the sofa. For the last hour and a half, we'd watched Stacey complete lap after lap of the Turkish circuit.

Aldric St Pierre had been taken out of the running after a malfunction with his car. Héctor Sanchez and Harri Linna had wiped out on their 23rd lap now that the track was wet. And Ottokar Keil was still in first, with Stacey tailing him pretty closely.

She was gaining ground with every lap, but she was running out of time. With just four laps left, she needed an edge. She needed to get in front of him and protect her position. Right now, she was having to play offence and it was costing her precious milliseconds.

Max yelped as she gained on the next corner, only to have to brake for a split second too long. Her back end slipped ever so slightly and the tension in the commentator's voice told me this was just as dramatic for him as it was for us.

I couldn't stand it. My mouth had gone dry and my hands were clenched into fists.

She just needed an *edge*. If Keil would just make the tiniest slip-up, the smallest miscalculation, it would give her the chance she needed to slip in front. But was that really going to happen?

I'd promised Max we'd have a Formula One party, even though he was now back living with Adrianna. She didn't mind, and had said it gave her a chance to have some much needed one-on-one time with Lily.

What had started out as a casual day on the sofa with all the best snacks had fast descended into the most tense viewing party in history. It had been a thrilling race so far, and I just knew it wasn't over yet.

"Come on, baby," I muttered under my breath.

"She can do it, Dad. She can do it." The utter faith my boy had in her was brilliant to witness. She'd always been his favourite racer, way before I'd ever met her. Way before she'd ever needed my services.

Another lap went by and she'd shaved off another second. But it wasn't enough. Why wasn't it enough? She was pushing herself, I could feel it. But at the same time, she was holding back. She was waiting. Waiting for the perfect opportunity.

Two laps left and there it was. Keil had a habit of going tight on the second to last corner. She'd been watching him, I was sure of it. She'd been watching his driving pattern, looking for weaknesses.

He went tight, like he always did. And she went wide. She inched past him as the corner ended and accelerated onto the straight, over-taking him at the very last second.

Max cheered.

"What an overtake!" he yelled.

"One lap left. One lap left," I chanted. Just one lap. She just had to hold on to that lead for one more lap.

She crossed the finish line to cheers from the crowd.

Max launched himself off the sofa, yelling at the top of his lungs.

"Yes!" I yelled, jumping up. We both pumped our fists in the air. Relieved and thrilled that she had done it. First place. My heart was bursting with pride. I couldn't wait to see her.

Max turned and threw himself at me. I caught him mid-air and squeezed him tight.

"She did it!"

"Of course she did," he said. "She's the best driver there is."

Chapter 27

STACEY JAMES

TURKISH GRAND PRIX

Sunday 10th October

She pulled into the pit lane to see her whole team jumping in triumph and celebrating her victory. Undoing the too-tight harness, she hoisted herself out of the car, her arms feeling like jelly. She was exhausted but the adrenaline coursing through her was giving a new wave of energy she didn't know she had.

The thrill of the win had her grinning from ear to ear. She rushed over to her pit crew, accepting a volley of high-fives and back slaps over the barrier.

She spotted Aldric St Pierre weaving his way through the throng of bodies. The moment he was within reach, he swooped her up into a bear hug.

"What a win!" he yelled.

Pulling back, she flipped open her visor. She caught sight of her Sporting Director, Eden Schneider, pushing the celebrating mechanics, and he didn't look happy.

She pulled her helmet off, instantly enjoying the feel of the cool drizzle on her skin.

Plastering a smile on his face for the cameras, Eden put a hand out. As she shook it, he pulled her in close and said, "Reckless. But brilliantly done. Please don't scare me like that again."

She breathed out a sigh of relief.

"Sorry," she said with a half-smile. "Thought it was worth the risk."

"Next time, listen to the radio."

She smiled and nodded, knowing full well she wouldn't. Her team was brilliant and they meant well, but they couldn't see what was happening out on the track. They couldn't feel how the car manoeuvred beneath her, couldn't get a sense of how things would play out. The overtake might have looked dangerous from the outside, but in the moment she'd been confident that it would work, without putting her or Keil at risk. She'd heard her race engineer, Kyle, tell her not to, that second would be enough for this race. But she'd chosen to ignore him anyway. She'd known she could do it and she hadn't been wrong.

After her post-race weigh-in, Sam appeared at her side. Silent and solid. A warm hand on her back reminded her she was out in the open, in the middle of a crowd. While the old fear was no longer there, her wariness remained.

She scanned the faces around her and began to make her way through the crowd, Sam calmly and resolutely carving a path for her.

A figure approached, still clad in their driving suit and helmet. She recognised the sponsors plastered across the helmet as the figure undid the strap and removed it. Ottokar Keil was smiling. Stacey couldn't help but smile back.

"What?" she said with a laugh.

He held out a hand. "I may have underestimated you, Stacey James."

She laughed and shook his hand. "Thanks, I think?"

"Never saw that coming. Thought I had you locked in second for the rest of the race."

"Well, that's what happens when you get comfortable."

He laughed. "Until next time," he said and turned away, still smiling, to head back to his own crew.

"Time to go," Sam murmured in her ear. She nodded her head and continued her way through the throng of bodies. From the corner of her eye, she saw a man standing a little apart from the others, a press badge hung around his neck. But he wasn't engaging in conversation with anyone. He was watching her. She locked eyes with him for a moment and he lifted a hand in a wave, a small smile on his lips.

"What—"

And then he was gone. A melee of bodies obstructed her view just for a second. She blinked and he'd disappeared. Almost as if he'd never been there in the first place. Did she imagine it?

In the conference room, holding a microphone, Stacey looked out at the reporters clamouring to have their voices heard. Faruk Kaya, the host, called for quiet.

"What a race," he said, with a strong Turkish accent. And there was a murmur of agreement through the room. "Ottoker, to have your lead taken from you at the very last moment, how do you feel?"

Keil smiled and lifted his microphone to his mouth. "Such a daring overtake, I'm happy to let Stacey have this one. She showed real skill out there on the track today and that's admirable."

"It was indeed daring. Stacey, we could hear your race engineer advising against the overtake, but you did it anyway. Why?"

She smiled and lifted her microphone. "I have a huge amount of respect for my engineers and my whole team. And yes, I did go against their advice out there today. Not something I usually do, I'd like to add. But in the moment I assessed whether there would be a risk to me or Keil. I'd followed his driving pattern for several laps, and was identifying any opportunities I could take advantage of. I saw one, and I took it. Had it felt like too much of a risk, I wouldn't have."

"Dare I say it," Faruk Kaya said. "But I believe Stacey James is back." There was a loud applause from the assembled reporters and that was when she saw him again. At the back. Lingering half in the shadows, not participating. He gave her a small nod of his head. Her breathing quickened and she didn't know if she was glad he was there, or if it meant something more sinister was about to happen. Was she in danger? Was there more going on than Jason had let on? Did Jason even know? He had to. She glanced at Sam, standing to one side. He frowned at her and she looked back towards where she'd seen him standing at the back, but he was gone.

She tuned back into the conversation.

"And Dima, only a few seconds behind Ottoker to the finish line. You must have witnessed Stacey's overtake. How did it look from behind?"

"It was certainly bold, that's for sure." The room laughed.

Stacey glanced at Dima Volkov from the corner of her eye. He was openly watching her, waiting for her reaction. She tried to ignore him, ignore the feelings his presence dredged up from the depths, but she couldn't dismiss the panic that crept into her chest. Her mind flashed back to last year. To gunshots in a soundproofed office. To dead bodies lying on the floor. And suddenly the room felt too hot, the walls felt like they were moving in. Was she having a panic attack?

She tried to concentrate on what was being said but she really couldn't.

"I'm going to open up to some questions. I can see a few keen faces in the audience."

Hands shot up into the air.

She looked at Faruk Kaya and tried to slow her breathing. She breathed in. Held it for a moment, and then breathed out again.

"Yes?" He pointed to a man in a navy suit in the second row.

She pushed thoughts of Volkov to the back of her mind. *Not now*, she told herself. She breathed in again, focusing on the reporter.

"Stacey, some might say your overtake was reckless. And recklessness costs lives. What's your response?"

She smiled graciously, trying not to let her irritation show. "There was nothing reckless about it. My overtake was a calculated manoeuvre. I took the risk to myself and my fellow drivers," she gestured to Keil and Volkov sat next to her, "into account before I executed the overtake."

"But—"

"Who's next?" asked Faruk Kaya.

"Yes?" He pointed to a brunette female in the first row wearing a tailored trouser suit.

"Stacey, you're paving the way for young girls who want to race. What do you say to that?"

"I think it's safe to say I've shown the world what women can do. Formula One is no longer a man's sport; we just need more women to take on the challenge. I have plans in place for how I can help with this."

She didn't know where the response had come from because she certainly didn't have any plans in place at the moment. But an idea had sparked in the back of her mind and suddenly she felt eager to see where it would go.

The rest of the press conference passed by in a blur before Faruk Kaya called an end to the questions and thanked the drivers for their time. Stacey stepped down from the platform and headed straight for Sam who guided her to her driver's room.

Once inside, a quiet calm descended.

"Bill is here," she said after a moment's breath.

"Cooper?" asked Sam.

The silence was almost deafening after the constant noise of the race and the media circus.

"So you didn't know?" she asked.

Sam frowned. "No."

Chapter 28

JASON HUNTER

HOME

Sunday 10th October

I heard the lock in the door and jumped up from the sofa. The front door opened just as I entered the hallway. I glanced upstairs, more out of habit than anything else, but the kids were with Adrianna and would be until their next visit. I'd waited up, and tracked Sam's live location from the moment he'd touched down and pinged it through to me. I was eager to see her. Maybe too eager. I hoped this wasn't a result of recent events. Was I being overprotective? Overbearing?

Stacey walked in, carrying her duffel bag over her shoulder. Sam followed, the expression on his face unreadable.

"Everything alright?" I had a weird feeling.

"Did you know?" she asked, glaring at me. This situation felt all too familiar and my mind flashed back to the time she'd stormed into my office after Gemma's death.

"Know what?" I asked, frowning.

"Bill. He was there. Did you know?"

I groaned inwardly. Why had he let her see him? What did he think that would achieve? The whole point of him tailing her was that he kept an eye on her from the shadows. Unseen. It had started when she'd insisted I reduce the number of people that accompanied her on race weekends. She said she was drawing too much attention, especially now that Liam was no longer an imminent threat – we hadn't heard from him since he'd disappeared on the night she'd crashed in the Lamborghini – and she didn't like to look weak.

Everywhere she went, I'd insisted she take multiple bodyguards, but it just wasn't necessary. And my overprotectiveness had been suffocating. So we'd reached a compromise. Sam would go with her. And only Sam. Except that that wasn't the case. Cooper had followed. I'd given him the details, sent him locations and he'd tailed her, made sure she was safe. I knew he had her best interests at heart, as much as I loathed him being around her. At least this way, I'd know where he was.

"He was just looking out for you."

She let out an exasperated sound and threw her hands up in the air.

"I'm gonna clock off now, boss," said Sam.

"Yes, of course. Go home. Enjoy a few days' rest."

He gave me a small nod and then lightly touched Stacey on the arm, a gesture I'd never seen from him before.

She stomped past me into the kitchen as Sam closed the front door behind him. I slid the bolt across and followed Stacey through the living room and into the kitchen.

"What the hell are you playing at?" she asked. Before I could answer, she continued, "He's a wanted man, Jason. Do you know how much trouble you could be in for just contacting him? Hayley would not take kindly to being lied to."

"I know, I know. When you wanted me to reduce the number of bodyguards you took with you on race weekends, I did. But it just didn't sit right with me. And if I've learnt anything from everything we've been through, it's to trust my instincts. I thought an extra pair of eyes on the lookout wouldn't hurt. He's good at what he does and nobody would know."

"How long has this been going on? This cosy operation of yours?"

"A few months." I paused. "How did you even find out?"

"He was standing at the back of my press conference with a journalist pass hanging around his neck," she said.

"Oh, for God's sake," I muttered. Silence filled the room. A heavy one laden with an unspoken argument. "I'm sorry. I really just wanted to keep you safe. I can't shake this feeling, and now with everything going on with Mickey, I feel like this is only the beginning."

She nodded. "I understand. I just wish you'd have told me."

"Would you have agreed?" I moved to stand behind her and wrapped my arms around her waist.

"No," she said and leaned into me.

"Exactly."

I held her, soaked in her smell, enjoyed her warmth. "You didn't even give me a chance to congratulate you," I said. She turned around in my arms, a huge smile on her face. "Eden wasn't overly happy with me. I mean, he was happy with the outcome, but not happy I'd gone against Kyle's advice. He's my race engineer."

"But it's just advice, right?"

"Kind of. I mean, you wouldn't turn left if your co-driver says right turn up ahead."

I chuckled. "Such a daredevil," I said, and leaned down and kissed her. She kissed me back and man she tasted good. I breathed her in, all of her, and relished being this close to her again. Her hand found its way to the back of my neck and held me there, pulling me impossibly closer. She pushed against me and I scooped her up, her legs wrapping around me. It felt like we'd been apart for weeks, not just a few days.

She pulled away from me, breathing hard, and asked, "Are the kids here?"

"No," I panted. "They went back to Adrianna."

"Good."

She wiggled free of my hold and I put her down. Taking my hand, she tugged me towards the door. We ran up the stairs, giggling like horny teenagers. By the time we reached the bedroom, we'd both stripped naked and fell onto the bed, kissing, tasting, exploring.

Chapter 29

JASON HUNTER

THE OFFICE

Monday 11th October

"You're late in today," said Lucy, watching me approach from across the room.

"Alright, Luce," I said, glancing around at our other employees. The main office floor was open plan and consisted of eight desks in total. Lucy's sat closest to my office door. The others were taken up with our tech guys and a few admins who helped out with paperwork, organising jobs and coordinating the teams.

"Let's not go broadcasting it."

She gave me a sly smile, picked up some papers on her desk and followed me into my office. Closing the door behind her, she leaned against one of the chairs that faced my desk. "Heavy night, was it?" she asked, almost unable to contain her laughter.

"Stacey got home last night."

"Oh I see," she said with a smirk.

"Get your mind out of the gutter, please."

"As if that's not what you've been up to."

I couldn't help the smile that spread over my face.

"Even so, I'd appreciate it if you didn't let all and sundry know. I've got a professional image to maintain now that I'm the boss."

"You've always been the boss," she said. "Adam wouldn't have been able to keep this place going without you. Funds and all."

I shrugged out of my coat and hung it up on the hook in the corner of my office. I knew what she was referring to. A few years ago, the company had some financial trouble. Adam had needed an investment partner, preferably a silent one, but before he'd openly advertised, I'd offered to give him the cash he needed in return for a stake in the business. I was happy for him to stay at the helm, but I would have more sway with the bigger decisions. I guessed it was this control that he resented me for.

I'd been able to keep the company on the straight and narrow ever since, kept it afloat and made the right decisions. But every time I'd voiced my opinion, controlled the direction, or exercised control in any way, I could see how much Adam hated me for it. I was a constant reminder that he was failing, and my interference wasn't welcome. It had been a difficult business relationship but we'd made it work as best we could. And now that he was dead, the business fell solely to me.

"What have you got for me?" I asked, changing the subject.

"Hayley called. Vance Cherry also called. And, believe it or not, Alik Gromov called."

"What did *he* want?" I asked, surprised.

"He wanted to talk about the opportunity to work together again."

"Is that what he's calling it?" I laughed. "We never worked together, I worked *for* him. Together implies there was something in it for me and there most definitely wasn't."

"I know, I know," she said, placatingly. "I'm just repeating what he said."

"Sorry," I held up a hand. It felt like I was saying sorry a lot at the moment.

She handed me some folders. "Here's the details of Iris Mccleary's tour, and the finalised contract ready for review."

"Excellent," I said, taking the folders. "Thanks Lucy."

"No problem. Give me a shout if you need anything," she said with a brief smile before leaving.

I dropped the folders on my desk and sat down behind it. Before I could do anything, I needed to phone Gromov and find out what the hell he was after.

He picked up on the second ring.

"Ah, Jason. I'm so glad you called," he said, his accent thick and heavy.

"I thought I made myself perfectly clear the last time we spoke?"

"Yes, yes you did. I still need a residential team, but that's not why I wanted to speak with you. Are you free for lunch?"

I sighed and tried to hold the frustration at bay. "Mr Gromov, whatever it is you want to say, you can do it over the phone."

"I would much prefer-"

"Alik," I said in a warning tone.

The line went silent and for a moment I wondered if we'd been cut off.

"I think we may be able to help each other." When I didn't reply, he continued, "I'm wondering if the name Sonny Serrano means any-thing to you?"

I felt my heart skip a beat at the sudden turn in direction.

"Should it?"

"Some... contacts of mine have been asking questions about a Son-ny Serrano. They seem to be under the impression that the two of you know each other. Especially as you were seen entering his club recently."

My mouth went dry at the implication.

"I don't know what you're talking about," I said.

"Come now, Jason. My contacts aren't known for their inaccurate information."

"I still don't know why you're telling me this."

"It was more to warn you. These contacts of mine are dangerous people, Jason. Something has been taken from them and they are very keen to get it back. Should it transpire that you have it, I can't guarantee you or your family would be safe."

"Are you threatening me?" I asked. My mind flicked back to the text message I'd received, and I could feel my temper rising.

"Of course not," said Gromov. "I'm simply warning a good friend."

"We are not friends," I said through gritted teeth.

"Well, perhaps we should be? I would be able to provide better protection than your Detective Inspector friend. My contacts are not known for their understanding nature, and this Sonny, whoever he is, has caused them quite a problem."

I hung up the phone, not wanting to listen to any more of his manipulations. He was toying with me, and I knew it, but I didn't think he was lying. In his own twisted way, Gromov was genuinely trying to look out for me. Why? I wasn't so sure. No doubt it would be a favour he called in later.

But he had given me a big piece of the puzzle, confirmed a suspicion; Mickey had taken something that wasn't his. It explained the safe, the ransacked office, and Adrianna saying that Mickey had been on edge in the weeks before his death.

The office felt overwhelmingly quiet as my brain whirled through the possibilities. What had Mickey stolen? Money? Jewels? Secrets? It would be impossible to guess without knowing *who* he'd stolen from. Perhaps Gromov would offer up a name, but I doubted it. I considered redialing his number but I knew he'd offered me an olive branch and I wasn't going to get any more for my troubles.

This added a whole new level of urgency to finding Mickey's killer. And now it seemed like I was responsible for returning whatever it was he'd stolen. Except I had no idea where to look, or who to ask.

Cameron.

I needed to speak to Cameron.

Chapter 30

JASON HUNTER

THE OFFICE

Monday 11ᵗʰ October

I knew that Cameron, whoever he was, would know a lot more about this whole sorry mess than we did, including who had murdered Mickey. Adrianna had said Mickey was on edge in those last few weeks. He'd been dodging phone calls from everyone, *except Cameron*. He knew something. Maybe they'd been in on it together.

My phone was still in my hand, and I was staring at the blank screen. I needed to revisit Club Dionysus, and *make* Cameron talk to me. I was sure just five minutes of his time would be enough to point me in the right direction, except it was highly likely that Cameron wouldn't want to help or get involved. He likely had his own issues to deal with. And yet, Gromov hadn't mentioned Cameron. Did that mean his contacts didn't know about him or that he just wasn't involved? I mean, I wasn't really involved but somehow my name had made it onto their radar.

I swallowed as my thoughts flicked to Max and Lily. This couldn't be happening *again*. I'd already put them in harm's way once when I was trying to protect Stacey from Liam, I couldn't believe I was doing it again. But this directly affected them whether I was involved or not.

If it wasn't me they were after, it wouldn't be long until they tracked down Adrianna and that would be worse.

I unlocked my phone and sent a quick text to Stacey. We were going to visit Club Dionysus, but this time, I wanted enough of a distraction that Gromov's 'contacts' wouldn't notice us.

Then I video called Hayley.

"I did wonder when you'd call me back," she said when her face filled my phone screen. I opened my mouth to reply but she cut me off. "Yes, I know, hi, how are you, isn't the weather nice? Do you want to hear what I have to say or not?"

"I literally didn't say a thing."

"You were about to."

I couldn't argue with that. "Did you manage to speak to the bag company?"

"Yes. Friday afternoon, and they've agreed to look into it but we don't have too much to go on. All we can send them is a grainy image of the bag from the CCTV and see if it matches any of their custom orders," she said. She shuffled in her seat and the camera angle changed.

She leaned back and I could see she was in the same boardroom as before. It was obvious she'd propped her phone up on something, maybe a laptop, because her hands suddenly came into view, holding a takeout cup. Over her shoulder, I could just about glimpse parts of the evidence board.

"I'm revisiting the footage from Budapest to see if the bag makes an appearance there. I don't remember it being there but that doesn't mean it wasn't. We weren't looking for it. And while it's not a guarantee on the timeframe, it gives us a narrower purchase window to work with."

"Makes sense," I said. I turned my chair to the left so I could look out at the London skyline.

"We're waiting on a search warrant to be able to complete a full exam of the shoot site."

"How long will that take?" I asked.

She shrugged. "Who knows? But without it, we can't collect any evidence. The lock on the door to the apartment had been picked. It's currently up for sale and vacant. The sales agent reported it to the police in order to claim for a new lock on the building's insurance."

"So he picks the lock of the apartment. Goes in and sets up. There's no distractions because the apartment is empty – that's one hell of a coincidence—"

"Tell me about it."

"What next?"

"We get the warrant, search the apartment and open it up to the SOCO team." She paused for a beat. "Have you figured out what's wrong with Cameron's number?"

"No," I shook my head. "Admittedly, I haven't really thought about it."

"Too preoccupied with the race?"

"A little," I laughed. "She did brilliantly. Did you see it?"

"Oh I saw it," she said and a smile finally broke through. "Only Stacey."

"Yeah, she got a bit of a bollocking for it too."

"I'm not surprised." Hayley laughed. "But going back to Cameron..."

"About that. I think I know why Mickey was murdered."

There was a pause.

"Go on," said Hayley.

I told her about the phone call with Gromov. About his subtle hints at the danger I was now in, and the wider implications.

"Who are these 'contacts'?"

"No idea. And as you can guess, he wasn't volunteering that information."

"Any idea what Mickey took?"

"Also no, but I'm guessing it was in that safe."

"Hmm." She went quiet as she pondered this new information and I let my eyes wander over the evidence board behind her. From this angle I couldn't see much; a few scribblings under the note about CCTV, a photograph of Adrianna's sticky note with Cameron's dud number and the end of a mapped-out timeline. "We need to get hold of Cameron," said Hayley interrupting my thoughts.

"Agreed. I feel like there's a lot of smoke and mirrors going on here, it's hard to tell what's true."

"I know what you mean."

"There's a lot of intentional misdirection. First, the killer shoots from a distance and then again up close. Mickey is some guy called Sonny. This number we have for Cameron doesn't work."

"And I don't know why Mickey would give Adrianna an emergency number only for her to not be able to use it," she said with a frown.

"No. I don't get it either. Mickey wouldn't have wanted to leave Adrianna in the lurch. He'd want her to have some kind of insurance policy."

"We need to think about this differently. We need to know what it is that Mickey supposedly stole, and whether there's any truth to that claim."

I nodded. "I do think Cameron is our best bet for that."

"Agreed."

We both went silent.

"Okay," said Hayley. "What if things were reversed? Put yourself in Mickey's shoes."

I stared over her shoulder, and then the penny dropped.

"What?" she said.

"What if things were reversed?"

"Yeah. I just asked you that," she said with a frown.

"No, I mean literally." I nodded to the photo of the sticky note on the board behind her. "What if things were literally reversed? What better way to disguise it?"

Hayley looked over her shoulder.

"Mickey would have wanted to give Adrianna a contact, someone he trusted, but he wouldn't leave something like that lying around, right?"

"I guess not."

"So what if the number is back to front?"

She continued to study the number on the board. It started with 077 and then ended 770. A clever ruse to look legitimate, but not dangerous should the number fall into the wrong hands.

A knock at the door interrupted us and Hayley's head whipped around. I could hear murmurings of someone else in the room. "I've got to go," she said to the camera. "The boss wants an update. Whatever you do, don't call that number."

"Well, you can't call it."

"Why not?"

"What do you think Cameron's gonna do if he gets a call from the police? He's already underground, and Mickey's dead. The guy will bolt and you'll never find him."

"I hear you, Jason, but it's too dangerous for you to follow up on this."

I made a non-committal sound.

"Promise me," she said. "Promise me you won't call it."

"I won't call it," I said.

Chapter 31

JASON HUNTER

HOME

Monday 11th October

"Sorry, why do I need to call it? Why can't you?"

"I promised Hayley I wouldn't. So you need to do it. Plus, he might respond better to a woman. Pretend you're Adrianna."

Stacey rolled her eyes at me.

"Really? You want me to role-play being your ex-wife?"

I winced. "You know what I mean."

She laughed. "Alright, alright."

She typed the 11 digits into the keypad, starting with the last number and working her way backwards. Then she hit the call button. The phone rang and rang and rang and then cut to voicemail.

She tried again but the same thing happened.

"Maybe he doesn't deal with anyone over the phone," she shrugged. "Shall I text him?"

"Why not?" I said. "What do we have to lose?"

Her fingers hovered over her screen as she contemplated what to write.

"Mickey gave this number to Adrianna, right?"

I nodded.

"And said to use it in an emergency?"

I nodded again.

She looked thoughtful for a moment and then started typing. She showed me the message.

Things are bad. I need your help. When can we meet?

Then she hit send before I could comment.

I opened my mouth to say something then thought better of it.

"What?" she asked, putting her phone on the counter.

"Nothing," I replied. "I like the earnestness."

"I'm not messing around. We need to see this guy, and soon—"

Her phone screen lit up and we both leaned forward to see an incoming message from an unknown number.

"Well, that was fast," I said.

Stacey scooped up her phone, unlocked the screen and read the message before turning her phone to face me.

Tonight. Club Dionysus. I will find you.

"You did say you wanted to go back there," she said with a smile. "Looks like we're going out-out tonight." And then she winked.

Chapter 32

JASON HUNTER

CLUB DIONYSUS

Monday 11th October

The club was alive. People milled about in the street, spilling out the door, while others queued behind a thick, red velvet rope. Music pulsed in the air, occasionally muffled when the entrance door swung shut. Two huge bouncers stood guard out front. A woman stood with them, holding a tablet and periodically speaking into the microphone attached to her headset.

Stacey's arm looped through mine as we made our way down the street. Her cerulean blue mini dress moved as she walked, making tiny little clicking sounds as hundreds of string beads swished together. Her long strides were calm, collected and sexy as all eyes followed her.

I stood up a little straighter as I noticed the crowds of people smoking outside bars and gathered in groups turned to look at us. She had that effect on people, and she knew it.

As we came to the entrance of the club, I was prepared to join the long queue of waiting patrons, but Stacey let go of my arm and marched straight up to the bouncers. She held the small silver clutch in front of her body and waved her other beautifully manicured hand in the direction of the tablet the woman was holding.

I risked a sideways glance at the two bouncers and recognised the one on the right from my previous visit. My subtle look didn't go unnoticed and he gave me a small nod.

"Miss James, what a delight," said the woman, smiling as she tapped her fingers on the tablet screen, her brown hair falling forward to partially obscure her features. "I didn't have you down as a guest on tonight's list but of course, accommodations can be made, I just can't guarantee a VIP booth."

Stacey flicked a finger over her shoulder. "Of course not. And I wouldn't expect you to. I really should have made a reservation. Although I do believe I have an appointment inside."

"Ah, I'll just let them know." The woman inclined her head and I assumed that meant she was letting Cameron know we'd arrived. Except Cameron wouldn't know to be expecting us, would he? Did he know Mickey had given his number to Adrianna? Or was he in the habit of taking random requests for help from unknown numbers? "Someone will collect you when they're ready." The woman looked up at us then with piercing blue eyes and gave us both a professional half-smile.

The bouncers parted enough to let us through. I opened the black door for Stacey who stopped to give a quick wave to those who'd recognised her in the queue and then we were inside, engulfed in darkness.

The music was louder in here, too loud for ordinary conversation. I took hold of Stacey's hand and led the way up the stairs where a soft pulsating light illuminated the stairway.

At the top, the entrance to the club was concealed by heavy drapes. I pulled them aside and gestured for Stacey to enter. I followed and was amazed at the transformation of the place. It had been impressive in the dim daylight but this was a whole other level.

The two huge statues by the DJ set were lit by uplights, making them seem even bigger, looming over the partygoers on the dance floor. Strobe lighting skittered through the air above our heads and the swathes of fabric that hung from the ceiling gently billowed.

The place was packed and there didn't seem to be any room to move, the dance floor just one heaving mass of bodies. We edged around the throng of people and made our way over to the bar.

It took a good fifteen minutes to get to the front, and then I had to wave to get a bartender's attention. He leaned forward and I yelled—"Two beers"—over the sound of the music. He stood up, held up two fingers and I nodded. Less than a minute later and I was squeezing my way back through the crowd.

I found Stacey casually leaning against one of the marble pillars dotted around the edge of the dancefloor. I handed her a beer and took a grateful sip of my own. Stacey took a swig just as the music changed. Her face lit up and her eyes swivelled towards me. I shook my head, mouthing 'no' but she took my hand anyway and dragged me into the crowd.

I wasn't a dancer, could not hold a rhythm to save my life, but I let Stacey lead me and it wasn't long until I found I was actually enjoying myself. Even here I could sense eyes turning to look at us, and I really hoped it wasn't because of my awkwardness. Who was I kidding, of course it wasn't. Stacey always commanded a room, but clad in her skimpy blue dress and killer heels, she was irresistible.

Suddenly the tempo of the music changed and I pulled Stacey into me. She wrapped one hand around the back of my neck, her nails gently caressing along my skin, making me shiver, while the other she placed on my chest.

She pulled my face down and I didn't need asking twice before our lips met in a crushing kiss. Her body pressed close and I could feel her hips grind against me. We moved to the rhythm of the music, forgetting there were hundreds of people around us. We were in a bubble, kissing without a care in the world. My left hand rested at the very bottom of her back where I could feel the outline of her underwear through the thin fabric of her dress. Suddenly my mind filled with images of removing them.

There was a tap on my shoulder. Our bubble burst and I jolted back to reality. The same bouncer from my previous trip, the one that had been standing at the door earlier, beckoned for us to follow him.

We weaved through the crowd. It was easy enough to follow his head as it bobbed above everyone else's. I gave Stacey's hand a squeeze, and she squeezed back.

Emerging on the other side of the dancefloor, the bouncer took us through a curtained doorway into a VIP area. Booths lined both sides of the room, all of which had their own curtained entranceways. He continued past them all to the very back where a wall of sequins hung, glittering in the dim light. He swept aside part of the wall to reveal a padded door covered in a rich red velvet with gold studs.

He placed a finger on the scanner embedded in the wall next to the door and it swung open. Looking back at us, he gestured for us to enter. I glanced at Stacey and then we walked in.

Chapter 33

JASON HUNTER

CLUB DIONYSUS

Monday 11th October

It was too dark to see the entire room clearly. A sofa was pushed up against the wall to my right, and the wall on my left was lit by the glow of at least twenty computer screens, all embedded in the wall. The top two rows of screens were split into four, each showing a CCTV livestream. The bottom row of screens showed analytical charts and timetables that were updating in real-time.

"Oh darling, don't you look delicious?" purred a voice. That's when I noticed a woman sitting in a large plush armchair that was strategically positioned to have a view of both the door we'd just come through and the bank of computer screens.

She stood up, her long limbs unfolding gracefully. She slowly sauntered towards Stacey, looking her up and down, and then began to circle the both of us. She had long, cherry-red hair that hung over one shoulder in gentle waves. It matched her cherry red dress that was cut tantalisingly low at the front and hugged her curves before flaring out at the knees.

"I absolutely *love* the dress," she said, her accent unplaceable.

"It's an original Sherri Hill," said Stacey, giving a quick twirl. The beaded fringes swung outward and then clacked together as she came to a standstill.

"Oh, I do love a Sherri Hill design," she said.

Now that she was closer, I could make out her features more clearly. Her eyes were bright, surrounded by smokey makeup that gave her a feline look. Her lips, also coloured cherry red, were full and mesmerising as she spoke.

"We're here—" I began, unsure what was happening.

"I know why you're here, darling," she replied, stepping around me and strolling back over to her armchair. She cast a quick glance at the computer screens before collapsing into the seat. "Although, I must admit I was surprised when the two of you showed up. Not exactly *who* I was expecting." She carefully crossed one leg over the other. The slit in the side of her dress fell open, revealing bare legs and creamy, delicate skin.

"Cameron?" asked Stacey.

"That's me, darling," she purred. "The name's Cameron Holly. And it really is a pleasure to meet the sensational Stacey James." She picked up a long, slender cigarette holder from the table next to her and lit it. The glow from the flame illuminated her face for the briefest of seconds before it was snuffed out.

"I was—" said Stacey, as speechless as me.

"Expecting a man? Yes, I know, darling. It's to be expected with a name like mine. One that I like to use to my advantage." She took a long drag on the cigarette and then slowly exhaled, blowing the smoke up to the ceiling. "The only question left is; do you actually need my help? Or was that simply a ruse to get a meeting with me?"

"A bit of both," I answered.

"Honesty. Good. I like honesty."

"You thought the message was from Adrianna?" I asked.

She inclined her head. "Oh look, I'm being rude. Take a seat. Please." She gestured towards the sofa. "Yes, I have been waiting for the poor soul to contact me." We both took a seat and Cameron swivelled the armchair so it was facing us, her back now to the bank of computer screens.

I hadn't noticed, but I realised that the bouncer had followed us into the room and was standing quietly by the door. So much for a quick getaway.

"That number you have, the one you sent the message to. It's only ever used to contact Mickey. So, you see, it could only be Adrianna who would contact me. I assumed Mickey would have given her some kind of insurance policy. Although I am intrigued as to why it was you who contacted me and not her." She took another drag on her cigarette while she waited for our answer.

"Mickey had written the number backwards. Adrianna brought it to me because she couldn't get it to work."

Cameron tilted her head back and laughed.

I glanced at Stacey, an eyebrow raised. She shrugged.

"Sorry, darling, sorry. It's just so like Mickey. Brilliant business partner, useless with life admin." She smiled to herself as she took another drag on the cigarette, slowly exhaling and watching the tendrils of smoke disappear into the darkness.

I wasn't sure how to ask what I needed to. I wasn't sure how Cameron would react. She seemed far too calm and... in control. That worried me. The fact that Cameron was a woman had thrown me off, and had me reevaluating everything.

"I haven't got all night, darling," Cameron purred, her voice like silk. She adjusted her chair slightly and glanced over at the screens.

"Do you know why Mickey was on edge before he died?" Stacey asked, cutting to the chase.

Cameron's eyes snapped to her face. "What do you mean?" she said but the purr was gone. She was trying to maintain her nonchalance but all of a sudden, her body seemed tense.

"Adrianna said he was acting paranoid. Would only answer the phone to you. Want to tell me what was going on?" I asked.

Cameron shrugged and took another drag on her cigarette.

"Okay. So we know he stole something—"

"And who told you that?" The friendliness seemed to evaporate completely and suddenly I had a good insight into how ruthless Cameron really was. While she liked to play the sassy seductress, there was definitely more to her.

"—something really valuable," I continued, ignoring her. "There are some pretty powerful people that are pretty pissed off. They're looking for Sonny Serrano—"

"Out," she barked. I sat up straight, eyes wide. "Not you," she spat at me. "Out," she said again and waved at the guard by the door. He did as he was told. "You have no idea what the fuck you are talking about, Jason Hunter," she hissed, leaning forward. "My *friend* is dead because of this."

"Don't you think I know that?" I shot back, my temper getting the better of me. "It's my ex-wife and my kids that are now in the firing line."

She blinked, opened her mouth and then closed it again. After a few moments, she sat back in her chair and took a final drag on her cigarette before stubbing it out in the ashtray on the small side table next to the armchair.

"Look," she finally said. "Mickey was in over his head. He shouldn't have done it. I tried to talk him out of it, but he promised me it wouldn't be traced back to him. A few weeks ago, he'd heard rumblings on the grapevine. Rumours that people were looking for him. They were pissed. Yes, mostly it was about Sonny Serrano. Very few people know that was his real name. Me, I'm assuming Adrianna, and probably his mother."

She got up from the armchair and crossed the room, approaching the sideboard I hadn't noticed standing next to the sofa. She bent down, opened the front door and pulled out three glass tumblers.

"Drink, darlings?" she asked.

"Sure," I said and got to my feet.

"Yes," said Stacey, who remained sitting.

I approached Cameron's elbow as she poured several fingers of whiskey into the three tumblers. Passing a tumbler to Stacey, I took the one Cameron proffered.

"Then what?" I asked.

Cameron downed half of her drink before she continued. "I believe you know Alik Gromov?"

My glass stopped halfway to my lips. "Are you fucking joking me?"

She gave me a wry smile. "I wish I was."

"What did he want?" asked Stacey, nursing her drink.

"He was looking for Mickey, hinting that he knew something had gone down, mentioned the missing—" she paused for half a heartbeat, "—item. Well, that was that. Mickey was really paranoid after that. I'd never seen him so worked up. It was like he'd taken drugs. But he hadn't," she added quickly. "What I mean is, he was wired. It tipped his paranoia over the edge."

I watched as she downed the rest of her drink.

"Cameron?" I asked slowly.

Her eyes met mine.

"What did Mickey take? And who did he take it from?"

Suddenly, she looked impossibly sad.

"I wish I could help you, darling," she replied as she poured herself another drink. "I really do. The last thing I want is more blood to be spilled. And those darling children of yours." She paused for a moment, then looked up at me. "Mickey loved those kids, I hope you know that."

I gave her a small smile and was surprised at the warmth it created in me.

She sighed. "Information. That's what he took. Incredibly valuable information."

"Valuable how?" asked Stacey from the sofa. Her eyes flicked to me as she considered what this could mean.

"It could get a lot of important people arrested," she said and she turned to look at the bank of screens on the wall.

"Like who? Who is it that Gromov knows?"

I could feel our welcome starting to wear thin.

"I've told you everything I know, darling. I swear it. I don't know who Gromov is working for. I mean, hell, I wouldn't be surprised if he was just trying to cover his own ass. You know what he's like." She gave a hollow laugh.

I placed my drink back on the sideboard.

"I appreciate you telling us all of this," I said.

"Just promise me one thing, darling."

"Yes?"

"I know you'll need to tell that police friend of yours. But leave me out of it. I have enough on my plate without the police sniffing around. My clientele are very sensitive to that type of intrusion."

I gave a small nod. "I'll do what I can."

She lifted her chin and regained some of her earlier composure.

"Actually," said Stacey, getting to her feet. "I just have one more question."

Cameron turned to face her, curiosity on her face.

"How did Mickey know Irhaa Lindberg?"

She raised an eyebrow, clearly surprised by the question and change of direction. "I believe *Professor* Lindberg was his psychologist on the inside."

Stacey opened her mouth to reply but something caught Cameron's attention on the top left screen. She strode forward, scooping up a small handheld controller from the table by her armchair. After a few clicks, one of the video livestreams took up the entirety of the screen and she frowned.

"*Fuck*," she muttered under her breath.

Chapter 34

JASON HUNTER

CLUB DIONYSUS

Monday 11th October

"What is it?" I asked, frowning. I stepped forward and craned my neck to get a better view of the screen. Someone had entered the club, and he looked important. Two burly guys in black suits flanked him as he surveyed the club in front of him. The pretty concierge from earlier suddenly appeared behind him and gestured towards the private room of booths which we had come through earlier.

"A very important patron. You need to leave. Now. If he finds out you're here, I'll be in a lot of trouble."

For the first time that evening, Cameron looked scared.

"This way," she said and gestured to the door. Outside we were reunited with our bouncer friend from earlier.

Plastering on her most dazzling smile, Cameron greeted the staff working between booths.

"We have a situation," she muttered to the bouncer and he nodded.

"Booth 3," he replied, his deep voice tinged with the Jamaican accent I remembered from my previous visit.

"Thank you, Damarae," she said, lightly touching his arm before sweeping forward with grace and confidence. We followed. "In here," she said, stopping next to a booth and sweeping back the curtain.

Sitting down on the plush cushions, I was surprised to see the booth wasn't empty. Wide, surprised eyes looked at us from across the space and Stacey clapped a hand over her mouth. I was speechless, stunned by this turn of events as much as our companion who was sitting next to a beautiful, bored-looking brunette.

"Dima?!" said Stacey, trying to hold back her laughter. The edges of my lips curled up into a small smile. It had been a while since I'd seen Dima Volkov up close and personal. Of course, I'd seen him on the track competing against Stacey but since Gromov's party over a year ago, our paths hadn't crossed. "What are you doing here?" she half-yelled. The music in here wasn't quite as loud as the dancefloor but it was enough to drown out the ability to overhear others.

Dima's shocked face turned into a scowl. "I don't think that's any of your business," he said.

I leaned back towards the curtain and peeked between the fabric, trying to catch a glimpse of Cameron and her new guest.

Stacey giggled. "I'm sorry," she said. "Just such a coincidence." Dima continued to scowl. "We didn't mean to... interrupt," she said, her eyes flicking to his guest.

"What are you two playing at?" he hissed.

"Nothing," I said without looking back.

"You better not be doing what I think you're doing. Did you learn nothing from last year?"

Stacey rolled her eyes. "We were just visiting a friend," she said dismissively.

"A friend you're now hiding from?" he asked. He reached across to the curtain and pulled it back enough to view the rest of the room.

"Can I help?" asked a waitress, appearing in the gap and blocking my view.

"More drinks, please," said Dima. "For the table." He twirled his finger in the air, indicating where we were all sitting.

"Of course," smiled the waitress and disappeared, the curtain swinging back into place.

"Bloody hell, Jason. You want to tell me why you're hiding from Alfonso Torres?" said Dima.

Stacey's eyes went wide. "Is that who it is?"

"Who?" I asked.

Dima rolled his eyes, a look of contempt on his face. "Your girl-friend is the biggest name in Formula One right now and you don't even know who he is."

"Just bloody tell me."

"He owns Formula One," said Stacey.

"What's he doing here?" I asked, peering out between the curtains again.

"Same thing we all are, I guess," shrugged Dima.

Stacey threw him a look and I let the curtain fall back into place.

"Sorry, but I'm not hiding from him. I don't know what the hell you two are playing at." He turned back to the woman practically trying to drape herself over him.

"I can understand why he's here," I said to Stacey. "It's a high-end place. But what I don't get is *why* he's here. Cameron seemed bloody terrified of him."

"What if he's one of the contacts Gromov was talking about?" said Stacey. She'd lowered her voice and glanced over to see if Dima could hear her. It appeared not, although I didn't trust the little weasel. I never had.

"Not here," I said, taking Stacey's hand and giving it a squeeze.

Chapter 35

STACEY JAMES

HMP BRONZEFIELD

Tuesday 12th October

Stacey handed her paperwork to the woman in uniform behind the desk who glanced down at it and then looked up at Stacey.

The woman gave a curt nod, then said, "Stand on the two red markers on the floor and look directly at the camera please." She waved towards where a camera was mounted at eye level.

Stacey did as she was told, trying her best to calm the fluttering feeling in her stomach. Her nerves were making her feel sick. Her mind was still reeling from the night before but she'd barely had time to process everything.

They'd left the club well past midnight but had been reluctant to talk things through in front of the taxi driver. Not that they'd thought he posed a threat, but they were fast realising that you couldn't be too careful.

Once home, Stacey had declared she was too tired to do anything other than collapse into bed.

But she'd barely slept, tossing and turning all night until her alarm went off in the morning. She'd tried on at least four different outfits, her nerves almost getting the better of her. Jason had gotten ready for work and wished her luck on his way out as she headed back to the bedroom to change for the fifth time.

And here she was. About to face her fears. Confront the one person she'd failed.

"I'll need a fingerprint." The woman gestured to the biometric scanner mounted on the desk. Stacey pressed her finger onto the small black box and waited. After a moment, the woman gave a nod and Stacey removed her hand.

After a few moments of tapping on keys on the keyboard and clicking on her mouse, the woman said, "Right, that's all sorted, love. Won't need to do all this next time, we'll just check against what we have on file for you."

Stacey gave a weak smile.

"Now, lockers are just there," the woman pointed to the other side of the room. Stacey turned to see a bank of square lockers. "You'll need to leave your stuff in your locker. Phones, keys, loose change, bags, it all needs to stay here. You can keep a bank card on you for the service counter. Then through here when you're ready," she gestured to the metal detector next to the desk, "and one of the officers will do a pat down search."

Stacey nodded nervously.

"First time?" the woman asked gently.

Stacey nodded again.

She gave a small smile. "It can be quite daunting. But you'll be fine. The inmates are always glad to see a familiar face. Once you're in the visitor's hall, you can buy yourself a nice coffee, maybe treat yourself to a bar of chocolate."

"Thanks," said Stacey quietly. She took a deep breath, then followed the woman's instructions, depositing her belongings in one of the lockers and walking through the metal detector.

Once on the other side, a second uniformed prison officer was waiting for her. He indicated for her to spread her arms and then proceeded to pat her down. "All good," he said and waved her through.

She walked through the final door, down the corridor and into a brightly lit visitor's hall. It was definitely not what she'd expected. There were no metal tables bolted to the floor, no metal chairs that made awful scraping sounds when they were pulled out, and no drab, oppressive walls. Instead, there were comfy seats dotted around the room in twos, threes and a few fours. A children's soft play area was off to one side and small kids gleefully climbed over each other and ran around.

Stacey headed to the hole-in-the-wall counter where a man thanked the woman serving him and picked up a tray laden with two coffees, a couple of chocolate bars and a packet of crisps. He gave Stacey a cordial nod as he turned away, and then did a double take. He headed over to who Stacey assumed was maybe his partner, and watched as he said something to her and they both looked her way.

"Hi, what can I get you?" asked the woman behind the counter with a friendly smile. Her hair was cropped short, making her round face look fuller. She must have been in her fifties, and she somehow made Stacey feel slightly less nervous.

"A cup of tea, please. Anything herbal, if you have it."

"I've got peppermint, green, rooibos, Earl Grey and chamomile. Take your pick."

"Peppermint's fine."

The woman busied herself with making the tea and Stacey glanced over her shoulder. The hall was relatively empty. A couple of families were sitting near the soft play and a few more couples were scattered throughout.

"There you go." The woman said, placing a mug on the tray. Stacey tapped her bank card against the payment machine and picked up the mug. She wound her way through the tables and chairs to find herself a seat.

Perched on the edge of her chair, she clutched the mug and nervously glanced around. Posters and colourful drawings decorated the walls, making her smile. A lot of energy had gone into making this place feel welcoming, and it definitely helped to calm her.

Barely a minute had passed when a figure sat down in the seat facing her.

"Hi Diane," said Stacey, forcing herself to look at the other woman.

Diane didn't reply. She was dressed in a pair of black leggings and a plain teal sweater. Her face was scrubbed clean of makeup and her hair was pulled back in a ponytail at the nape of her neck.

"How are you?" asked Stacey.

"I've been better."

Stacey winced. It was a stupid question to ask, of course it was, but she was nervous. Diane had been backed into a corner by Liam's evil manipulations. Weighed down with the guilt that she believed she was responsible for Gemma's murder, Diane had been backed into a corner by Gromov and ended up laundering money in order to pay her debt. All because Stacey had treated her like a dog, had made comments and belittled her at every opportunity.

The silence felt heavy between them. Stacey's stomach was tying itself in knots. Her mouth had gone dry and her brain had gone blank.

"Can I get you a drink?" she eventually asked.

Diane sighed. "Stacey, what are you doing here?"

She looked down into her mug of peppermint tea. What *was* she doing here? Facing up to her anxiety, dealing with her problems, doing as Professor Lindberg had suggested.

"I wanted to apologise."

Diane's eyebrows shot up but she didn't reply.

"I'm sorry," she said quietly, forcing herself to look Diane in the eye. "I feel responsible for you being here. I was horrible to you. I don't even know why. But I wanted to say sorry for that, for every time I made you feel awful, for everything that happened." She couldn't quite bring herself to spell it all out, but she hoped Diane would think it was enough. Suddenly Stacey wasn't quite sure what she expected to gain. Absolution? No, not possible. Forgiveness? Maybe.

Hope slowly began to bloom in Stacey's chest. Hope that she would be able to put everything behind her. Hope that she could be forgiven, that things could get better, that she could repair her self-esteem and move on from what had happened with Diane.

"Is that it?" asked Diane.

Suddenly the ball of hope popped and the weight of it sat heavy on her shoulders.

"I shouldn't have come. I'm sorry. I didn't—"

Stacey stood up, the mug of peppermint tea still clutched in her hands.

"Sit down," sighed Diane. Stacey did as she was told, ashamed at how meek she'd become, and how much she needed this woman's approval. "I'm just a bit surprised to see you, that's all. Even more surprised to get an apology, I can tell you. I mean, it's been a while. Why now?"

"I—" Where did she begin? It felt like so much had happened since Diane had been arrested, but at the same time, nothing quite as monumental as having her whole life put on hold and serving time for a crime she was blackmailed into committing. "I'm trying to be a better person."

Diane studied her for a moment and Stacey wondered what she saw. The old Stacey felt long gone. There were glimmers of her confident, sassy nature, mostly either when she was behind the wheel or when she was with Jason. When she felt safest.

"I'll have a latte," said Diane eventually.

Stacey recognised a peace offering when she was offered one and jumped at the chance. "Of course. Anything else?" She placed her mug on the table.

"A packet of crisps would be nice."

Chapter 36

STACEY JAMES

STACEY'S APARTMENT

Tuesday 12th October

After visiting the prison, Stacey desperately needed some alone time to process everything and decompress. She'd felt tense all morning, her skin feeling too tight for her body, but the relief at having visited Diane almost outweighed the overwhelming sense of guilt she still carried. Guilt about treating Diane so badly. Guilt that she'd been such a trigger. Guilt that she was the reason people had died.

Professor Lindberg had assured her that things would get better with time and the guilt would start to fade. She just needed to work on forgiving herself.

She decided to head over to her apartment and check in on things. It felt like ages since she'd been there. It had once felt like such a sanctuary for her, but since Liam, Jason's house had become that sanctuary. She spent almost all of her time there when she wasn't racing.

The racing season was hard work. It took a tremendous toll on her physically, mentally and emotionally. In between her demanding training sessions, she was flying to countries all across the world and was expected to perform in extreme circumstances under tremendous pressure.

Everyone assumed that racing was all adrenaline and glory, but the G-force that pressed down on her body as she raced left her feeling like she couldn't breathe. The adrenaline was usually enough to keep the panic at bay but having now been home for 36 hours, the exhaustion from it all was catching up with her. And the added emotional toll of her visit to see Diane certainly wasn't helping.

Dropping her keys on the kitchen island, she glanced around the immaculate open plan kitchen space. A cleaner came in twice a week, even while she was at Jason's. So the place was completely spotless.

On the plane ride home, she'd thought more about what she'd said at the press interview. There was definitely a lack of female representation both on the track and behind the scenes. She was getting tired of being the only female racer, tired of the pressure and scrutiny for simply being a woman. And she'd begun to think about how she could encourage more women to enter the world of Formula One. How she could provide the financial support and backing that was in short supply.

She'd chatted with Sam about it almost the whole way home, bouncing ideas off him. And while he wasn't able to provide much insight, it was helpful to simply have someone to talk things through with.

On the counter next to her coffee machine was a neatly stacked pile of mail. Most of her mail was redirected through to a PO Box; her personal address was definitely not something she'd give out for the press or some crazed fan to get hold of.

Been there, done that.

So really, all she ever received were adverts, bills – why did the water company never just send an email like every other 21st century provider, no matter how many times she asked? – and anything she ordered online.

She quite liked the routine of flicking through the mail. So many things in her life were controlled by the media, by her career, by her fame, that it was nice to do something mundane. It was one of the reasons why she loved being with Jason and his kids so much. With them, she was just Stacey. Stacey who just so happened to be really good at racing, and a mean competitor when it came to the PlayStation.

She flicked through the stack on the counter; a leaflet for a new pizza place that's opened in the neighbourhood, a couple of charities looking to appeal to the goodwill of the homeowner, an estate agent looking for high demand properties and another internet company telling her about the new fibre optic set up in her area.

That's when she saw it.

Weirdly, it looked a little frayed around the edges, like it was old, or had been carried around for a while. But somehow that didn't seem right either. On the front was an iconic mosque that took up most of the photo. A gorgeous fountain with clear blue water spraying out of the top sat in the foreground. In the bottom right corner, in a cursive script, were the words *Greetings from Istanbul.*

Stacey's mouth went dry and her stomach clenched. It was just a postcard. But something in the back of her mind was trying to tell her this wasn't just a postcard. It was a calling card.

She turned it over, noticed the Turkish postmark in the top right-hand corner and the messy scrawl of letters taking up the centre space.

A small sob escaped her lips as she clamped her hand to her face and a feeling of despair washed over her.

Chapter 37

JASON HUNTER

THE OFFICE

Tuesday 12th October

"What did I tell you?!"

Hayley stood on the other side of my desk, her hands flat on the surface as she leaned forward and yelled at me.

"I told you not to call the number! I told you, Jason. And I made you promise. You lied to me."

"Technically, no. I didn't call the number."

"Don't throw semantics at me," she spat as she pushed off the table and marched over to the windows. I watched her shoulders heave up and down as her anger roiled off her in waves.

I didn't dare break the silence. In fact, I couldn't remember a single time she'd ever been so angry with me. Sure, I'd seen her annoyed, but this felt like a whole new level.

"I brought you onto the crime scene," she said quietly. "I stuck my neck out for you, Jason. And how do you repay me? You disobey a direct request."

Suddenly I felt guilty. She was right. She had put herself on the line for me. I had no right to be involved in this case. Last time, I'd been too close to not be caught up in it. But this time was different. God knew how many rules, how many laws she might have broken getting me access to Adrianna's apartment when Mickey's body had only just been removed. And while she'd been cagey about some areas of the investigation, she'd actually been quite forthcoming with where they were at.

A small voice in the back of my mind told me that it was only because it was in her best interest, but I ignored it. It was still one hell of a risk to invite a civilian to be privy to information in an ongoing murder investigation.

Shit, I hadn't really thought about it like that. What if Hayley lost her job because of me?

"I'm sorry," I said quietly. "I didn't do it to purposely annoy you. I just felt like we were on to something. And like I said on the phone, if the cops had called, Cameron would have clammed up."

My words faded into the silence between us. Hayley didn't acknowledge that she'd heard me, staring out of the window instead. I waited, hoping she would forgive me, promising myself I'd never put her in this position again, but wondering if I could truly keep such a promise.

Finally, after what felt like an age, she turned around.

"In future, we talk these things through," she said. I nodded. She let out a breath. "After I hung up on you, I got an absolute bollocking from my boss. The whole 'bringing civilians onto the crime scene' thing did not go down well. Even after I argued that you're consulting on this case. That seemed to get me some breathing room, but he's not happy. So we need to be careful."

I nodded again, her earlier outburst making more sense now.

"When we get this guy, I don't want him to go free on a technicality," she added.

"Agreed."

She walked back over to my desk and collapsed into one of the chairs that sat facing me. She leaned forwards, her elbows on her knees. "Tell me everything that happened."

I did, and I spared no details. I felt like she deserved at least that.

An hour later, after I'd told Hayley everything that had happened, and she'd quizzed me until my brain felt fried, she finally let up. Leaning back in the chair, she stretched her legs out, crossing them at the ankles. She looked out the window again, this time thoughtful, a frown on her face.

"Are you sure that's who it was?" she asked, glancing back at me.

"Dima was pretty sure. Stacey recognised the name but hadn't put two and two together. I Googled him this morning and it's definitely the same guy."

"Well, it's not a crime to go to a club."

"No, I know. It was just the way Cameron reacted to him that made the whole thing weird. Like she was terrified of what he might do. I get that the guy's wealthy and probably throws his weight around a little. But this was something else. She was genuinely scared of him."

Before Hayley could reply, the door to my office opened and Stacey appeared, her face anxious and her body tense.

"Hayley, you're here. Good." Without hesitating, she strode up to my desk and slammed her hand down in the middle of it. When she took her hand away, underneath it was a rectangular piece of card with a picture of a large mosque on the front. "That slimy, relentless bastard," yelled Stacey.

I arched my eyebrows, surprised at her anger. Looking down at the postcard on my desk, I picked it up and flipped it over, worried about what I might find. Nausea rolled through my stomach as I read the words on the back. Then my anger rose.

"No more fucking around," I said to Stacey. "We reinstate your protection detail. And as for racing events, you're not going anywhere without a full escort."

She let out a frustrated huff but didn't argue with me. She knew it was in her best interest and she knew I wouldn't budge when it came to her safety.

"What is it?" asked Hayley, leaning forward to get a look at the card. I handed it to her and watched her face as she turned it over, reading the words on the back.

What a pleasure to see you racing again.

Yours,

Liam

Her eyebrows shot up and her eyes flicked to Stacey, then me.

"Where did you get this?" she asked.

"At my apartment," replied Stacey, fury still clear on her face. "It was with my other mail."

"Is this the first time he's contacted you since...?" she let the words trail off.

"Yes," said Stacey through gritted teeth. "I didn't think he would resurface, and especially not like this." She gestured to the postcard.

"What do we do?" I asked, looking at Hayley.

"I think you have the right idea," she said, looking at me. "Increase Stacey's safety detail, don't give him the opportunity to get close. Although it looks like he's being smart, keeping his distance. I take it you didn't see him in Istanbul?"

Stacey threw a quick glance at me before saying, "No, I didn't see Liam."

"What was that?" she asked, looking from Stacey to me and back to Stacey again. She waved a finger in the air between us. "What just happened?"

"Cooper was there," I said with a sigh.

"Cooper?! As in Bill Cooper? Wanted by the Metropolitan Police?" said Hayley, sitting up straight in her seat. Stacey nodded. I could feel Hayley's annoyance start to grow again. "And you didn't think to mention this before now?"

I opened my mouth to say something and then closed it again, not sure how to defend myself without dropping me further in it. I wasn't planning to tell Hayley about the burner phone, or the fact that I'd asked him to be there in the first place.

"Did he make contact?" asked Hayley.

"No," replied Stacey. "He just made sure that I saw him. Twice."

Hayley leaned back again, mulling this over. "Any idea why?" she asked after a brief silence.

Stacey shrugged. "He was always quite protective, I guess he was just keeping tabs on me. And what better way to do it than at my races? It's not exactly like he can enter the country and knock on my apartment door."

"I guess." I could tell she wasn't satisfied with this answer.

Stacey glanced in my direction but thankfully didn't say anything else on the matter.

Hayley puffed out her cheeks and then exhaled. She was tense, I could see that. Stressed, most likely. She'd failed to make any headway with Mickey's murder so far and I'd gone and threatened to sabotage the whole investigation with my trip to see Cameron.

"Am I okay to take this?" she asked, holding up the postcard.

"Be my guest. It's not like I want to keep it as a memento," she said and rolled her eyes. "What have I got to do to get rid of this guy?" Stacey looked at me as if I'd have all the answers.

"I don't know," I shrugged.

"It's still an open case," said Hayley, laying a reassuring hand on Stacey's arm. "Which means we're still gathering evidence against him. While I can't promise anything right now, I'll do everything I can to nail the bastard."

Stacey nodded, not looking convinced. And I couldn't blame her. In the 14 months since Liam had almost killed her, since he'd tormented her and almost ruined her racing career, they hadn't gotten any closer to catching him. It was no surprise she was in therapy. Liam had put her through hell.

A knock at the door interrupted us.

"Sorry to interrupt," said Lucy, poking her head in.

"Jason, Divya is waiting for you in the boardroom. Apparently, the interviews are about to start."

"Ah, shit," I said, standing up from my chair. "I've got to go. Hayley, let me know if there's anything else I can help with. And I'll keep you updated on my side." She nodded in acknowledgement. "And I'll see you at home this evening," I said, giving Stacey a quick kiss as I came around my desk.

"Alright," she said and gave me a quick smile, calmer than when she entered.

We vacated my office.

"Fancy a coffee and a catch up?" Hayley asked Stacey. "I've still got time, and I feel like we're overdue."

"Oh yes," replied Stacey. "And cake. I've got an intense workout planned for this afternoon so I need to carb load."

Hayley laughed. "Not sure they're the right kind of carbs."

"A girl can treat herself," she replied with a devilish grin.

I watched them walk towards the bank of elevators on the other side of the office before heading towards the boardroom.

Chapter 38

THE GUNMAN

SOMEWHERE IN LONDON

Tuesday 12th October

The room was dark. The gunman lay on a sofa on one side of the room, his arms behind his head, eyes closed. He'd been dozing on and off for the last couple of hours whilst he waited. The room was warm, almost too warm, and he was starting to feel uncomfortable in his t-shirt. He frowned, and then opened his eyes, looking up at the blank ceiling above him.

"Have you got anything yet?" He pulled himself into a sitting position and looked across the room at the figure hunched in front of a bank of computer screens.

Three screens sat on the desk, gently curving around the figure in the middle, while another dozen screens were mounted on the wall above. Some showed live CCTV, one was what looked to be a military-based computer game paused mid campaign, and a few more showed black screens covered in programming code.

"The de-crypter will take a few more minutes."

The gunman got to his feet, stretched and approached the desk. His large frame leaned over the figure to peer at the computer screen.

"Do you mind?" she snapped.

"Sorry." He held up his hands in a placating gesture and gave the hacker a little more space.

She was the third hacker he'd given the memory stick to in the last week. The previous two had tried to break through the layers of protection but had simply ended up getting locked out.

Sh4rkByt3, as she was known online, had come highly recommended but she wasn't cheap, and he was loath to part with so much cash up front. But he needed to know what was on that damn memory stick. If Gromov had been desperate enough to hire him, it was obviously valuable. And if two hackers had failed already, someone had gone to extreme lengths to keep this shit secure.

"Here we go, let's see if it's managed to get through the last of the defences."

She dragged something over onto the screen to her right and he watched the loading bar as it slowly, painfully, extracted whatever information was being so well protected. He watched the percentage number tick upwards. It reached 60%. Then 70%. The seconds crawled past. Then it hit 80%.

"Come on," he muttered under his breath.

The girl next to him, who couldn't be any older than 16, drummed her fingers on the desk as she waited, her head propped on the fist of her other hand.

"How long does this usually take?" he asked, gesturing to the screen.

She shrugged. "Depends."

He rolled his eyes. Helpful.

They both watched the screen, waiting. 95%. He leaned closer. This was it. He was about to find out what all the rich boys were fighting over. He was about to be in possession of something that would make him a lot of money. He was confident he could sell whatever it was to the highest bidder. Maybe it would be enough to retire on. Buy a nice place somewhere in the Caribbean and finally give up being a gun for hire.

99%.

Suddenly the screen filled with new windows opening, one on top of the other. It looked like an explosion on the screen, each one containing new information. Lists, numbers, names. What the *hell* was he looking at?

"Shit," muttered Sh4rkByt3.

"Does this make any sense to you?" he asked.

She looked up at him, her eyes wide and her mouth open. "Where did you get this?" she whispered.

"I can't tell you that," he replied gruffly, looking back at the screen.

Her dark eyes didn't leave his face. He could feel them boring into him as he tried his best to ignore her and focus on what was in front of him.

The windows were still opening. Some looked like documents, others looked like datasheets. Whatever it was, it was a goldmine.

Finally, the program seemed to finish its processing and the windows paused where they were. Sh4rkByt3 looked at the screen. She moved a few of the windows so they were side by side and suddenly he realised what he was looking at. And shit, it was not good.

"You're either one powerful sonofabitch or you're about to be murdered," she said quietly.

In front of him was a ledger of transactions. It only dated back a few years, but it was enough to give a clear picture of what was going on. It seemed to be a ring of purchases and transactions. That in itself wasn't the most shocking part. It was the names attached to those transactions; politicians, celebrities, business people, most of which were in the public eye. And he didn't doubt that every single person on this list had money and power.

But *what* were they buying? That was unclear. The transactions were matched to codes. Some were sequential, others weren't.

"What are we looking at?" he asked, dreading the answer.

"This," she gestured to the screen, "is a blockchain ledger for NFTs."

"NFTs?" he asked. "What the hell are they?" He hoped they weren't drugs. He didn't want to be involved with that kind of crap.

"They're called non-fungible tokens," she explained. When he didn't reply, she continued, "Basically, they're digital assets. They can be anything; music, art, files. But this, here, that you're looking at, is the black market of NFTs. It looks like some powerful and important people are moving their money around using NFTs."

"As in money laundering?"

She nodded and he paled. While he could definitely sell this information on, it suddenly put a huge target on his back.

"Now, are you gonna tell me where it came from?" She paused for half a second. "Actually, you know what, I don't want to know. I value my life too much. But I can tell you now, I definitely didn't charge you enough for this job."

She was right. This was more than he'd anticipated, and whilst he was keen to have some dirt on Gromov, this might be a bit too out of his league.

What was he supposed to do now? And how was he supposed to stay alive?

Chapter 39

JASON HUNTER

THE OFFICE

Tuesday 12th October

I spent all afternoon locked up in the boardroom with Divya. True to her word, she'd managed to find an impressive collection of women with experience in personal protection. Some had done bouncer work with their SIA licences, others were ex-military, and some were just starting out. Those were the ones with the most fire, and they reminded me so much of Gemma.

Not all of the interviews had been in person. At least half of them had been done via video calls. After all, we operated internationally, so it made sense to recruit internationally too. But also, we prided ourselves on only hiring the best in the business, and they weren't all going to be British, or local.

"Thoughts?" asked Divya.

"Brilliant. I can't believe you managed to pull this together so quickly," I said.

"A lot of them are on temporary contracts at the moment and looking for their next job. That works in our favour."

"Of course," I said. It was definitely a sentiment I'd picked up on throughout the day. And despite our recent bad press, it was clear that our company name still meant something.

"Any idea on how many you'd want to hire?" she asked.

"Give me a day or two to think it over. I want a couple of two-woman teams, and maybe some bigger ones. But I need to check in with Vance Cherry about Iris and her tour. I'll need to finalise the security contract for that so I have a clear idea of how many we need on a permanent basis. It may be that we have a couple more on temp contracts. Not ideal, I know, but it's a start."

"So, thinking about 6? 8 maybe?"

"I think so."

"I'll speak to Rose in Finance and see what she says budget-wise," said Divya, making a note.

"Good thinking. We need to be a bit careful on spending while the rebrand happens."

"No problem."

We both looked down at the notes we'd made throughout the day.

"Anyone stand out?" asked Divya.

"I like Aysha. Lauren's got a good skill set. And Neve."

Divya nodded, putting an asterisk against the three names. "Well, that gives me something to work with for the moment. Let me know when you've decided who you want."

I nodded and stood up. "Excellent work, Divya. Thanks."

She gave me a brief smile before going back to scribbling furiously in her notepad and I left her to it, heading back to my office.

Chapter 40

JASON HUNTER

IMANI'S HOUSE

Tuesday 12th October

Adrianna was surprised to see me on the doorstep of Imani's house, even though I'd texted to say I'd pop by on my way home. Maybe she was just so unused to seeing me follow through on what I said I'd do that it was a shock when it happened. The thought hurt. Had I really been that much of a shitty husband to her?

"Hey," I said, suddenly unsure of myself.

She didn't meet my eyes, obviously still embarrassed about trying to kiss me on Thursday evening. To be honest, there was so much history between us – not to mention two kids – that I was almost surprised it hadn't happened sooner, and that it wasn't me who'd made the move. It's the stupid, dickish type of thing I'd half-expect a drunken me to do.

"Oh no, you don't," I said with a laugh.

Her eyes shot to my face. "What?" she asked, pulling the sleeves of her hoody over her hands, not a gesture I'd ever seen her do before.

"I'm not gonna let you suddenly make things awkward between us. Do you not think we've both been through enough?"

She gave me a small smile. "Coffee?" she offered.

"Please." I stepped over the threshold and followed her down the immaculate hallway and into the kitchen. It was a beautiful space, as was the rest of Imani's house. But it felt sterile, unlived in.

"Daddy!" shrieked Lily as she came barrelling into the room and threw herself at me. I scooped her up and covered her in kisses as she squealed with delight. I popped her on the kitchen counter while Adrianna made us both a coffee.

"How's school been, sweet pea?"

"Oh, good," she said. "Miss Crisp has been showing us all these cool animals, and we've been learning about them."

"Oh yeah?"

She nodded enthusiastically.

"Which one is your favourite so far?" I asked.

She looked thoughtful for a moment and then said, "Tiger, because I like their stripes." I saw Adrianna's smile from the corner of my eye as she stirred one mug and then the other.

"Tiger? What about a zebra?" I asked. "They have stripes."

She giggled and shook her head.

"Okay. My favourite would have to be the whale 'cause he's the biggest."

Lily giggled again.

"Alright you," interrupted Adrianna, turning to us and tucking a loose strand of hair behind her ear. "Go play with your toys. I need to speak to your dad."

Lily nodded and I helped her down from the countertop. "Will I see you before you go?" she asked.

"Of course," I replied. "I'll come and find you." Satisfied with my answer, she darted out of the room.

Once she was out of earshot, Adrianna turned to me. "I'm sorry about the other night," she said.

I waved a hand as I accepted the mug. "Honestly, completely forgotten. You've been through a lot recently. Speaking of which, how are things?"

She picked up her own mug, cupping her hands around its warmth. "I'm getting there. It still feels really raw and unreal, but you know..." She shrugged.

"Have you got stuff sorted for the funeral?"

She nodded. "The coroner is releasing the body tomorrow and the funeral will be held on Friday."

I nodded, unsure how to respond.

"Our Family Liaison Officer has been great. Really supportive and understanding, and giving me all the information I need to make plans," Adrianna continued, filling the silence.

"That's good." The words felt lame as they left my mouth, so I distracted myself by taking a sip of the coffee. It was hot, too hot, and I felt it scald my tongue as I swallowed.

"Did you get anywhere with Cameron's number?" she asked.

"No," I shook my head. I don't know why I lied, but it was an instant decision and I didn't regret it. The more Adrianna knew about what was going on, the more stressed she'd be and right now, that was the last thing she needed. The last thing *I* needed. I needed her to keep it together for the sake of the kids. And until I knew exactly what was going on, I didn't want her to know any more than she had to.

We stood in silence for a moment, both taking tentative sips of our drinks. I'm not sure if she knew I'd just lied to her but she didn't call me out on it or ask any follow up questions.

"Was there something in particular you wanted to talk to me about?" she asked.

I shook my head again. "Not really. I just wanted to check in and see how you're doing. See how the kids are doing."

She nodded, as if she understood my protectiveness. Maybe she did.

"How's Stacey?" she asked.

"Yeah, good. Really good, actually. She's doing well this season."

"I'm glad to hear what happened last year didn't ruin things entirely."

"Not quite," I said with a half-smile. I paused. Why did things feel so damn *awkward?* "I best be off," I said, placing my still-full mug on the counter. "I just wanted to check in, make sure you're okay. I'll go say goodbye to the kids." I made to leave and then paused. "Oh, and Adrianna," I said, turning towards her. She looked up at me. "I don't know exactly what Mickey had got himself caught up in, but if anything out of the ordinary happens, no matter how coincidental, I want you to call me, okay?"

She frowned and then nodded.

Chapter 41

STACEY JAMES

PROFESSOR LINDBERG'S OFFICE

Wednesday 13th October

"How are you doing?" asked Professor Lindberg, leaning back in her chair.

"Better," replied Stacey, and then added, "I think." Where had all this uncertainty come from? She used to be so decisive, so assertive. She knew it was because of Liam, because of what had happened last year. And she hated him for it.

"I'd say so," said Lindberg with a smile. "I saw your race. What you did out on the track."

Stacey gave a small smile. "I got into a lot of trouble for that."

Lindberg smiled back. "When was the last time you felt that in control?"

"When I'm racing," she answered without hesitation. "Whenever I'm racing, I feel in control." And she realised it was true. When she was behind the wheel, she didn't agonise over the decisions she made, didn't feel this constant anxiety in the pit of her stomach.

"Do you want to talk about yesterday?" asked Lindberg.

The quick change in conversation threw her off balance. The honest answer was no. She didn't want to think about it. Didn't want to pick through the conversation again. She'd already done that in her head more times than she cared to count.

She stood up and walked to the window, suddenly feeling on edge, and wondering where to begin. Looking out at the quiet residential street below, she felt calmer, less like she was trapped in a box with no way out. She took several deep breaths. Focusing on breathing in through her mouth and out through her nose, just as Lindberg had taught her to do in times of stress.

"I think it went well," said Stacey, turning to look at Lindberg. "We were both able to say our bits, get stuff off our chest, and while I don't think all is forgiven, I feel like we can move forward."

"That's great," said Lindberg enthusiastically, a smile lighting up her face. "I know you blame Liam, but Diane was a large part of it all too. Were you able to apologise to her for the way you treated her?"

Stacey slowly walked back over to her chair and then sat down. Unsure how to respond, she looked down at her hands and nodded. But it didn't stop a wave of guilt from sweeping over her.

She hadn't realised she'd been doing it at the time, hadn't realised she'd been so awful. Diane had brought it up once, pointed it out to her and suddenly she could see it. Saw how she spoke to her. How she became a different person when Diane was around. She didn't know why Diane seemed to bring it out in her. Jason might have even pointed it out to her once. And it was her behaviour that had tipped Diane over the edge, made her believe she was responsible for Gemma's death, got her embroiled with the Russians, blackmailed into money laundering. All because of Stacey.

She buried her head in her hands and let out a rush of breath.

"It's okay, take your time," said Lindberg.

Stacey concentrated on her breathing, on reigning her emotions back in.

"I feel exhausted," she said. And she knew she looked it too. She thought she'd be able to welcome a good night's sleep, be able to finally rest and recuperate, but instead she just felt emotionally drained.

"It can take its toll. You took some big steps forward yesterday. You confronted a lot of stuff that's been weighing you down. I bet you felt relieved when you walked out."

"Yeah, I did." And it was true. When visiting hours were over and the inmates were asked to return, Stacey had felt lighter than she had in months. Diane had given her the briefest of smiles and held out her hand as a gesture of a new friendship. Batting it aside, Stacey had pulled her into a quick hug before saying goodbye.

"What comes next?"

Stacey frowned. "What do you mean?"

"What comes next?" repeated Lindberg.

Stacey thought for a moment. How did she answer that? Truthfully, she had no idea what would come next, but she knew that wasn't an answer that would satisfy Lindberg.

She'd promised Diane she would visit again, and soon. That was something. And then there was her racing academy. She'd finally worked up enough courage to write up a business plan and actually think about how it would work, and she was excited about it.

She'd only gotten this far in her racing career because of scholarships, and even then she'd been turned down plenty of times simply for being a woman. The assumption she wouldn't be able to keep pace because of her gender had been a barrier she'd come up against time and time again. She didn't want that for others. She wanted to create a supportive pathway for those wanting to get into the industry.

She told Lindberg all of this. And as she talked, she could feel the passion rising in her, taking hold. It had been a long time since she'd felt so fired up about something. Sure, she'd had glimmers of it out on the track but those moments quickly faded away, leaving her feeling empty and hollow.

When she finally paused for breath, she saw that Lindberg was smiling.

"What?" asked Stacey.

"It's good to see your enthusiasm," she replied.

Chapter 42

JASON HUNTER

HOME

Wednesday 13th October

I tipped the saucepan of pasta into the colander in the sink.

"How was it?" I called over my shoulder.

"Ugh," groaned Stacey, appearing in the doorway to the living room. "Draining. It always is. We talked about my visit to see Diane."

"All good, though, right?" I said, turning to look at her.

"Yeah." She caught her bottom lip between her teeth and even from this distance I could see how hard she was biting it.

"What's wrong?" I asked with a frown.

"Lindberg thinks I hold Diane responsible, which I guess is true, but then I hold myself even more responsible, right? Because it was me that drove her to it all in the first place. If it wasn't for me, Gemma would still be alive, Liam wouldn't have been able to manipulate her so easily—"

"Stop," I said, approaching her and placing a hand on her shoulders.

Stacey looked up at me. Her eyes were brimming with tears that threatened to spill over. I knew she blamed herself, hard not to when it was your body double who died, but everything that had happened was entirely Liam's fault and I thought she knew that. A part of me felt annoyed at Lindberg for leading Stacey down this path.

"You can't think like that," I said, taking hold of her hand. "Liam's the one who is at fault. He manipulated everyone, Gromov included. And you can't blame yourself for what he did. There's no guarantee that things would have happened any differently. Even if Gemma hadn't died, someone else would have."

She nodded but didn't meet my gaze.

"All you can do now," I said, placing a finger on her chin and tilting her face up, "is to put it behind you and move forward. You've done the right thing in going to visit her, and hopefully she sees that and appreciates how hard that must be for you. Then it's up to her whether she accepts your apology or not."

She studied me for a few moments before nodding again and giving me a weak smile.

"I don't know what I did in a past life to deserve you, Mr Hunter," she said. I leaned forwards and gently kissed her.

"I'd love to know," I said as I pulled away and she chuckled.

The sound of sizzling punctuated the quiet. "Shit!" I said, letting go of Stacey and turning around to face the hob. I dashed forwards, turned the gas off and frantically began to stir the sauce.

Satisfied it wasn't completely ruined, I served up the drained pasta and then topped it with my homemade tomato and basil sauce.

I placed both dishes down on the kitchen island. Stacey pulled one closer so it sat in front of her, then scooped up some of the pasta and twirled it round on her fork.

"So," she said after a while, dragging the syllable out. "How were the interviews yesterday?"

I swallowed what was in my mouth. "Yeah, good. A few promising ones in there."

"That is good news. Kinda wish you'd thought of this back when I came on board. It would have been great to have protection in the style of a couple of girlfriends."

I laughed, but it also made me realise that Stacey didn't really have too many friends. Wherever we went, she knew almost everyone but I hadn't once heard her talk about a real friend, or even seen her hang out with someone who wasn't involved in her racing world.

"I can't take all the credit," I said. "It was actually your idea."

"Yeah?" she asked.

I nodded.

"Do I get a cut of the profits?" she said with a smirk.

"I tell you what," I said. "I'll treat you to a date night."

"Oh Mr Hunter, you do spoil me," she said and lightly tapped me on the wrist.

I shook my head. She was such a flirt and I loved it.

"It's actually got me thinking," she said, suddenly more serious.

"About what?"

"Well, there aren't many women in Formula One. In fact, it's just me. But that isn't for a lack of trying. There are a lot of female racing teams in other divisions, other competitions. And then there's the engineers, mechanics, personal trainers; plenty of women doing those jobs too. So where are they in Formula One?"

"That's a good question." Finished eating, I scooped my bowl and fork up, rinsed them off in the sink and placed them to one side, ready to be loaded into the dishwasher later. "What's the answer?" I asked, opening the fridge and pulling out two beers.

"What about a Formula One school? Women only. It could cover all areas of F1 and give industry appropriate training alongside its own driving school?"

I placed a beer on the counter in front of Stacey and opened the second.

"I think it's a great idea," I said, perching back on my stool. And it was true. I could see it now; creating the next generation of women racers who disrupted the industry like no-one else had done before. "I think you're onto something."

"Yeah?"

I nodded as I took a swig of beer. "The Stacey James Academy," I said, waving my hand in the air like I could see her name in lights.

She smiled, finished off her last bite of food and then dropped her bowl and fork in the sink.

"I like it."

"Me too," I said, placing my bottle on the counter and pulling her into me.

Chapter 43

Jason Hunter

Home

Wednesday 13th October

We spent the evening curled up on the sofa watching a Chris Pine movie about bank robberies. It was the perfect slice of normality I didn't know I'd been missing. For a couple of blissful hours, it felt like the chaos of the last week was just a distant memory.

My arm was around Stacey's waist and she leaned back into me. I'm sure it was so she could stay warm, but I didn't mind. I loved to hold her. It was a comforting routine we'd built up over the last year but since Mickey's death, all normality seemed to have gone out the window. Which was to be expected, considering the circumstances, but it still gnawed at me.

The credits rolled onto the screen and Stacey picked up the remote, going back to the Netflix home screen.

"What are we gonna do about that Alfonso guy?"

"Alfonso Torres?" asked Stacey, her head whipping around to look at me.

I nodded.

"There's nothing we can do," she said with a casual shrug, looping an arm around her knees.

"That's never stopped us before," I said with a smile. Her eyes flicked to me and then back to the TV screen. "What?" I asked.

"I know what that fight with Hayley was about," she said, not looking at me. She concentrated on flicking through our TV choices, but she wasn't pausing long enough on anything to read it.

"I'm not suggesting we go rogue behind her back. I was thinking more along the lines of brainstorming some constructive ideas." I could see her roll her eyes. "Hey," I said and nudged her. She laughed, putting the remote down and turning to look at me.

"Okay. What do you want to do?"

"I want to find out what the hell is going on. What's got Cameron so worked up about Old Fonso being in her club?"

"And how do you propose we go about doing that?"

"Absolutely no idea," I said. "You know more about him than I do, what do you think he was doing there?"

She looked thoughtful for a moment before shrugging. "The guy's rich and it's an exclusive club. Seems like that's exactly where he would be."

"Okay, what about Lindberg and Mickey's lucrative side hustle?"

I could sense her starting to get frustrated. "What are you talking about?"

"Well, Lindberg knows who Mickey is. She says it's to do with his community service, and in all honesty, she's probably telling the truth. At least that's how they met. But what if Lindberg was actually supplying prescription drugs to Mickey who then distributed them via the club? Do you think Alfonso could be in on that?"

"That feels far-fetched to me. Considering how much Torres makes from Formula One, why would he need to dabble in low level drug dealing? Even if he's just taking the profits. That seems too risky. And if I was him, I definitely wouldn't be seen in the one place I have affiliations," said Stacey, easily destroying my theory.

"Besides," she continued, "we don't actually know that's what was going on between Lindberg and Mickey, and Cameron wasn't able to confirm anything like that was happening."

"She's hardly going to confirm her club is a known drug den, is she?"

"You're basing this theory on coincidences. If you want to help Hayley, you need something a lot more concrete. And dropping Cameron in it like that is not going to earn you any favours."

"True," I replied. Damn, she was good.

We sat in silence for a moment and Stacey went back to flicking through the movies on Netflix.

"What if it's related to what Mickey stole?"

She paused and looked at me.

"What if that's why Cameron was worried?" I continued. "It's obvious she knew what he was doing. How could she not? And maybe Alfonso has been throwing his weight around there before."

"That would make sense," she said.

"Gromov said his contacts were powerful people. Power more often than not means money. And those with a lot of money have a lot to lose. Most of them have done questionable things to get to where they are."

"That brings us back to the same old question we can't answer though, doesn't it?" said Stacey. "What on Earth did Mickey steal?"

Chapter 44

JASON HUNTER

THE OFFICE

Thursday 14th October

"It's so good to see you again," I said, holding open the door to the boardroom. "And thank you for making the trip," I added. I gestured to the seats. "Tea? Coffee?"

"A peppermint tea, if you have it," said Iris McCleary.

"Coffee. Black, no sugar, for me," said Vance Cherry. They both took a seat while I passed their drinks orders on to Lucy who graciously headed to the kitchen.

"When we last met, I mentioned a female-only team."

Iris nodded eagerly, her delicate features lighting up with a smile. "I love the idea. A more subtle way of offering protection. I don't want to be hidden behind burly figures. It's not good for the paparazzi and it's not good for the over-eager fans either. It tells them I've heard them."

"Exactly." Lucy appeared at the door. I opened it and took the tray from her with my thanks. Placing the tray on the boardroom table, I passed out the drinks. "So, earlier this week I met with a few individuals who I thought would be a good fit for the job. And as they'll be with you for the duration of your tour, it's important you feel comfortable with them."

Iris nodded and took a sip of her peppermint tea, the end of the teabag dangling over the side.

"For today, we'll go through profiles, get your first thoughts and then we'll arrange an informal meeting where you can let me know if they make the cut or not."

Iris nodded again. Vance, surprisingly, stayed quiet.

I opened up my folder on the table and handed across the first profile.

"This is Aysha. She's 5 foot 1. Small but mighty. Military trained, she's served in Iraq and Afghanistan. Not for the Brits though; she's American."

Iris studied the photo in the top right corner of Aysha's profile sheet and then nodded her head. I handed across the second profile.

"Lauren is SIA trained. She has experience working as a bouncer for a number of different clubs in London, and has been hired as personal protection on a freelance basis in the past. She's trained in Taekwondo and packs a mean punch." That made Iris laugh.

I passed across the third profile.

"Neve is also British but she grew up in Hong Kong. Her parents work for the British Consulate there. She can speak four languages; Chinese, English, Spanish and Arabic."

From the corner of my eye, I could see Vance watching Iris and the look on his face made me think he was impressed. Had he seriously thought so little of me?

I ran through a few more of the faces I'd interviewed with Divya before sitting back, satisfied I'd given her enough to choose from.

"So, what do you think?" I asked, taking a sip of my lukewarm coffee. I tried hard not to pull a face.

"They almost feel overqualified," she said with a small smile.

"We pride ourselves on only hiring the best in the industry."

She nodded, looking at the faces spread out on the table in front of her.

"How many would you say she needs?" asked Vance. It was the first time he'd spoken since we'd sat down. The last time we'd met, he'd insisted on speaking for Iris for most of the meeting. Now I was wondering whether that was an act, and this was the real Vancy Cherry.

"I'd suggest four, if we can find four you're happy with," I said. "It means we can rotate teams to be two on and two off. Ultimately, it's up to you and who you feel comfortable with. We can work with a smaller team if we need to."

Iris nodded. "Can I take these away and think about it?"

"Of course. We've got a couple of weeks until the tour starts, so ideally, I'd like to get this locked in by the end of next week."

Iris nodded again. For someone who made a living by using her voice, she sure was quiet. It never failed to amaze me how the famous name in the limelight didn't always match the real person behind the scenes. Stacey was a perfect example of this; she was still her usual bubbly self in the media, but behind closed doors, she was definitely battling with her own demons, and last night had been an eye-opening moment. I wondered how Iris felt when she adopted her on-stage persona. Did it make her feel more confident? Did it feel like she was being herself? I found it hard to reconcile the quiet, calm girl before me with the bouncing, larger-than-life popstar.

Chapter 45

JASON HUNTER

THE OFFICE

Thursday 14th October

A knock at the door interrupted me. I looked up to see Zack poke his head in.

"You got a minute?" he asked.

"Sure," I gestured to the chair opposite my desk and leaned back. I needed a break anyway. I'd been rota planning which always gave me a headache. It was difficult juggling as many contracts as we did, and each one had its own unique needs. I would have handed it over to Richard but he was tied up with new client meetings and Divya needed to know how many new hires I wanted. Which made this a priority.

Zack entered my office, leaving the door slightly ajar behind him which told me it wasn't anything confidential.

"I just wanted to show you the new mockups. Make sure you're happy with them before I give them the go-ahead."

"Exciting times."

Zack smiled. "I think you're gonna like it."

I didn't doubt it, but he had my curiosity piqued. I'd already seen a few concepts from him and liked the direction it was going. In fact, the last time we'd sat down together, his vision had been exactly what we needed.

"I've emailed you a couple of links. If you could put the first one up on the board, I can talk you through it."

I did as he asked, and powered up the whiteboard projector. The wall opposite my desk came to life and mirrored my laptop screen. I opened the link in the email which loaded a website preview. Zack gave me a few minutes to familiarise myself with the new site. It was sleek, stylish and featured casual photos of the team, including a few of Sam in action. I smiled. It was great.

"I love it," I said.

Zack took me through the site page by page, showing me the new styling, the new brand positioning and the new functionality of the site. It was more than I could have hoped for, and I was confident it would help fix our current image.

Hawk Security was written in gold in the top left-hand corner of the screen, intertwined with an outline of a hawk. The rest of the site was mostly black, with gold used to accentuate different elements. Even the photos were black and white, giving it a professional feel.

"Who took the photos?" I asked.

"Me," said Zack casually.

"They're really good," I said, surprised.

"Thanks." He grinned. "The hardest thing was trying to get a few willing participants to model for me."

I laughed. "Yeah, I bet. God knows how you managed to talk Sam into it," I said, nodding towards the screen where Sam was holding open the door to a sleek black car while looking over his shoulder.

"Let's just say I owe a few favours around here now."

I laughed again. "Well, it looks great."

"Super. If you click the second link in that email, I can show you our socials."

I did as he asked and he walked me through the new look and feel of our social channels, with the proposed tone and content for each. Once he was done with that, he then showed me mockups for business cards, office signage and any other collateral he could think of. I had to hand it to him, the man had done a thorough job.

I couldn't help but wonder why Adam had never let Zack do this before. It was obvious we could have done with an update for a while, and Zack clearly knew what he was doing.

"So have a look at it all, let me know if there's anything you want to change and if you're happy, I can set a go-live date."

"Great. This is amazing work, Zack. Thanks."

He gave me a small nod of satisfaction before leaving.

Chapter 46

JASON HUNTER

THE OFFICE

Friday 15th October

There was a knock at my office door and I looked up to see Lucy enter. Her usual cheery demeanour had vanished and she seemed nervous. I frowned.

"Lucy, what's up?"

"I've just had an email from FixRecruitment."

"Everything okay?"

"They've decided to cancel the contract."

I blinked, taken aback for a moment. "What? Why?"

"Well, I gave them a call, and Serina was quite reluctant to talk to me but she basically said they'd had someone get in touch who has explicitly told them to not work with us."

"What?" My voice was now full of disbelief. I almost couldn't believe what Lucy was telling me, but it was clear she wasn't done yet.

She bit her bottom lip for a half second, almost as if she was debating whether or not she should continue. "I pressed her for more details but she said she couldn't go into it, just that there would be consequences if they did proceed with the contract. And then she hung up on me."

I was speechless. It was literal sabotage.

"I'll call her."

"I really don't think—"

"It's fine, I'll call her. I'm sure it's just a misunderstanding."

"Jason, she's blocked our number. I've had a follow up email requesting we don't contact them again."

I dragged my hand over my face in frustration and then sat back in my chair. What the hell were we going to do? I'd been relying on that contract to help keep things afloat. To get the reputation of the business moving in the right direction again.

The more important question was who in hell was behind it? My mind flickered back to the anonymous text I'd received. Was this what they were talking about? Was this the price I was meant to pay?

My phone started ringing on the counter and I glanced down to see Vance Cherry's name light up the screen. I had a sneaky suspicion this was about to go from bad to worse.

"Thanks Lucy," I said.

She gave me an apologetic smile before leaving, closing the door behind her.

I picked up the phone.

"Who the hell did you piss off?" said Vance, skipping the pleasantries.

I pinched the bridge of my nose with my thumb and forefinger.

"Let me guess," I said. "Someone's been in touch to tell you not to sign the contract and threatened you about it?"

Vance laughed. "Got it in one."

"Fuck's sake," I muttered. "Can you tell me who?"

"None other than the office of Mayor Britland himself."

"Are you fucking joking me?" I said, almost dropping my phone. What the hell did the Mayor of London have against me? Gromov had warned me that powerful people were angry, but I'd just assumed we were talking about the rich and famous, not the politicians running the country.

Which meant the Mayor of London was involved in whatever it was that Mickey had done. Or taken. Maybe it was the Mayor he'd stolen from. I was so confused, I really didn't know what to think.

"What did you tell them?"

Vance laughed again. "They tried their hand at a little blackmail, but they don't seem to know that there's no such thing as bad publicity and I really couldn't care less." I chuckled at that. Of all the people to have a blasé attitude towards this, it had to be Vance. I'd warmed to him at our last meeting, and suddenly I felt grateful.

"Can you forward me what they sent you?" I asked.

"Of course. Pretty shitty play, if you ask me. But I ain't getting involved. We've spoken to god knows how many security firms now and Iris has flat out refused every single one of them. I'm not gonna tell the girl the one professional she liked is now off limits. The contract still stands, but if I was you, I'd sort this shit out pretty quickly before it turns nasty."

"Noted. I have a friend in the police. I'm gonna phone her as soon as we're done talking."

"Well, best of luck to you. I'd love to go for a pint some time and hear all about whatever it is you've been up to. I'm sure it's all above board." He laughed again. "I'll forward the information over now."

I hung up the phone, bewildered and fuming.

True to his word, an email appeared in my inbox from Vance within minutes. I opened it up and began reading. I could barely believe my eyes. He'd been right. It was direct from the Mayor's office and outlined some concerning discrepancies about my business and how we operated, including a reference to what had happened with Gemma and Stacey the previous year.

Vance had actually sent me a chain of emails. Because he'd replied to the initial outreach saying he appreciated the input and concern but assured the Mayor's office he'd done his due diligence in requesting a contract with me and was prepared to take the risk.

This clearly wasn't the reply that had been expected because the follow up email, whilst still perfectly polite, felt a lot more sinister. And the more I read it, the more I was sure it was a subtle threat. That's obviously how Vance had read it too. He'd mentioned something about blackmail but there was nothing in the email thread to indicate that, so maybe he'd received a phone call; much easier to cover up and much harder to prove.

Chapter 47

ADRIANNA BIANCHI

KENSAL GREEN CEMETERY

Friday 15th October

The sight of the coffin being carried on the shoulders of six of Mickey's friends almost broke her. These were people she'd invited into her home, had shared meals and drinks with while Mickey told stories and laughed, always larger than life. Now they carried his lifeless body to its final resting place and it felt like something inside her was tearing open.

She stood by the side of the empty grave, waiting. Waiting for the pain to go away, waiting for it to subside enough that she could breathe, waiting for the moment when she would wake up and realise it was all just an awful dream. But it didn't seem like that was going to happen any time soon. She was trapped in this nightmare and all she wanted to do was scream.

The coffin inched closer and it seemed to take a millennia for it to finally reach the graveside. It was lowered into the ground with care and precision. Was there really much more she could ask for?

Part of her wanted to keep her head bowed, to give in to the grief, but Mickey's voice in her head told her to look up, to stay strong, to show the world that fire in her that he loved so much. No matter where he was, he'd still be right there with her. So she did just that and looked resolutely ahead as the tears streamed down her cheeks. She knew it would ruin her makeup, but she didn't care.

A flash of colour in the corner of her eye made her turn, and she stared at the red-haired woman standing next to her. Whilst all the other mourners were clad in black, she stood bold in cherry red. Her hair, her lips, her dress, even the fascinator and attached veil were a deep cherry red.

The woman reached out and took Adrianna's hand silently, squeezing it in comfort and then turned to face the grave as one of Mickey's friends stepped forward to deliver the service. It wasn't long; Adrianna didn't have the stomach for a long, drawn-out goodbye. Her beloved Mickey was dead and no amount of lamenting would change that.

The whole thing passed by in a blur of grief and it felt like only minutes later when the crowd of people began to disperse. Most approached her to pass on their condolences and she nodded wordlessly, accepting each one with a silent 'thank you' while the gaping hole in her chest seemed to grow.

The woman in red stayed by her side, unmoving, until the last person had said their goodbyes and the gravediggers crept forward to pour the dirt over her husband's coffin.

"Come along now, darling," said the woman. "I think you need a stiff drink and a good cry."

Adrianna let herself be led away. As she turned around, she caught sight of a tall, burly man standing in the corner of the graveyard, under a tree, his eyes fixed on them. There was nothing particularly memorable about him and she would have completely missed him had he not tilted his head in a solemn nod of respect. The woman in red stiffened. Before she could do anything else, he turned on his heels and left, his backpack bobbing between the gravestones.

Chapter 48

Jason Hunter

Adrianna's penthouse

Friday 15th October

I was sitting in my old BMW, looking up at the fancy houses and apartments of Holland Park. My phone was pressed against my ear while I waited for Hayley to pick up. I didn't have to wait long.

"Hi Jason, how are you? It's been a while? How are the kids? Oh, good news. What can I do for you?"

"Are you gonna do this every time I call?" I was too tense to join in with her banter today. The phone call from Vance Cherry that morning had thrown one hell of a curveball my way and I wasn't happy. Of course, I'd tried phoning the Mayor's office after. I wanted to speak to the bastard, confront him if possible, but knew it was unlikely to happen. I settled for leaving a terse message with his PA who assured me he'd be in touch as soon as he could.

As if.

"If you're gonna bust my ass for not being polite, then yeah, probably."

"I had a phone call this morning," I said.

"From who?" Her voice was suddenly serious and I knew she'd picked up on my mood.

"In fact, I had two. One from a client who's cancelled on me. And the other from a client who's been threatened by the Mayor's office."

There was a silence on the other end of the line, followed by some rummaging. The background noise disappeared as the sound of a door closed.

"Jason, what the hell are you talking about?" said Hayley, urgently. I imagined she was now back in her cramped office with the door shut, pacing up and down.

"The client who cancelled told Lucy they'd been warned off us. And when my other client politely told them he'd still be using us, he was threatened."

"What's this got to do with the Mayor?"

"It was his office who sent the damn emails."

"Are you sure it wasn't someone pretending to be him? A hacker, maybe?"

"I don't know, Hayley," I said exasperated. "Do I look like an IT technician? Whether it's real or not is beside the point. Someone has an agenda."

She didn't answer for a moment.

"Is this the first time anything like this has happened?"

My mind flicked back to the text I'd received and I hesitated before filling her in on all the details. She needed to know, especially if it was connected to Mickey's death. It could be important.

"You should have told me sooner."

"I know, I know. There's been a lot going on."

"Send me a copy of the text, and the emails if you have them. I'll speak to our tech team, but it's likely we'll need access to your phone."

"Sure, sure." I watched a woman and her dog walk down the street. "One more thing," I said.

"What?"

"I actually wanted to know if Adrianna's place was still taped off?"

"No, it was released last week. We're done processing so no need to keep it locked down. Did Adrianna not tell you?"

I hesitated for a moment. Depending on when exactly her apartment restriction had been lifted, it could have coincided with her coming over to the house and then trying to kiss me.

"It must have slipped her mind," I said. "It's Mickey's funeral today."

Hayley's tone changed and I could hear the remorse in her voice. "I know. I was hoping to swing by and pay my respects but things kinda got away from me today."

"In all honesty, that might be a good thing. She's still on your suspect list, right?"

"Until I can rule her out or someone else steps into the frame, yep."

I made a mental note: I needed to do more to establish Adrianna's innocence.

"Right, I'll forward those bits to you now," I said after a beat.

"I'll keep you in the loop," she promised.

I ended the call and climbed out of my car into the crisp October air. I didn't really get why people always said Autumn was the best time of year. I knew a large part of the appeal was getting cosy when things started to get cold, but I definitely didn't enjoy the sudden drop in temperature. And now, as the wind rustled around me, I pulled my coat tighter, wishing I was somewhere warm.

Entering Adrianna's building, I gave a friendly nod to the resident trying to corral two small children into their winter coats. She didn't return my greeting, staring at me with a frown creasing her forehead. I guess that was to be expected considering someone had recently been murdered in the building. Strangers were unlikely to be welcome.

I took the lift to the top floor and followed the familiar hallway to Adrianna's front door. I thought about knocking but I knew she was at Imani's, with no intention of coming back here any time soon.

Instead, I pulled out my keys and found the silver, unused key to Adrianna's apartment. She'd given it to me about a year ago, when we'd settled into a happy truce after Stacey's ordeal. At the time it made sense, so I could pick up or drop the kids off around their school schedule should she be busy. Except I'd never had cause to use it, until now.

I slipped it into the lock, slightly surprised she hadn't thought to change the locks after Mickey's murder. But then if she hadn't come home yet, it would be far down on her list of priorities right now. The lock clicked and the door swung open.

Walking into the familiar apartment, there was an eerie quiet that had settled over everything. The lights were off and a weak autumnal sun filtered through the windows. I noticed that the white rug that had been soaked in Mickey's blood was gone, and the floor looked bare.

I wasn't sure what I was hoping to find here, but I figured looking around Mickey's office again wouldn't hurt. At least now we knew why Mickey had been killed. I thought back to the crime scene and how his office had been upturned. The theory was the killer had been looking for something, and now I knew that was true. So *what* was it that Mickey had taken?

I moved further into the apartment, knowing that I was violating Adrianna's trust and privacy with every step.

Before I was even halfway to the office, something small and solid collided with the back of my head. I winced, let out a yelp and spun around only to be clipped in the face by another flying object. My hand flew to my face in pain and I felt a warm liquid on my fingers.

"Jason!"

Flinching at the sound of my name and wary of another attack, I looked up to see Adrianna leaning over the upstairs railing, her hand raised above her shoulder, clutching something that looked like a small projectile.

"What the hell are you doing?" I yelled, pulling my hand away from my face to confirm it was blood coating my fingers. Whatever she'd thrown had split my eyebrow. Had there not been enough blood spilt in this apartment?

"What the hell are *you* doing?" she countered. "This is my apartment."

Ah. She had me there.

"Sorry, I didn't think you'd be here."

"Obviously." She rolled her eyes and her expression of surprise turned to annoyance.

"I wanted to see if the police had missed anything."

"What? Because suddenly you're better than the police, are you?" She descended the spiral staircase and approached me through the open plan kitchen. She clutched a worn stuffed teddy in her hand.

"More like looking for inspiration." I looked around to see what it was she'd thrown at me. I spotted two of Max's toy Hot Wheels cars on the floor.

"Sorry about that," she said, gesturing to my eyebrow. She walked over to the sink, placed the bear on the counter to one side, pulled off a sheet of kitchen paper and ran it under the tap. "You startled me," she said and placed the damp paper towel to the cut on my face.

"I didn't think you were home yet, otherwise I would have knocked."

"Well, technically, I'm not. I just wanted some space."

And that was when I put it all together. "The funeral," I said, feeling like an insensitive idiot. Adrianna was clearly trying to process her grief in private.

She nodded, swapped her hand for mine and went back to the teddy on the countertop.

"I just wanted to have a look through some stuff. Just being sentimental more than anything," she said quietly and held up the bear as if that explained everything.

"How did it go?" I asked.

"I'm not sure I can use the word 'good'. That doesn't feel right. I mean, it was fine. Nothing went wrong, everyone had such nice things to say about him."

The room fell silent as she continued to examine the stuffed teddy and a lone tear trickled down her cheek. I thought back to the weeks Stacey was in hospital after the crash where Liam had kidnapped her from Gromov's party and the anguish that I'd felt. The anxiety and constant turmoil over whether or not she would survive. I couldn't even begin to think about how I'd feel had she not made it through.

"I should go," I said. "Leave you in peace."

She looked up at me and swiped the tear away. "No, it's fine. Stay. What was it you were looking for?"

"Are you sure?"

"I'll just wallow in self-pity otherwise, and I think I've done enough of that today."

I studied her face and then nodded. "How about I boil the kettle?"

"That would be great," she said and gave me a small smile.

Shrugging out of my coat, I laid it over the back of the sofa and headed into the kitchen.

"I met Cameron today," she said.

"You what?" I said, turning to face her, kettle in hand.

"I met Cameron. She came to the funeral."

"Did she now?" I muttered as I made the drinks.

"I really like her. She was quite close with Mickey by the sounds of it. Professionally speaking, that is," she added.

I made a noncommittal sound, not wanting to let on that I'd already met her.

"She told me that she spoke to you," said Adrianna with a sigh. I looked up, worried, but she had an amused look on her face. I placed a mug of herbal tea on the counter in front of her and she scooped it up to cradle in her hands. "I just don't know why you wouldn't tell me."

"I don't want you getting caught up in his mess," I said.

She looked down at her mug, frowning, and for a moment I thought I'd upset her.

"I just feel like the less you know, the better. When I know exactly what's happened, I'll tell you. But there's no point worrying you with every lead I'm following up."

"I guess," she said and shrugged.

I took a sip of my drink, unsure of what to say next.

"Oh I know what I was meant to tell you," she said. "You told me to tell you if anything strange happened."

"And?" I watched her face carefully, wondering where this was going.

"There was a guy at the funeral. He wasn't with everyone else, and I only noticed him at the end. Me and Cameron were the only ones left. I turned around and he was standing way back, watching."

I frowned. "Did you recognise him?"

"No." She shook her head. "Never seen him before."

"And he didn't approach the graveside or anything?"

She shook her head again and sipped her tea. "He kinda nodded at me as if I should've known who he was. Cameron got a bit weird. And then he disappeared."

"Anything else?"

She shrugged. "The whole thing was weird and I can't say I was really paying attention. He was wearing a rucksack which seemed odd. Who'd bring a rucksack to a funeral?"

"Rucksack?"

"Yeah, a big thing, kinda square."

"And Cameron recognised him?"

"I think so. I mean, I didn't ask her about him, I was a bit distracted."

"Of course, of course," I mumbled, my brain working at a million miles an hour. Had the man who killed Mickey shown up at his funeral? And why? Everything we knew about the shooter so far indicated her was nothing if not professional. The man was practically a ghost. He was a gun for hire, so it's not like he was emotionally attached to his victims. Unless Mickey was different? Did he know Mickey personally?

I was running through different scenarios in my head as to why the gunman might decide to show his face in such a public place.

And then I suddenly had a horrible thought.

Was he a message from Gromov's supposed 'contacts'? Was he following my family? Was he *meant* to be seen?

"I think you should speak to Hayley about this."

"Really? Do you know who he is?"

I weighed up whether I should tell her. On the one hand I didn't want to freak her out, but then she'd already caught me out with the Cameron thing and I didn't want this to come back and bite me in the ass.

So I decided on honesty as the best policy.

"I think he could be Mickey's killer."

Adrianna sucked in a sharp breath and her eyes went wide. Her hand flew to her mouth and I instantly regretted saying it. Today had been his funeral for god's sake.

"I'm sorry, I didn't mean to—"

"It's okay," she said, interrupting me. "I shouldn't have asked."

"I obviously don't know for sure, it's just a hunch."

Adrianna nodded.

"But if you saw what he looked like, this could be huge. You might be able to ID him, which means Hayley might actually be able to catch the guy."

Adrianna nodded again. This time she seemed more confident, as if suddenly she'd realised we could get the bad guy.

I drained the rest of my mug and put it on the counter. "Do you mind if I take a look in Mickey's office?" I asked.

"Go ahead," she said and waved in the direction of the corridor.

Chapter 49

JASON HUNTER

ADRIANNA'S PENTHOUSE

Friday 15th October

I headed down the hallway and entered Mickey's office. The place looked exactly the same as when I'd first visited. Papers, glass and debris littered the floor, the door to the safe was still wide open, and the leather chair behind the mahogany desk was torn to shreds.

A small part of me had thought the clean-up crew would have been in here, but I knew they mostly dealt with bloodstains and bodily fluids instead of general tidy up. And perhaps Adrianna hadn't wanted them in here. It had been Mickey's sanctuary after all.

I looked around, unsure where to start. Unsure what it was I was actually looking for. Instinctively, I headed to the safe. Logic would say this is where it was hidden. It made sense for Mickey to lock away something so valuable in his safe. His hidden safe, I reminded myself as I looked at the bookshelf next to it.

"What are you looking for?" asked Adrianna, making me jump.

I turned to see her standing in the doorway, leaning against the frame.

"I'm not sure," I answered honestly. "Do you know the combination to the safe?"

"It's biometric," she said.

Interesting. So that's not where he kept it. He wouldn't risk Adrianna coming across it and putting her in even more danger.

I was starting to get a feel for the way Mickey thought. Or at least, I think I was. He clearly valued Adrianna and the kids above anything else, and I think he would have been kicking himself for putting them in harm's way.

Which made me think. Perhaps he was trying to offload whatever he had onto someone else. Was he using it to blackmail someone? Maybe that's how it had started, that's what he'd wanted to do originally, but when he realised the danger it was putting his family in, he needed to change tact.

As a theory, it wasn't bad. And gave me an idea on how or what to search this place for.

I closed the safe, confident that Adrianna would be able to open it again if we needed to, and slid the bookcase into place.

Adrianna let out a gasp. My eyes shot to her, still in the doorway and I saw she was looking at the wall where the bookcase had been just a moment before. I turned around to see giant, angry letters carved into the wall.

THIS ISN'T OVER

Without hesitating, I slipped my phone from my pocket and took a photo, wondering who the message was intended for. Surely Mickey was already dead when this was done. How else would someone have been able to gain access to the office? It had obviously been there since before the police cordoned the apartment off, as the safe was still open and blocking the bookcase from moving.

So that left three possible scenarios: Adrianna could have written this on the wall herself. She'd already admitted to having access to the safe, but it seemed highly unlikely. Unless she'd murdered Mickey herself or hired the guy that did it, and staged everything up until now. A theory I knew Hayley was still working with, but one I couldn't believe. Adrianna's grief felt real, and I couldn't see a motive for her to kill him.

The second scenario was that Mickey had written these words himself, though the motivation behind that idea was very unclear. Was he working with the killer? Did he know the killer was coming? Did he want to freak them out, knowing that he'd likely be dead? I didn't really buy it.

The third scenario, and certainly the most likely, was that the killer wrote this. The letters were angry, gouged into the plasterboard of the wall. In too much of a rush to look around for a pen, clearly. Although I can't imagine writing on the wall in a ballpoint would have the same effect. But why? He must have written the message before he discovered the safe, which meant he didn't have what he'd come here for. But then he must have found the safe, and whatever had been inside it.

Unless it was for show. A lot of what had transpired since Mickey's death had been misdirection, smoke and mirrors. Cameron was a great example of that. No-one had a clue she was a woman, not even Adrianna.

I honestly had no idea how Hayley managed to do this on a daily basis. All this thinking in circles was starting to make my head hurt. And no matter how many times it felt like we were making progress, new avenues opened up a never-ending sprawl of questions.

I leaned closer to the wall, inspecting the lettering, trying to work out what the killer had used to carve the words. From this angle, I could see the roller mechanism on the bookcase more clearly. Perhaps the killer had searched the room, gotten frustrated, and then seen the runners for the bookcase when he was carving the message, realising it was hiding something.

While that seemed like logical reasoning, and a plausible sequence of events, it still left a bunch of unanswered questions. Like, how the hell did the killer get into the safe in the first place? It didn't look like it had been tampered with.

"Who else would have been able to get access to the safe?" I asked, turning to face Adrianna. Her arms were folded across her chest as she watched me.

She frowned. "No one. Just me and him."

"I'm trying to work out how the safe was opened," I said, gesturing to the bookcase that now hid it from view. "It doesn't look like it's been broken into it. In fact, it's working perfectly fine. I've just locked it. So how did the killer get into it?"

"I don't know." Then she looked suspicious. "Are you trying to insinuate—"

"No, no," I said, holding up my hands. "I'm just trying to answer the questions."

She was still frowning at me. "Well, I don't know," she said with a huff.

I decided to leave it at that for now. I didn't want to piss Adrianna off; I may still need her help. And I didn't honestly think she would know anyway.

"What's this that's broken?" I asked, pointing to the large chunks of glass on the floor.

"I'm not sure," she said, and looked around the room for the source.

"What about the papers?" I picked a few up off the floor and handed them to her. She tentatively stepped forward and took them from me. She glanced through them as I scooped up a few more.

"These look like business deals," she said.

"Why don't you take a seat?" I said, gesturing at the desk. "I'll pass them to you and you tell me if anything looks strange."

She nodded and did as I suggested, gingerly sitting in the torn leather chair that seemed to swallow her up.

We worked in silence. Me picking up and organising the stuff strewn everywhere while Adrianna read through the papers. Nothing seemed to jump out as unusual. Although little of it made sense; business deals and club paperwork mixed in with the usual life admin of credit cards and household bills.

"I don't know what this is," she said, breaking the silence and holding up a piece of paper. She handed it to me and I scanned the page. It was an invoice from a company called Vault Bank. And it was paid nearly two weeks ago.

I quickly Googled the company name on my phone to discover they offered safety deposit boxes. I showed it to Adrianna.

"What would Mickey need a safe deposit box for?" I asked.

"I have no idea," she said, looking shocked. I felt a little guilty because the more we dug into this, into Mickey's secrets, the more Adrianna would question if she really knew the man she'd married.

I looked at the invoice again. If I was a betting man, I'd say that whatever Mickey had taken was currently hidden away somewhere at Vault Bank.

Chapter 50

JASON HUNTER

SOMEWHERE IN KNIGHTSBRIDGE

Friday 15th October

The rain splattered onto the windscreen as I drove down Brompton Road. Throngs of people rushed around, sheltering under umbrellas and the hoods of their jackets. Harrods was busier than ever, with people pouring through the doors. It seemed the typical British weather wasn't too off-putting for tourists and locals.

We turned down one side street and another, the crowds thinning as we traveled. I parked the car and we climbed out, both of us pulling the hoods up on our coats. I looked up at the discreet sign displaying the letters 'VB'.

"You ready?" I asked, turning to see Adrianna nod. "After you." I opened the door and gestured for her to go in. I followed close behind.

Inside was small and compact. A receptionist sat behind a small desk, a fresh vase of flowers next to him. The room was sparsely decorated and could barely fit more than four people.

Adrianna approached the desk and cleared her throat.

The receptionist, a man in his early thirties, looked up and gave us a warm smile.

"Welcome to Vault Bank. How can I help you?"

"I'm looking to access my husband's safe deposit box."

"Do you have the access card?"

Adrianna glanced at me before turning back to the receptionist. "I'm afraid I don't," she said. "He, erm, he died recently."

"I'm so sorry."

"Thank you," she whispered and then handed the invoice over. "I found this in his possessions. I don't have an acccss card, I'm afraid."

The receptionist took the piece of paper from Andrianna. He looked at it for a few moments before typing away on his keyboard.

"Do you have any ID?"

"Of course," she said and rummaged in her handbag, pulling out her purse. She handed him her ID, and he glanced quickly at it before handing it back.

"That's fine. Mr Serrano has you listed as a nominee on his account which means you're able to access his safe deposit box. But I will need to charge an administration fee of £15 to cover the cost of issuing a new access card."

"Of course, of course."

The receptionist did what he needed to on the computer, then pulled open a drawer to his left and took out a new, plastic card, the same size and shape as a bank card. He indicated for Adrianna to pay using the terminal on the chest-high counter before tapping the new access card on the little machine in the corner of his desk.

Handing the card to Adrianna, he said, "Excellent, that's all set up for you. Your box number is 5129. There is a table in the vault where you can open it but if you would like somewhere more private, we do have a private viewing room that's available on request."

Adrianna nodded.

"Just go on through when you're ready," he said and gestured to a door in the wall next to his desk.

"Thank you," she said. "How do I—" she trailed off.

"Just place your finger on the biometric scanner."

She nodded. "Do you need my fingerprint first?"

"Nope, it's already set up in the system," he said with a glance at his screen and a nod of confirmation.

I frowned. Weird. How had Mickey managed to set up Adrianna's biometrics without her knowing?

"Oh, okay." She placed a finger on the scanner next to the door. It beeped once and then the door clicked open. I made to follow but the receptionist stopped me.

"I'm afraid it's named box holders and nominees only. There are no other names on this box so I can't let you through."

I looked at Adrianna and gave her a small nod. "No worries. I'll wait out here."

"I won't be long," she said quietly and then disappeared from view.

Unwilling to be cooped up in the tiny room with the receptionist, I walked back out onto the street to find the rain had stopped. It was times like this I wished I still smoked, just for something to do with my hands.

Instead, I dug them into my coat pockets and looked up and down the street. It was deserted.

I stared down at my watch, watching the minutes tick by as I wondered how Adrianna was getting on. Would she find what we were looking for? Would she finally have the answer to all the questions surrounding Mickey's death? I didn't know whether I should be worried about how clueless I was right now. We had absolutely no idea what Mickey might have in his safe deposit box. No idea what he'd taken from Gromov's contacts.

I was more interested in why Mickey was still using his old name. Was he doubling up his identities so he could get away with more shady dealings? Cameron had said he'd changed his identity at 18 but if that was the case, why was he setting up safe deposit boxes under his childhood name?

A woman appeared from one of the residential buildings a few doors down, pulling the door closed behind her. She glanced my way before heading down the street away from me, back to Brompton Road.

"Hey," said Adrianna, appearing at my side. I turned to face her.

"And?"

She looked disappointed and my stomach sank.

"It was empty."

My mouth dropped open. "Are you joking?"

"No. I opened the box on the table and there was nothing in it. No paperwork, no hidden identity cards, no nothing. It was completely empty."

"Why would he keep an empty safe deposit box?"

Adrianna shrugged. "I don't know."

"We need to go speak to Hayley," I said, pulling my phone from my pocket.

Chapter 51

JASON HUNTER

HAMMERSMITH POLICE STATION

Friday 15th October

Hayley looked at me incredulously.

"Let me get this straight," she said. "You found an invoice in Mickey's office for a safe deposit box?"

Adrianna nodded. She hadn't said a word since we'd stepped into Hayley's office. I was assuming it was because she was nervous. The last time she'd spoken to Hayley it was as the prime suspect in a murder investigation. So I could understand her apprehension.

I, on the other hand, was wondering if I'd crossed the line again and whether we were about to witness another Hayley explosion.

"Then what?" she asked, looking at me.

"We decided to visit, see if Adrianna could get access, or at least some information. You know, being his widow and all." Hayley nodded. "Turns out she was a listed nominee on the account. Mickey had already added her fingerprints."

"How?"

Adrianna shrugged. "I don't know," she said. And I realised just how much she was saying that at the moment. Whether it was genuine or not, she was starting to sound like a broken record and it was becoming frustrating. She'd already lied to me once and it made me wonder how much she actually knew, whether she was being truthful now.

"So what was in it?" asked Hayley, looking from Adrianna to me and back again.

I glanced at Adrianna, knowing Hayley wasn't going to like the next bit. It felt like we'd taken a huge leap forward and then several steps back all at the same time. Just more unanswered questions.

"It was empty," said Adrianna.

Hayley frowned. "Empty?"

Adrianna nodded.

Hayley let out a sigh. "This case is ridiculous," she muttered.

"So I was thinking," I said, trying to see the positive in all of this, keep us moving forward instead of settling on the drawbacks. "Can you get hold of the access list? You know, all the people that have accessed that specific security box in the last month? It might tell us when Mickey emptied it. Assuming he put something in it in the first place."

Hayley nodded. "I can certainly have a word, but they might not give up any information without a warrant which will take some time."

I nodded.

"Oh, and Adrianna had something else she wanted to share," I said.

Adrianna looked at me wide-eyed, panic suddenly bubbling up.

"The funeral visitor," I said gently.

"Oh. Yeah," she said, understanding what I was getting at. She quickly recounted the information about the man at the funeral. The mention of the rucksack piqued Hayley's interest, and she bent over her computer, pulling an image up on the screen to show us.

"Did it look like this?" she asked.

Adrianna studied the picture of a rucksack on the screen before nodding. "I think so. I can't be a hundred percent because he was quite far away and I wasn't paying that much attention to it, but it's definitely similar."

Hayley nodded, swinging the computer screen back round to face her. "Okay," she said. "I want you to work with one of our sketch artists and do your best to recreate his face. I've had a list of customers back from the rucksack company," she said to me. "They've given me a handful of names in the UK that I need to check out but I wouldn't be surprised if he was using an alias."

I nodded. "Progress, at least."

"Adrianna, are you able to hang around while I get hold of a sketch artist? It would be better if we could do this today while it's still fresh."

"Sure." She turned to look at me. "Will you be able to get the kids from school?"

"Of course. Actually, why don't I get Stacey to pick them up and I can give you a lift home when you're done?"

She nodded. "That works."

"How long will this take?" I asked.

Hayley shrugged one shoulder. "It'll be a few hours at least."

Chapter 52

ADRIANNA BIANCHI

HAMMERSMITH POLICE STATION

Friday 15th October

"In here," said the uniformed policeman, gesturing to the door.

Adrianna thanked him and stepped into a family room. There were sofas up against two walls, a low coffee table in the middle and a box of books and toys in the far corner. The room was painted in a soothing shade of blue with orange floral decals.

A man in his late fifties with greying hair and glasses sat on the sofa to the right. He was busy pulling items out of his rucksack and laying them on the coffee table. He looked up at Adrianna's entrance and smiled.

"Hi," he said. "I'm Darwin. Like the biologist but not as old." He chuckled at his own joke, stood up and held out a hand. Adrianna gave him a wry smile and shook his hand. "I'm a residential E-Fit specialist."

"E-Fit?" asked Adrianna with a frown.

"It stands for Electronic Facial Identification Technique. We're going to create an electronic resemblance of the man you saw and pass it along to Detective Inspector Irons for the investigation. Like the old school sketch artist, but just digital. It's much quicker," he added in a conspiratorial whisper. Then he clapped his hands together. "Before we get started, I'm gonna grab a drink. Want me to get you something? Tea? Coffee? Water?"

"A coffee would be great."

"No problem. Make yourself at home and I'll be back in two ticks." He slipped out the door, leaving her alone.

She looked about again, taking in the worn carpet, the artificial potted plant in the corner, and the squashed sofa cushions before perching herself on the edge of the sofa along the far wall.

True to his word, Darwin returned a few minutes later carrying two steaming takeout cups. He placed one in front of Adrianna and settled down onto the other sofa.

"Okay," he said, full of enthusiasm. "Let's get cracking, shall we?" He picked up the iPad on the coffee table and flipped the cover open. He tapped about on the screen a little and then pulled out a pen. "First thing's first," he said. "Can you describe the man you saw? Just start with the basics; you know, hair colour, skin colour and we'll see how we go."

Adrianna did as he asked, recalling as many details as she could. It was tough. She'd only seen the guy for a split second, and from a distance.

When she was done describing as much as she could, Darwin suggested they take a break. He fiddled and sketched on the iPad and she left him to it, venturing down the corridor in search of another coffee.

She wandered back into the family room ten minutes later, a coffee in each hand, and placed one on the table in front of Darwin.

"I wasn't sure how you take it," she said and then fished in her pocket, pulling out some miniature pots of long-life milk and sachets of sugar.

"Ah, thank you, my dear. Excellent timing, too. I think we're almost ready."

Adrianna raised an eyebrow. "Ready for what?"

He turned the iPad around to face her. On the screen were nine different faces.

She sat back down on the other sofa and he handed the iPad across to her.

"I want you to take a look and let me know which one is the closest. They're not perfect, they're only a starting point, so don't fret. We'll need to make some changes."

Looking down at the nine artificial faces in front of her, she thought back to the man she'd seen. What had he looked like?

One by one she looked carefully at each of the faces. One was too angular, a couple had the wrong face shape, and one looked an awful lot like her grandad, which made her wince. But there was something about faces three and eight. They weren't a perfect match but there was a close resemblance. She glanced between the two faces again before pointing to face number three.

"I think this one," she said.

"Great," said Darwin. He tapped on the face and it filled the screen. "So, tell me what's not quite right, and I'll do my best to fix it."

She thought for a moment. "Squarer in the jaw."

Darwin took the tablet from her for a moment and when he handed it back, there were nine faces again, all of which were the same except they had varying jawlines.

"That one," she said instantly, pointing to the fifth face. Darwin swapped the new jawline in and Adrianna nodded.

They worked like that for another hour, Darwin carefully teasing details from Adrianna's memory. It was thorough and detailed work. By the time they were done, Adrianna was sure the E-Fit likeness was of the man she'd seen at the funeral.

"Great work," said Darwin, pleased with the outcome. "You did brilliantly."

Adrianna smiled shyly.

"I'll get this over to Detective Inspector Irons. Before you go, I'll need you to sign a witness statement describing the process we've been through here."

"And that's it?"

"That's it."

"Will Detective Inspector Irons be able to catch him from the image?"

"Tricky to say," said Darwin, beginning to pack away his things. "It might not be an immediate payoff, but it will allow her a better chance of finding out who he is. Once she has a name, she can track him down and then ask him a few questions."

Adrianna nodded, unconvinced.

"I still need to speak to your friend who was there. Cameron, is it?"

Adrianna nodded again.

"We can compare the likenesses you both produce and see if that gives us a better idea of who we're dealing with."

"What if they end up looking completely different?"

Darwin shrugged, unbothered by the idea. "It happens. It's not ideal, of course, but eyewitness recollections are notoriously unreliable, so we make do with what we have."

Chapter 53

JASON HUNTER

HAMMERSMITH POLICE STATION

Friday 15th October

I finished going through the addresses of the UK-based Battle-pouch customers and handed the sheet of paper back to Hayley. I'd highlighted the ones that could be our man, mostly because they were either PO Boxes, which hinted at someone wanting to keep their identity a secret, or they were a male that fitted our demographic; white and middle aged. Of course, if he was smart, which we knew he was, it was likely he was using a completely fake ID altogether, but at least it was a starting point.

"Sorry to trouble you, thank you for your time," Hayley said into the phone and hung up. She looked at me. "Another no." Reaching for the sheet of paper, she crossed out the next highlighted name.

"Unlikely he's gonna have ordered it to his home address, right?"

"Unlikely," agreed Hayley. "But I've got to check every lead."

I nodded in understanding, even if it was incredibly frustrating. It felt like we were wasting time phoning through the list of addresses when we knew it would lead to a dead end.

"I think I'll get Webb to follow up on this," she said, sitting back in her chair.

I nodded in agreement. It wasn't how I wanted to spend my time either.

"Do you trust her?" she suddenly asked, breaking the silence.

"Who?"

"Adrianna."

"Yes," I said without hesitation.

"Hmm," said Hayley, unconvinced. It was the same argument we'd been having since Mickey had been killed. "But you didn't go into the vault with her, right?"

"No. I wasn't allowed access."

"Let's assume for a moment she's telling the truth—"

"She is," I said through gritted teeth, my temper rising.

"Yeah, alright," she said, waving a hand at me to placate me. She leaned further back in her chair and put her feet up on the corner of her desk. "How did the killer get to the safe deposit box before you?"

I shrugged. "I'm guessing the access card was in the safe in Mickey's office."

Hayley looked at me, suddenly more alert. "So he finds the card, then searches the office to see what it's for. Finds the invoice and puts two and two together?"

"Something like that. I just don't know how he'd get past the biometric scanner. It's unlikely he was able to fake being Mickey."

She dropped her tatty old Converse from the corner of the desk and started clicking the keys on her keyboard. A few moments later, her eyes darted across the screen, and her body tensed.

"Here," she said and pointed to the screen.

"What?"

"Residue on Mickey's finger."

Suddenly I understood what she was talking about. "It's how the killer got biometric access."

She nodded. "The autopsy report said there was residue on Mickey's fingers, specifically on the fingerprint area."

"Ah shit. So the killer took a fingerprint sample using a type of glue or something. Maybe wood glue?"

"I'd need to get the forensics team to test it," she said.

"And from that he recreates Mickey's biometric pass. He'd be able to lay the sample over the top of his own and hey presto, he's in."

The reality of it hit us.

"Would that really work?" she asked. "It feels too Hollywood."

I shrugged. "It depends on the sophistication of the system, but there's a fair amount of research into how easy it is to steal biometric data. It's a lot easier than people think, and there's a pretty high success rate in fooling security systems. If it failed, he had the access card as well and could potentially blag his way in. Attempt number two or three might work and he'd be away. I'm guessing he got lucky and it worked on the first try."

"Shit," she said.

My phone vibrated in my pocket. Expecting it to be a text from Stacey saying she was home with the kids, I was surprised to see it was a text from an unknown number. And then my stomach sank, remembering the last message I'd received.

"What is it?" asked Hayley.

I looked up to see she was watching me.

"Another text," I said.

"Show me," she said.

I turned the phone around so she could see the text notification on my home screen.

"Open it," she said, getting up and coming around the desk to look over my shoulder.

Opening the text, there were only four words:

Time is running out.

And then I saw the photos that had been attached. One was of Adrianna at Mickey's graveside, Cameron stood next to her, both of them with their heads bowed in grief.

The second was a bit blurry but there was no denying who was in it, or the threat it conveyed. It was a picture of Max and Lily, taken from their school gates.

I looked up at Hayley in horror.

"I'm on it," she said, rushing around to the other side of her desk. She picked up the phone and started ordering a check in at the school, as well as my address. Then she called the tech team to see if they'd be able to get a trace on the source of the message.

After a few minutes, she put the phone down.

"That's the best I can do," she said.

I gave her a small nod.

"Does tech want my phone?"

"Drop it off on your way out," she said.

I nodded again, feeling numb.

I dialled Stacey's mobile and she picked up on the second ring, assuring me everything was fine and they were at home, safe.

"Okay, good," I said into the phone.

"What's going on?" she asked.

"I'll explain when I get home," I said and hung up.

There was a tentative knock at the door and we both turned to see Adrianna in the doorway.

"All done?" I asked.

She nodded.

"That was quick. Okay let's get you home." I stood up from my chair and stretched.

"Before you go," said Hayley, looking at her computer screen. A few more clicks and then she beckoned me around her desk. I obliged and Adrianna followed. "Do you recognise him?" she asked, gesturing to the screen. In front of us was the electronic face Adrianna had created with the E-Fit specialist. He was quite plain-looking. Square-ish in the head with a short haircut and deep-set eyes. I didn't recognise the face.

In fact, I'm surprised Adrianna was able to describe him at all. He was so ordinary, the kind of man that's almost instantly forgettable. Which made sense. If you went around killing people, you wouldn't want to be memorable.

"Sorry, don't think I've ever seen him before."

"It was a long shot," sighed Hayley. "I'll circulate this and see if anyone recognises him."

"I still don't get why he was there in the first place."

"Some murderers enjoy watching the effect of their actions."

"I get that, but this isn't your usual murderer. He's a hitman for hire and I highly doubt he goes to all of his victims' funerals. If he was the same guy that killed Gemma, he didn't make an appearance there."

"That you know of," said Hayley. "He could have been at the back and you just didn't notice."

"True." The thought made me shiver. I remembered Gemma's funeral like it was yesterday. Had this guy been lurking somewhere at the back? Had he been hanging back and watching us all? Would I have even noticed? I didn't like the thought. What else had I missed?

Chapter 54

JASON HUNTER

HOME

Friday 15th October

I'd taken Adrianna home and picked the kids up from mine on the way. Not only had Stacey picked them up from school, but she'd helped them with their homework and cooked their dinner too. I was starting to forget what life before her was like.

"Was the E-Fit any good?" asked Stacey, twirling a half-full wine glass on the countertop whilst I ate a microwaveable pasta meal.

I shook my head. "I didn't know him."

Stacey looked thoughtful for a moment. "Should we maybe run it by Bill?"

"That's a dangerous game and you know it."

She shrugged, avoiding eye contact with me. "Makes sense if they're in the same industry."

Not wanting to get into an argument, I changed the subject. "I had another text."

Stacey looked at me wide-eyed. "Is that why you phoned me all panicked about where we were?"

I nodded and told her about the photos.

"Shit," she said. "You don't even have what they want."

"I know," I groaned. Pushing down the feeling of panic that was slowly creeping up my throat, I reassured myself that the kids were fine. The police had informed the school of a potential threat and I'd sent a couple of guys over to Imani's house to keep watch.

"How was your day?" I asked, not wanting to dwell on it. There was little I could do about it right now, and Hayley was helping as much as she could. I needed to focus on finding whatever it was that Mickey had stolen.

"My PT put me through my paces. Said I'm losing focus with my fitness and I need to get my head back in the game."

"Talk about tough love."

"That's why he's one of the best," she shrugged.

I finished off the pasta meal, rinsed the plastic tub and dumped it in the bin. "Oh, I didn't even tell you the most interesting part," I said, spinning around to face her.

Stacey's eyebrows shot up. "What?"

"We visited Mickey's safe deposit box."

She frowned. "Hold up. You what?"

And so I filled her in, starting with my trip to Adrianna's apartment, the cut to my eyebrow which she then inspected with a concerned look, the invoice we found, the message on the wall, and our visit to Vault Bank. When I was done, Stacey was still frowning.

"You have had an eventful day," she said. "What's next?"

I shrugged. "Hayley's going to look into who else might have accessed the box between when Mickey died and now. The working theory is that the killer stole Mickey's fingerprint using a kind of glue and was able to just walk right in."

"You're kidding?" she said.

"I wish I was."

"And we still don't know what was in there?"

I shook my head. "I'm guessing Mickey felt it was safe enough where it was, but how could he anticipate someone going to such lengths? It wasn't listed under his real name, so it's not even like it was traceable to him."

"Unless the killer knew who he really was."

"Maybe."

We sat in silence, mulling things over. It reminded me that we needed to retest all of our security systems and upgrade them where necessary. We didn't rely on fingerprint biometrics often, if at all. It was the easiest biometric data to steal, so I avoided it as much as possible. But if this guy had managed to walk into a safe deposit vault that easily, who knew what else he might be able to do.

Chapter 55

Dima Volkov

Gromov's mansion

Sunday 17th October

He stood in the classic wood-panelled office he'd come to know so well over the years. He'd lost count of how many times he'd been called in to be admonished or praised by Gromov. Each time, a sense of dread sat heavy in the pit of his stomach, and this time was no different. While he was grateful for Gromov and his sponsorship – he wouldn't be racing if it wasn't for him – he didn't condone his actions or the ruthless way he conducted business.

After watching Diane be backed into a corner and forced to launder money last year, something had changed in Dima. He was no longer the silent, sulky presence he once was. His closest friend was currently in prison, broken from the way that Gromov had misused her, and he wanted to bite back.

With the scandal at the party where several people had been shot and killed in this very room, where Stacey had been kidnapped and had almost lost her life in the brutal car crash that followed, he was feeling overwhelmed. It was just all too much. While Alik Gromov might believe he'd gotten away with it, Dima Volkov was very much still holding him accountable.

"Your performance this season has slipped," said Gromov in Russian, not looking up from his desk. From this angle, Dima couldn't see what it was he was doing, nor did he care. He rolled his eyes and it was almost as if Gromov heard the action because his head snapped up and his eyes narrowed. Dima's stomach clenched with nerves. "What do you have to say for yourself?" he barked.

Despite himself, Dima winced.

"It's been tough this year. The racing conditions have made things... trickier. And reckless driving seems to be rewarded."

Gromov eyed him suspiciously before nodding. "That's true. Stacey shouldn't be racing."

"I didn't say that," he replied quickly. The last thing he needed was Gromov taking out the competition of his own accord. "All I meant was usually there would be some kind of penalty, but it seems Stacey is bringing in too much publicity for them to punish her."

"I'll have a chat with Alfonso. See if we can't do something about that." Then as if realising he'd given Dima a pass on his current performance, he pointed at him. "That doesn't mean you can slack off. I want to see you at the top of the podium for this race or there will be consequences."

Dima gritted his teeth and gave a curt nod before dismissing himself. Gromov had never threatened him before, which meant things must be bad. He walked out of the office, his hands balled into fists at his side, and marched down the corridor, out the front door and slipped behind the wheel of his Porsche 911 GT2.

Slamming the door closed, he gripped the steering wheel, his knuckles turning white. He was tired of being Gromov's pet, tired of being managed, of being dictated to, of being a *toy*. And how *dare* he threaten him? All he had ever done was work so damn hard all the time, sacrificing any hopes of a social life. All he had ever done was deliver; deliver, deliver, deliver. Had he not delivered enough? He was at the top of his game, for fuck's sake. He was racing with the best in the world. And everyone *knew* who he was. What more did the old bastard want from him?

Letting out a shaky breath, he started the engine and drove out of the estate.

There was someone he needed to speak to.

Chapter 56

JASON HUNTER

THE OFFICE

Monday 18th October

I still hadn't heard from Hayley. It had been three days since Adrianna had given her description of the funeral visitor. Three days since we'd discovered the Vault Bank safe deposit box. Three days since it felt like we'd taken one step forward and two steps back. Another dead end.

I'd even picked my phone up from the tech team in the hope that I'd bump into her. And when I'd asked at the desk, I was told she wasn't in the building. I'd tried calling her afterwards, but it'd gone straight to voicemail.

I knew Cameron was next on the list to sit with Darwin and provide her description of the funeral visitor, but I doubted Hayley would be able to get through to her. I didn't dare contact her and risk burning that bridge. Who knew when Cameron might be useful.

My mobile rang, interrupting me. I looked up from the CVs spread out on the desk in front of me and scooped my phone up.

"Yes?" I said as I answered.

"Divya needs your decision," said Lucy.

I sighed. My brain had been too preoccupied all morning. I'd promised Divya I'd make a decision on the new recruits and she wanted it now. If we took too long, we'd risk losing the best to other offers. It was a fast-paced industry and freelancers didn't like to hang around.

"I'm looking at them now."

"Good, there's only so many times I can get rid of her."

I chuckled. "I'm doing it, I'm doing it."

I hung up and opened Divya's email. She'd outlined enough budget on current contracts for one permanent two-person team, plus an additional four on temporary contracts for Iris McCleary's tour.

So that meant I needed six names from the list of fifteen we'd interviewed. I'd highlighted Aysha, Lauren and Neve to Divya on the day we'd interviewed them; they'd definitely impressed me.

Since my last meeting with Iris, Vance had emailed me to confirm which of the profiles Iris had liked. I was unsurprised to see Aysha and Neve's names included. And I could see why she'd chosen Mollie and Suriani too. They both had long, brown hair and were incredibly pretty. They looked young, carefree and the same age as Iris herself which might have been why the singer chose them. Not the usual serious ex-military, ex-police type I was used to seeing in this line of work.

I had said she needed to feel comfortable with whoever she chose and these two looked like they were the sort of people she normally hung out with, which in the grand scheme of things would actually be a good look. The whole point of having a female-only team was to provide Iris with covert protection.

I combined Vance's list of names with my own and sent it across to Divya. One job done. Now I just needed to work out who was threatening my family.

Chapter 57

STACEY JAMES

CLUB DIONYSUS

Monday 18th October

Walking into the empty club, Stacey was greeted by the same Jamaican bouncer who'd escorted her and Jason the last time she'd been here. This time, however, he gave her a friendly smile. He eyed Sam, who stood a step behind her, before gesturing for them to follow.

She expected to head towards the claustrophobic room with all the computer screens but instead Damarae led them past the bar and up more steps to a mezzanine floor that overlooked the main dance floor. Here there were more booths and another bar.

Cameron occupied the booth closest to the bar, her laptop open on the table in front of her.

"Hello darling," she said when she spotted Stacey, rising from her seat. The red evening dress was gone, replaced by a classy red jump suit that cinched at the waist and cut off mid-calf. It had a low-cut neckline that drew the eye to the single red gemstone hanging on a chain around her neck. Cameron embraced her and kissed her on both cheeks. "What a delight," she drawled. "Please." She gestured to the bench on the opposite side of the booth.

Stacey slid in and Cameron closed the lid of her laptop, pushing it to one side.

"A friend of yours?" she asked, nodding towards Sam who had positioned himself far enough away that they could talk privately. He was still in her eyeline so if she wanted out of there, he wouldn't hesitate in doing something about it.

"A necessity when Jason isn't around."

"Men," laughed Cameron.

Stacey could have sworn she saw a smirk flicker at the corner of Sam's mouth.

"Damarae, darling, could you fix us some drinks?"

The bouncer nodded and then headed behind the bar.

"To what do I owe the pleasure, Miss Stacey?" she asked.

Stacey suddenly felt nervous and wondered if this had all been a terrible idea. And yet, she wasn't sure who else to turn to. If Mickey had trusted Cameron enough to protect Adrianna, then she felt like that was enough of a character reference, even if she did barely know the woman.

"I have a business proposal."

"Oh my," said Cameron, her eyebrows shooting up with surprise. "Now this *is* unexpected."

Damarae reappeared at the table and placed two martini glasses in front of them.

"Ah, thank you darling," said Cameron, scooping one up without hesitation and taking a sip. Stacey moved hers to one side but didn't drink any.

"I want to open a Formula One academy for women. Drivers, engineers, pit crew, you name it. But female-only. And I want your help. Specifically, your business management skills," said Stacey, the words pouring out in a rush. This isn't how she'd planned to pitch it at all.

Cameron slowly smiled. "Tell me more," she said.

Reaching into her bag, Stacey pulled out her iPad and opened up her business plan. She spent the next 20 minutes talking Cameron through every detail of her idea; everything from the application process to the work placement.

When she was done, she sat back, leaving the iPad in the middle of the table, and took a sip of her drink. It was delicious. Unlike any martini she'd ever tasted.

"It's all about the alcohol, darling," said Cameron without looking up from the iPad. "The more expensive it is, the better it tastes."

"It's amazing," said Stacey, taking another sip.

"Kors Vodka, darling. The best vodka in my opinion. And the only one I ever drink." She picked up her own drink and took a sip, savouring the taste. "I do have one question," she said, her eyes on Stacey. "Why have you brought this to me? I mean, I'm flattered, darling, for sure. But you hardly know me."

"That's true. But it's no different to me hiring a business manager that I don't know. You've run this place with Mickey," she gestured around her at the club, "and now you're running it on your own, so you clearly know what you're doing. I'm not asking you to invest. I'm asking you to be an employee, to manage it while I'm racing, to keep the day-to-day running smoothly."

Cameron took another sip of her drink and leaned back in the booth, watching Stacey carefully.

"I want to build an all-female space. At the academy, that is. And perhaps when I retire, launch an all-female racing team."

"That's quite ambitious."

"Doesn't mean it can't be done."

"Of course not, darling. What has Mr Hunter said to all of this?" She gestured to the iPad on the table and watched Stacey's reaction over the rim of her drink.

"We've not discussed it in that much detail yet, but he likes the initial concept."

"So he doesn't know you're here trying to hire me?"

Stacey shook her head and Cameron didn't look surprised. Although Stacey wasn't sure why she'd expected any different. It would take a lot to catch Cameron off guard. Like Alfonso Torres suddenly turning up at her club unannounced.

"Can I think about it?" asked Cameron.

"Of course. I mean, these plans aren't finalised, they're just a starting point. Something I've been working on when I get some spare time. But I want to launch as soon as possible. Maybe have something in place by the beginning of next season."

"Stacey, darling," said Cameron, getting to her feet. "You never cease to amaze me." She smiled, showing a full set of bright white and perfectly straight teeth.

Stacey also got to her feet, sensing this meeting was coming to an end.

"Thanks, I think."

Cameron chuckled and then embraced her, kissing her on both cheeks. "Damarae will see you out."

"Just one more thing."

"Yes, darling?"

"Why did Alfonso Torres spook you so much? What's going on with him?"

Cameron's smile suddenly disappeared and Stacey feared she'd asked the wrong thing. Had she gone too far?

"That sleazeball has an entitlement issue," she said after a moment. "He's threatened to shut us down, and worse, on more than one occasion. Mickey long gave up trying to reason with the man and instead just put up with his antics. As a woman, I have even less sway. Sexist pig." She muttered the last part under her breath.

"You looked like you'd seen a ghost the other night."

Cameron plastered an artificial smile in place. "Alas, some of our patrons are less than desirable. But I do what I can."

"Does it have anything to do with what Mickey stole?"

Cameron's eyes fluttered to Damarae who had stepped back a few paces when he realised their conversation wasn't quite finished. Stacey was confident he was far enough away that he couldn't hear their conversation, but Cameron's nervousness was putting her on edge.

"Can I offer you some advice, darling?"

"Of course."

Cameron grabbed her by the hand and pulled her close so their faces were only inches apart. Stacey saw Sam step forward but hesitated when he realised she wasn't going to hurt her.

"Be careful who you go asking questions about. People like Alfonso Torres are mad with power and won't hesitate about playing dirty to get what they want." Her fun, carefree attitude was gone, replaced with a vehemence Stacey didn't think she was capable of. "And if you're not careful, you'll end up just like Mickey. Or worse."

Stacey went to say something but Cameron cut her off, and let go of her hand, her normal lazy drawl back in place. "I tell you what, darling, why don't you come back and see me another time? I'll text you about it."

Glancing over at Sam, Stacey was sure Cameron was trying to give her a covert message. Was she trying to say this conversation wasn't over? Or was she just trying to get rid of her?

Chapter 58

JASON HUNTER

HOME

Monday 18th October

I stepped through the door to the sound of the shower running upstairs. Assuming it was Stacey, I called up but there was no reply. She was probably singing along to the radio or something. Sometimes she liked to listen to a podcast or an audiobook. No idea why. She once told me it was because it helped her unwind and allowed her to relax without feeling idle. I guess that's what happens when you're constantly under pressure to perform; sitting still was not something Stacey James was good at.

I dropped my keys on the kitchen island and pulled a beer from the fridge, taking note of how empty it was looking. I barely had time to do the food shopping these days. Although, come to think of it, I'm not sure I'd actually ever been good at food shopping consistently. Of course I'd been to the supermarkets, but that was more on an ad-hoc basis because I suddenly realised the fridge was empty and the kids were coming over for the weekend.

When I was married to Adrianna, she was more than happy to be a stay-at-home mum which meant she took care of everything, including the food shop. One of the reasons we'd ended up getting divorced was because she'd felt under appreciated. And what that really meant was that she wanted a housekeeper to do the food shopping for her.

These days, I relied on online delivery - honestly, I don't know where I'd be without technology – but it was clear we were overdue. I pulled a second bottle out of the fridge and placed it on the kitchen island, opening both of them.

"Oh, hey."

I looked up to see Stacey standing in the doorway to the living room, a towel wrapped around her body and another around her hair.

"I thought I heard you come in."

Beads of water still clung to her skin and she gave me a lazy smile. She beckoned me with a finger and then disappeared from view. I let out a low chuckle and followed.

***

When I reappeared downstairs, the beers still sat untouched on the kitchen island. I picked one up and took a sip. Stacey padded in, barefoot, a pair of joggers slung low on her hips and one of my t-shirts swamping her. I handed her the second bottle and she gratefully took it, kissing me on the cheek as she pulled herself onto the stool next to me.

"I went to see Cameron today."

I almost choked. "You what?"

"I've asked her to help me with my academy project."

"What? Why?"

Stacey shrugged. "She's a smart woman, knows how to run a business. I could do with one of those."

"Did Sam at least go with you?"

She rolled her eyes. "Of course he did." Then she added with a grumble, "Sam goes everywhere with me."

"Why Cameron? You barely know her."

"You know, that's exactly what she said."

I could feel myself getting annoyed at her flippancy. It was something I noticed she did quite often. She tested my patience and pushed my boundaries. Part of me knew it was because I tried to keep her too contained but the other part of me found it frustratingly childish.

My phone buzzed just as there was a gentle knock at the front door. I pulled it from my pocket to see a notification from the camera system I'd installed in the summer. A tall, willowy figure stood at the door and she glanced nervously over her shoulder.

"Who is it?" asked Stacey.

"Not sure," I said with a frown, getting up from my stool.

"Are you expecting anyone?"

"No," I called over my shoulder as I headed through the living room and into the hallway. Opening the front door, Cameron stepped inside without an invitation.

"Hello darling," she breathed and then disappeared in the direction of the kitchen.

A little stunned, I scanned the street before quickly closing the door behind her. What the hell was Cameron doing *here?* And how on Earth did she even know where I lived? Actually, that last bit was less of a shock. It was surprisingly easy to find out where someone lived and I didn't doubt Cameron had access to systems she shouldn't. Stacey was probably right to ask for business help from her.

I walked back into the kitchen to find Stacey had opened a bottle of wine and was pouring two large glasses. I grabbed myself another beer from the fridge instead.

"Cameron, what are you doing here?"

She wasn't all dressed up like the last time I'd seen her, but she still looked glamourous in a red jumpsuit and ruby crystal covered trainers. It was something Stacey was good at too; dressing casually but in a way that still seemed sophisticated.

Cameron took the glass of wine Stacey offered and took a large gulp.

"I couldn't speak too openly at the club. Damarae is a sweet thing but I can't risk him knowing too much. That's what got Mickey killed in the first place, right? Knowing too much."

"What got Mickey killed was theft. He stole what wasn't his."

Cameron waved a hand at me dismissively.

"That was just an excuse."

"What are you talking about?" asked Stacey.

"Is this house secure?" asked Cameron, turning to me, her eyes wide. And that was when I noticed it: she was scared.

"Yes. Cameron, what's going on?"

She took another gulp of wine followed by a steadying breath.

"Mickey was laundering money for people. And I mean big people."

"Alfonso Torres big?"

Cameron nodded.

"He was acting as a third party to help buy and sell NFTs."

"What are NFTs?" asked Stacey.

"They're like digital assets," I said, my eyes not leaving Cameron's face. "And they've become quite collectible. Think of them like digital artwork."

"He was trying to raise some cash for the club. It wasn't desperate, but we needed it. He needed it. So he did a few favours, and before you know it, he was in so deep that he couldn't get out. He told Alfonso he was done, told the others the same, that they'd have to find someone else to move their dirty money around, but Alfonso wouldn't take no for an answer. I'm sure the others were the same. So Mickey decided to take matters into his own hands. He created a blackmail file with evidence of everything."

"He what?" I said, stunned, the enormity of the situation crashing into me. No wonder Cameron had been terrified when Alfonso Torres had turned up at the club.

"I thought he'd stolen something," said Stacey.

Cameron paled and nodded. "He has all the digital keys."

"All of them?" I asked, incredulous.

"All of them," whispered Cameron.

The room fell silent. Without the keys, Alfonso and whoever else he'd been moving money for wouldn't be able to access any of it. There could be millions tied up in a crypto wallet somewhere and there'd be nothing they could do about it. It's not like they could request new keys. It didn't work like that. Once the keys were gone, they were gone.

No wonder Mickey was in a world of trouble. The guy was a walking target. It was only a matter of time before someone delivered his head on a silver platter. That explained why a hired hitman had taken him out. In fact, I wouldn't be surprised if there had been a bounty on his head.

And it also explained why I was receiving threatening text messages. Someone clearly thought I knew what Mickey was up to, and thought I had the keys.

This was bad.

Like *really* bad.

How long would it be before the text messages escalated? I already had clients being pressured into cancelling contracts, photos of where my kids went to school. What would be next?

"Cameron," I said gently, confident I wasn't going to like the answer to my next question. "How many people has Mickey screwed over?"

"A lot," she whispered.

Fuck. This was not good. I dragged a hand over my face, hoping this was all a dream.

"But Alfonso doesn't know where his key things are?" asked Stacey.

Cameron shook her head. "I think he suspects it was Mickey, which is why he keeps showing up at the club, but I don't think he knows for sure. Mickey did it all under his original name thinking it wouldn't be traced back to him, but I don't know what went wrong." She let out a small sob and Stacey reached for her hand.

Alfonso appearing at the club must have been what spooked Mickey in the first place. Adrianna had said he'd been nervous in the weeks before his death, and then suddenly he was extremely paranoid about everything; wouldn't answer his phone, was constantly on edge and started to get snappy with the kids. The stress of it all must have been killing him.

"Were any of the people he laundered money for from the Mayor's office?" I asked.

Cameron and Stacey both stared at me, but I was watching Cameron, trying to see if I could spot a lie. Stacey turned to look at Cameron just as she nodded.

"Mayor Britland himself," she said quietly, looking down at her hands, her voice barely more than a whisper.

This just kept getting better and better.

"What was in the safe deposit box?" I asked.

Cameron looked up at me. "A memory stick," she said.

Chapter 59

BILL COOPER

JASON'S HOME

Monday 18th October

He lowered the binoculars and lit a cigarette, the end glowing in the darkness. It was late. He'd seen Cameron arrive a couple of hours ago. Watched her glance nervously over her shoulder and then enter Jason's house.

He was sure Jason had seen him, but he hadn't acknowledged him. He'd watched as he'd glanced down the street, scanning for anyone who might have followed and then closed the door.

Subtle.

He'd thought of Jason as a bit of a schmuck in the past, but he'd tested the house before settling down in his current vantage point, and he hadn't detected any weaknesses in the security setup. If anything, it looked like Jason had upped his game since the debacle with Liam. Which was just as well if Stacey was spending 99% of her time here.

The look on her face when she'd seen him in that press room had been both amusing and enlightening. He'd long ago come to terms with the fact that things wouldn't work out with Stacey. With his profession and her ambition, they were just incompatible. It didn't mean he no longer cared for her. But he knew it wasn't reciprocated.

He wasn't a fool. And his sense of obligation to keep her safe remained. Especially since Jason had already looped him in on every race this season. Jason had needed eyes and ears on the ground, even if he had to stoop to less-than-legal means to achieve it.

Stacey would be flying out again in just two days and he'd be following once again. Keeping his distance but keeping her safe, as always. At least, that was the plan. But sometimes plans changed.

The only reason he'd come back to the UK was a rumour on the grapevine. There had been murmurings about something big. Powerful people were angry.

He'd tried to dig around, find out what he could without raising too much suspicion, but to do that he needed to be here, talking to people face to face. And so far, he hadn't liked what he'd heard. Jason's name had come up. It was likely that he was the next target, but the way he'd been going about his business the last few days, it didn't look like Jason even knew. Which likely meant his sources had got their wires crossed somewhere.

Someone had mentioned some dangerous information. But the location of it was still unknown. He had a hunch he might know who was responsible. After all, he'd seen the ruthless style of Mickey's murder before.

Chapter 60

JASON HUNTER

THE OFFICE

Tuesday 19th October

I paced in front of the floor to ceiling windows. The view was stunning, the sky a clear blue, but I didn't see it. I was angry. Fuming. Absolutely livid. How could Mickey have been so careless? It was one thing to endanger his own life but another to endanger the lives of my kids.

And now here I was, the next target, with no way out.

I needed to tell Hayley what we'd learned, but that came with its own set of complications; I couldn't tell her it was Cameron who'd given us the information, but I knew she would push to find out how we knew. What's more, I was too angry to explain it in a calm and rational manner.

I knew it. I just *knew* Mickey was a crook. A two-faced, lying, gambling, cheating bastard. If he was alive, I'd be tempted to kill him myself. Part of me had wanted to believe he'd changed. Adrianna was clearly so in love with him, and it seemed he'd genuinely cared about Max and Lily, but I just couldn't seem to get my head around his behaviour. Why risk it all?

That in itself seemed to be an issue. Why would Mickey risk it all? He'd already changed his identity once, and now he had a family he seemed to really care about.

I stopped pacing and looked out the window.

What if Mickey was being blackmailed first? What if Alfonso had known his true identity and had used that against him? It made more sense with everything I'd learned about Mickey since his death. Whilst once upon a time I would have assumed he was just another prick, Adrianna seemed to really believe that he was a changed man.

It was definitely a narrative I preferred. The thought of Mickey knowingly and willingly putting my kids in danger made me want to punch a hole right through the goddamn window.

"Think, *think,*" I muttered, prodding my temples with my fingers.

We'd missed something. Missed something *huge.*

Mickey had managed to pull together a blackmail package that was potentially worth millions. Depending on how much he was laundering and who for, we could be talking tens of millions, maybe even more.

I felt my phone vibrate in my pocket. Pulling it out, the screen displayed a call from a withheld number. I swiped to answer and pressed the phone to my ear.

"Mr Hunter, I believe you have something that belongs to me." The voice was slightly mechanical, definitely distorted. My heart began to race. This couldn't be a coincidence, could it? Cameron had only visited last night. Was someone watching the house? Had they seen her visit me? Was Alfonso keeping tabs on her in the hope it would lead him to the memory stick?

Shit. Shit. Shit.

"I'm sorry, who is this?"

"Don't play games with me, Mr Hunter. You won't like the consequences."

"I honestly don't know what you're talking about."

"Very well. This isn't over."

Before I could reply, the line disconnected. That last bit stuck in my head. *This isn't over.* They were the exact same words that had been carved into the wall of Mickey's office and I suddenly felt very, very cold.

Chapter 61

JASON HUNTER

HOME

Tuesday 19th October

The phone call this morning had put me on edge all day. So much so that I'd texted Cooper from the burner phone in my office, asking him to come back to the UK. He'd replied pretty quickly with a thumbs up emoji which was as annoying as it was unhelpful.

I'd texted again, hoping he'd give me a clue as to what that meant but he hadn't replied. The phone sat on the kitchen counter, and I couldn't take my eyes off it. I needed him to answer.

It was late when I finally heard Stacey come through the front door. Not wanting her to see the phone, I slipped it into one of the kitchen drawers just as she appeared in the doorway.

"Good day?" she asked.

"Yeah, pretty good," I said, turning to face her. *Shit.* I don't know why or where it came from, but the lie slipped from me before I could stop it. In fact, I did know why. I didn't want her to worry. I didn't want her to be freaking out about my safety when she was just three days away from her next big race. I didn't want to be responsible for her losing focus.

"Have you heard from Hayley?" she asked.

"Nothing yet. I'll follow up tomorrow. Still figuring out how to tell her about what Cameron said."

"Yeah, I get that," she said, opening the now-full fridge. "Although, I don't think you can leave her out of it, if I'm honest. Things have gone far enough as it is." She studied the shelves of food in the fridge before closing the door. "I'm not sure what I want," she said, slumping onto a stool.

"I can rustle something up," I said, grateful for something to do with my hands as I began pulling ingredients from the fridge.

"Have you made any progress with the missing memory stick?"

"No. It's been winding me up all day."

"I knew it would," she said. "That's why you should have called Hayley."

"I know, I know," I said, waving a hand over my shoulder. And in all honesty, I couldn't say exactly why I hadn't. Sure, I'd had a busy day, been driving myself crazy trying to piece everything together. I'd spent some time trying to find a way to get FixRecruitment back on board, to no avail. I even did some digging into what the Mayor's office might be up to. Not that I found anything. "I'll call her first thing tomorrow," I said, turning to get more bits from the cupboard.

Stacey was looking at me with an eyebrow raised.

"I promise," I said.

Chapter 62

STACEY JAMES

SOMEWHERE IN CHELSEA

Wednesday 20th October

Wednesday 20th October

Stacey sat in her usual chair, with Professor Lindberg opposite, a pen and her usual notepad propped open on her knee. Looking out the window, Stacey wondered where to begin. Things felt vastly different today. Seeing Diane was almost a distant memory. A lot had changed in a week and she almost felt like an entirely different person.

"How's your week been?" asked Lindberg.

Stacey glanced over and saw that her therapist was watching her.

She sighed. In an hour's time she'd be heading to the airport and flying halfway across the world for her next race. She really didn't need her head being a mess.

"I made a start on my business plans for the academy," she said. What she really wanted to talk about was the fact that Mickey had been laundering money for the rich and famous, including the head of Formula One and the Mayor of London. And when he'd wanted out, he'd created a master blackmail file that contained all the cryptokeys needed to access the laundered money.

She tried to focus on the here and now, anchoring herself in the moment, but she could sense the walls closing in, feel her breathing speeding up and her heart beginning to race. All of a sudden she couldn't catch her breath and her vision began to swim.

She saw the outline of Lindberg lurch forward but she didn't know why, couldn't see what she was doing. Darkness pushed in around the edge of her vision, swallowing her and sucking her deeper as a roaring sound filled her ears. Her stomach felt queasy. The pounding in her head was persistent and she couldn't breathe. There was a weight pressing down on her chest, making it impossible to fill her lungs.

After what felt like an age, the blackness started to recede and her vision slowly came back. She was looking at the floor. Specifically, her feet that were firmly planted on the plush cream carpet of Lindberg's office.

The pounding in her head started to ease. Suddenly, her chest expanded and she sucked in lungfuls of air.

"Slow down, hold the breath before letting it out if you can," she heard Lindberg say, her voice distant and muffled. That was when she noticed the warm hand on her back, rubbing in a circular motion with a steady pressure.

Her lungs took another gulp of air and this time she tried her best to hold it, to slow her breathing and her racing heart.

Slowly, she sat up, surprised when a tear dripped off her chin and into her lap.

"It's okay," said Lindberg softly, reaching for the box of tissues she kept on her desk. She passed them to Stacey who took one and wiped at her cheeks.

"What—?"

"You had a panic attack," said Lindberg, frowning. "I feel like there's something you're not telling me."

Stacey shook her head.

"Just my next race," she lied.

Chapter 63

JASON HUNTER

THE OFFICE

Wednesday 20th October

I'd promised Stacey I'd call Hayley, so that's what I was doing.

Closing the door to my office, I hit 'video call' and propped my phone up on my laptop.

"Hey, how's it going?" said Hayley. Her video stream took a second to appear, and when it did, I had a perfect view of her chin and could see right up both her nostrils.

I couldn't help but laugh.

"I know, I know," she said. "I'm juggling a few bits. Just give me a minute."

I glimpsed her identity card and then heard the beep of access being granted before she opened the door and continued walking.

"Want me to call you back?" I asked.

"No, no, I'm almost there."

The phone was dropped onto a table and all I could see were the white ceiling tiles and strip lighting. Then, the phone was scooped up again, this time at face height as Hayley walked down the corridor, taking a sip from a takeout cup.

She elbowed open her office door and kicked it shut behind her.

"What's up?" she asked.

"You're not going to like it," I said, suddenly feeling nervous.

Now I had her attention and her eyes narrowed. "What's happened?"

I jumped straight in and told her about Cameron's visit. I didn't name Cameron specifically but it wouldn't take much for Hayley to guess who. And I conveniently left out that this had happened two days ago. I didn't need her on my ass about obstructing the investigation.

"Oh my god," she said, when I finished, her head in her hands, her takeout coffee long forgotten on the desk. She dragged her hands down her face as she tried to process this new information.

"That's not all," I said.

She looked up at me sharply. "What do you mean?"

"I've had a phone call."

"A phone call?"

"Like the texts, but a phone call. Distorted voice, nothing of note, but it was a threat. I'm worried things are escalating."

"In all honesty, I'm not surprised. If this memory stick does exist, it could be the key to millions of pounds and people are gonna be *pissed*."

"I know."

"What the hell was he thinking?" she asked.

"I have no idea. The blackmail I can understand, but the cryptokeys are something else."

"I'm wondering if these people – whoever they are – didn't know about the cryptokeys until *after* Mickey was killed."

"How come?" I asked, trying to follow her line of thinking.

"Well, it would be pretty damn stupid to kill the guy who has access to all your money."

"Good point."

"And still no idea where this memory stick is?" she asked.

I shook my head. "But I'm guessing that's what was in the safe deposit box."

"Yeah, I'd agree with that," she nodded. "We got confirmation that Vault Bank allowed a visitor entry the day after Mickey was killed. He passed the biometric scanners with no problem."

"He? So definitely the killer?"

"Most likely. He could have sent someone in for him, but it's looking likely. The guy wore dark clothes and a baseball cap, so the camera footage isn't much use. We're just tracking down the receptionist that was working that day. We're hoping he'll confirm Adrianna's E-Fit is the same guy."

"Fingers crossed. Sounds like progress."

"It is, except all this money laundering shit makes things a lot more complicated. I'm gonna have to get the fraud team involved on this." She let out a frustrated sigh.

This case just kept getting more complicated. At least now I was confident that Cameron had told us everything she knew.

All we had to do was find the memory stick, wherever it may be. I just hoped it hadn't been sold to the highest bidder already, and that the powerful, money-hungry people of London who thought I had it weren't going to kill me in the meantime.

Chapter 64

JASON HUNTER

THE OFFICE

Thursday 21st October

"I was expecting you to call me, not show up in person," I said, beckoning Hayley through the door and closing it behind her.

"I felt a face-to-face meeting was long overdue."

"Sure. You manage to find out anything more on your side?"

She didn't reply straight away, instead walking over and lowering herself into one of the visitor chairs that faced my desk. Frowning, I sat down in the second one and half-turned to face her.

"Not much I'm afraid." She shrugged.

I wanted to tear my hair out. With no idea who exactly was after me, I was at a loss. I had the Mayor's office sabotaging my client contracts, someone sending threatening text messages and now the phone call on top of everything else. Someone really did have it in for me. Whether that was the Mayor or a third party, it didn't matter because the outcome didn't change; I didn't have it.

Hayley shifted in her seat, suddenly looking awkward. "I've actually come about something else."

"What?" I asked, a sense of apprehension crawling up my spine and tickling the nape of my neck.

"There's a search warrant for your office and home."

"What?" I almost shouted, stunned.

Hayley winced. "I don't know why. But I do know they'll come knocking today. I'd say they're looking for something specific, but that in itself is weird. They would have needed some kind of tip off."

"Are you saying this a setup?" What the hell was going on? Cancelling my business was one thing, but putting out a search warrant was another. Was this a message? A threat? Was it the Mayor? Someone else? The person sending the texts showing me how they could control and disrupt my life?

"I'm saying it's weird. And unusual."

"For fuck's sake," I huffed. This was *bad*. How would I explain the police being here to my employees? And god forbid the media got a hold of it. What a great story that would be. After the scandal that had followed everything last year, everyone in the team had worked damn hard to pull us out of the gutter and it finally felt like we were turning a corner.

"Look, I need to go," said Hayley, standing up. "I can't be seen here, not when they show up. If I am, I won't be able to help should things go south."

"Should things go south?! What does that mean?" I threw my hands up in the air, trying desperately to keep the panic at bay.

Hayley leaned towards me, one hand on the arm of the chair. She spoke quickly, her voice low as if she didn't want to be overheard, though we were the only two people in the room. "If there's a search warrant, it means they have probable cause. Someone's going to extreme lengths to cause havoc in your life, so whatever tip they've given to the police, I wouldn't be surprised if there's evidence to back it up."

"What evidence–?"

"Whatever they want," she shrugged. "Let's face it, people this powerful can plant whatever they like. There's not much I can do in advance, really all I can do is try and help should you get arrested—"

"Arrested?"

"Worst case scenario. Basically, make sure you know who you're gonna call if they get the handcuffs out."

"You think I need a lawyer?"

"It wouldn't hurt to have someone helpful on speed dial."

I dropped my head into my hands and stared at the floor. This could not be happening.

"I'm sorry, Jason," said Hayley, placing a hand on my shoulder. "I wish I could do more but it was enough of a risk warning you in the first place."

"No, no, I get it," I said, lifting my head. "The worst bit is I can't fix it."

Hayley frowned. "How do you mean?"

"They think I have the memory stick, Hayley. This isn't going to stop until they get it. Or I end up dead. And considering I *don't* have it, we both know which outcome is more likely."

"I do not want to hear you talking like that," she said. "Think of your kids. Think of Stacey."

"It is them I'm thinking about. Remember the school photo? They're thinking about them too."

"I'm sorry, Jason, but I really do need to go," she said, glancing over her shoulder through the glass walls and across the open plan office, almost as if she was expecting a SWAT team to burst in at any moment. "The kids are safe and the school is on high alert. Stacey is in Austin with Sam and out of harm's way. Let's sort this mess first, then deal with the threats."

I nodded. "Thanks for the heads up."

I walked her to the door and watched her head to the bank of elevators.

"Lucy," I said as I watched Hayley press the call button and then wait.

Lucy's head appeared above her desk partition. "Yes?"

"We're going to get a visit from the police shortly. They'll be wanting to search the office and we'll need to be as accommodating as possible."

Lucy glanced towards the elevators as Hayley disappeared from view and then back to me, a frown creasing her forehead.

"What's going on?" she asked.

"I've got no fucking clue."

Chapter 65

JASON HUNTER

THE OFFICE

Friday 22nd October

I closed the door to my office and sat down in the chair behind my desk. I had no idea how long I had until the police came storming in here. From the way Hayley had been talking, I could assume it wouldn't be long.

And so I needed a game plan. Someone was turning up the heat, and I needed to pay them back in kind. But how?

Hayley had mentioned making sure I had a lawyer. It was clear she was expecting the police to find whatever it was they were meant to be searching for. It may already have been planted, but it was more than likely some mole would be bringing it with them.

The thought of being locked up in a cell while my life was picked through for some imaginary crime made me grimace. Adrianna and the kids needed me now more than ever. Stacey needed me. This business needed me. And I hadn't even done anything *wrong*.

Worse than that, I'd be a sitting duck for whoever it was that had put a target on my back, which meant I was a guaranteed dead man. So I needed to do whatever it took to get myself out of this mess and show these bastards I wouldn't roll over that easily.

Hayley's exact words hadn't been to phone a lawyer. No, she'd said *it wouldn't hurt to have someone helpful on speed dial.*

Pulling my phone out of my pocket, I scrolled through my contacts list until I came across the number I was looking for. They answered on the first ring.

"Ah, Mr Hunter, what can I do for you?"

"I'm wondering if your offer still stands?" I gritted my teeth, hating myself for stooping so low.

"Why, of course. Anything for an old friend," Alik Gromov said smoothly.

The thought of what I was about to do sent a shiver down my spine. But I didn't have a choice. Not really, not if I wanted to keep my life together and have any chance of finding this memory stick. I refused to be sidelined by people with too much power. At least this way I was able to take control of the situation.

"Then I need you to act fast."

Chapter 66

JASON HUNTER

THE OFFICE

Friday 22ⁿᵈ October

Just as Hayley predicted, a couple of detectives with a team of uniformed police officers arrived at the office with a search warrant. I didn't get in the way, knowing it would only make them more suspicious.

Instead, I'd stood by and watched them methodically search every inch of the office. My employees had been gathered in the main open plan space and stood in groups, whispering amongst themselves. I knew Lucy kept glancing my way, but I just did my best to ignore her. I didn't want to speak to anyone right now.

The door to the elevators opened and Alik Gromov stepped out, flanked by two bodyguards I'd never seen before. Both were huge, burly men who looked like they'd be more comfortable on the rugby pitch than in a tight-fitting suit.

I watched him approach, leaning heavily on his cane with every other step, as the lead detective, Gallagher, held up a bag of white powder. *Talk about cutting it fine. Pun* not *intended.*

"Jason Hunter, you are under arrest for the possession of Class A drugs." There was a collective gasp from everyone standing in the open plan space.

"You can't do that," said Richard.

"You can't arrest him," said Lucy.

"You do not have to say anything. But it may harm your defence if you do not mention when questioned something—"

"No, thank you, gentlemen," said Gromov.

The two detectives turned around at the sound of his voice.

"Excuse me?" asked Gallagher, clearly annoyed at the interruption. I don't know what I'd ever done to him, but I could have sworn he was enjoying this whole escapade far more than he should have.

"Not today. You'll find your search warrant has been voided and my client is not to be taken into custody today. That," he gestured to the bag of drugs still dangling from Gallagher's hand, "is part of an awareness training program and has been sanctioned by the Metropolitan Police. Apologies for the misunderstanding."

Frowning, Gallagher turned and walked a few steps away, dialling a number as he went while his colleague simply stood and scowled at both me and Gromov.

Gallagher grew animated as he spoke on the phone, gesticulating wildly whilst trying to keep his voice hushed. He hung up the phone with a scowl and strode back to us.

"Apologies for the inconvenience, Mr Hunter. We'll see ourselves out."

His colleague turned to look at him, his mouth agape.

Whatever Gromov had done had clearly worked and while I was relieved, a niggling voice in the back of my mind told me I was going to regret it.

Chapter 67

JASON HUNTER

THE OFFICE

Friday 22nd October

"What did you do?" I asked as I watched the police vacate the office.

"I called in a favour."

"Friends with the Chief of Police now, are we?"

He turned to look at me. "I don't like your tone."

I sighed. "Let's go into my office," I said, gesturing behind me just as Richard made a beeline for me. "Not now, please," I said in a low voice to Richard. He nodded and changed tact, heading towards the kitchen instead.

"Can I get you anything?" asked Lucy, appearing at my side.

"No, thanks."

She gave me a single nod and then went over to her desk as if the last couple of hours hadn't happened.

I walked into my office. Gromov was already seated in front of my desk, his two bodyguards stationed outside and his cane resting against his chair.

"Looks like I got here just in time," he said. "It's much trickier to get you out of these things once they have you arrested."

"I'm sure it is," I muttered.

"I promised you my protection, and that is what you will get," he said with a smile.

"At what cost?"

Gromov frowned. "I don't know what you mean."

"What is it going to cost? This protection? You said you needed my services again, what do you want?"

"Oh, it is free."

"No, it's not," I replied. This conversation had taken an unexpected turn and I did not like where it was going. "Nothing in this life is free."

"See, that's why I like you, Jason," he said, now grinning again. "You're very smart."

I held back the frustration as best I could. It wouldn't do well for him to see me getting wound up, he'd only play on it.

"There's no *monetary* cost, as such. But I'll call in a favour when I need to."

It felt like I'd been hit with a sledgehammer. The reality of my situation was quickly sinking in and it was bleak. I knew taking Gromov up on his offer would cost me, but somehow I'd thought he was just after an exchange. Personal protection for his playing the system. How did I not see this coming? Being indebted to Gromov was the worst possible outcome of today. I think I would have preferred prison.

"Is there a time limit on that favour?" I asked, trying to make light of the situation.

Gromov was no longer smiling. "I'll be in touch," he said and stood up.

Chapter 68

JASON HUNTER

HOME

Saturday 23rd October

After the chaos of the police search, the previous day had been a complete write off. And considering Stacey was in Austin with Sam, some uninterrupted hours at the office were exactly what I'd needed to distract me over the weekend.

I dragged my tired body through my front door, hating how early it got dark. The house was almost pitch black and it was barely 5pm. And yet, there was a soft glow coming from the living room, as if one of the lamps had been left on.

Frowning, I followed the source of the light down the hallway and into the lounge, stopping short at the sight of the man sitting in the chair by the window. The gun was steady as he pointed it at me.

I froze, unsure what to do next.

The man looked familiar but I wasn't sure where I'd seen him before. His face, at least the half of it I could see in the lamplight, was remarkably plain, almost unmemorable. He had cold, dark eyes that bored into me and I didn't even want to consider the possibility of a struggle. The guy was huge. Even sitting down, he managed to fill out the entirety of the chair with well-defined muscles. I wasn't small myself, but I knew he would dwarf me.

"You know, for a guy who works in security, it was far too easy to get into your house."

I frowned. He had a point. The motion sensor cameras I'd set up hadn't alerted me that anyone had visited. He'd disabled them, picked the lock and made himself at home. Unless he'd come in a different way? Perhaps through the back, but I'd set cameras up there too.

"How—?"

Before I could finish, he flicked the gun towards the sofa. "Sit."

"What the hell are you doing in my house?" I asked, thankful the kids weren't here.

He didn't reply. He didn't even move.

"Look, whoever you are, I don't have what you're looking for." That got his attention, and he quirked an eyebrow up. "I don't have it," I said again for emphasis. "And I don't know where it is."

"Just sit," he said.

And that's when I realised why he looked familiar.

I sat down on the sofa, placing an arm along the back and crossing my legs, feigning a casualness I definitely did not feel, my heart thundering in my chest.

After a moment's silence, I said, "So, what were you doing at the funeral?"

He didn't reply.

"I know serial killers enjoy watching their victims be buried, but I didn't figure a professional like you would stoop that low."

The gun didn't waver but he did crack a smile. "How?" he asked.

"Man of few words? Alright, I'll play along. The police have an E-Fit of you."

He seemed to consider this. "The wife?"

"Enough people saw you there. You weren't exactly subtle."

He gave a small nod. "True."

"So why were you there?"

He looked past me, as if he was weighing up his options.

"Why are you here?" I asked. He was sitting in my living room, holding me at gun-point and yet the man had the audacity to stay silent. I wasn't dead yet, so I had no doubt that he needed something from me. I assumed that he was after the memory stick. Or had been sent by whoever had contracted him to kill Mickey in the first place.

The thought made me go cold.

It was highly likely only one of us was going to walk out of here alive.

Chapter 69

JASON HUNTER

HOME

Saturday 23rd October

"You know," he said. "People have started asking questions about you."

I tensed, not liking where this was going.

"And those same people are under the impression that you have something incredibly valuable."

I didn't reply. Denying it would only make me seem more guilty.

"Something that doesn't belong to you," he said, his eyes not leaving my face. "But I know you don't have it."

I wasn't sure if I should feel relieved or not.

"So why are you here?" I asked.

"I still have a job to do." He shrugged a shoulder as if killing me was a mere inconvenience, just another task in his to-do list for the day.

"You make a habit of chatting up people you're about to kill?"

He chuckled.

"I figured you were more of a 'kill from a distance' kind of guy. I mean, that was your MO with Mickey. And Gemma."

He frowned.

"Stacey. On the podium of the Hungarian Grand Prix last year. Except it wasn't Stacey."

"A job is a job," he said.

I scoffed. That wasn't an answer, it was an excuse.

He sighed, as if dealing with a petulant child. "Jason, what do you want from me?"

"Shouldn't I be asking you that?" I said.

"I'll see myself out," he said and stood abruptly.

"What? You're leaving?"

"You know, you should try not to ask so many questions," he said and walked out into the hallway.

I was speechless. What the hell was going on? The guy broke into my house, held me at gunpoint, and was leaving? What was he playing at?

"Look, just tell me why you came," I said as he opened the front door.

"I needed to make sure you were here," he said over his shoulder before disappearing into the darkness of the street.

I watched him go, panic swelling up inside of me. Why did I need to be here? I pulled my phone out, ignored the camera notification for the front door – so he hadn't completely disabled my security system – and called Adrianna.

The kids were tucked up in bed and she was watching a movie with Imani.

"Can you go check on them for me, please?"

"What? Jason—"

"Please," I said as I clutched the phone to my ear, desperate to hear that my kids were okay. I walked back into the living room with the intention to pick up my car keys and drive over the moment Adrianna replied.

"They're fine," she whispered. "Both asleep. Max is all curled up and Lily is sleeping with her mouth open."

The tension in my body lessened.

"Thank god," I whispered.

"Jason, what' going—"

"I'll explain everything in the morning. I need to call Stacey."

I dialled Stacey and it rang once before I hung up, realising she'd most likely be on the track. Instead, I dialled Sam. He answered on the first ring.

"Boss?"

"Where's Stacey?"

"Racing."

"Everything okay?" I tried to keep my voice steady and even.

"All good."

There was a pause as I tried to think about what the gunman might have meant, who might have been the target. I mean, if he was here, who was doing his dirty work?

"Boss, you alright?" asked Sam.

I hesitated. "Yeah, fine. Just checking in. She doing okay?"

"She's doing great," he said and I could almost hear the smile in his voice.

"Amazing. Thanks, Sam."

"Sure—"

I didn't let him finish before I hung up the call and dialled Hayley.

"This better be good," she said when she answered.

And that's when I saw it. A small envelope on the chair where the gunman had sat.

"Sorry, I—" I let the words trail off, distracted by what he'd left behind. "I'll call you back," I said and hung up.

I picked up the envelope. It was blank and lightweight. Whatever was inside was pretty small. I opened it and tipped the contents into the palm of my hand. My heart almost stopped. I couldn't believe what I was looking at. And more importantly, I had no idea why it had been given to me.

A small, black memory stick.

Chapter 70

JASON HUNTER

HOME

Saturday 23rd October

I knew it was Mickey's before I even plugged it into my laptop. Knew without a shadow of a doubt what I was going to find on it. And yet, that still didn't prepare me for what I saw.

Opening the memory stick drive, a pop up appeared on the screen.

Call it a gift, or a curse. I didn't know who else to give it to.

The message disappeared after a few seconds and I was left staring at a folder filled with endless documents. I opened the master file at the top and was presented with a list of what I assumed was every document in the folder.

Worse than that, next to every file name was a date and *who it belonged to*.

Fuck.

What was Mickey *thinking*? I knew this was bad. Knew this was a shit load of trouble from the start, but I didn't realise the extent of it. No wonder I was being targeted. If I thought someone had this kind of dirt on me, I'd be pretty pissed too.

I grabbed a beer from the fridge and settled on the stool at the kitchen island, my laptop open in front of me.

And suddenly I knew why the gunman had delivered it to me. No matter what I did with this information, my life was going to get a hell of a lot worse. Planted drugs, threatening texts and cancelled client contracts were just the beginning. Things were gonna go bad, and fast.

I was a walking dead man.

My phone buzzed on the counter next to me and Hayley's name flashed on the screen.

Ah shit. I'd said I'd call her back and hadn't.

"Hey," I said as I picked up.

"Want to tell me what's going on?"

I hesitated. Did I tell Hayley? Realistically, what could she do? The search warrant had made it clear that the police weren't as trustworthy as they first appeared. I needed a contingency plan before I just handed it over. And it definitely wasn't safe to keep it at the house.

Now I knew why Mickey had the safe deposit box.

"Sorry, I thought I had something. Just doing some online re-search."

"Well, how about you tell me why Alik Gromov showed up at your office yesterday and managed to make the search warrant go away."

"I don't really want to go into it."

"Jason, please tell me you didn't do anything stupid," she said.

"You told me to have someone helpful on speed dial," I said, using her own words.

"I meant a lawyer or legal counsel. Not Alik fucking Gromov! Jesus Christ, Jason. What have you done?"

"I haven't *done* anything," I said, getting defensive. I didn't like her accusatory tone. And yes, in hindsight it wasn't the smartest thing I'd ever done, but in the heat of the moment I'd panicked. And all a lawyer was going to do was represent me while I was being questioned. At least Gromov had stopped them from arresting me in the first place.

At what cost?

I pushed the thought away. There was no point dwelling on it. What was done was done. And what Gromov wanted would eventually come to light. I just had to hope it was legal.

"Look," I said. "I didn't have many options. And if this thing with the Mayor is related in any way, I'd have been in more danger sitting in a police interrogation room than walking around the streets of London."

Hayley gave a non-committal sound, clearly unconvinced by my rationale.

Me too.

"Have you made any progress with the E-Fit?" I asked, changing the subject.

"Not yet. I'm working on it. I'll give you a call, okay?"

"Sure."

She hung up. I knew it was just an excuse to end the call. I knew doing a deal with Gromov was like making a deal with the devil, but what I didn't know was why Hayley was so bothered by it. Was it going to create issues for our working relationship? I hadn't thought of that until now. If I had ties to Gromov, it might mean that she'd be unable to rely on my help in future.

Looking at my computer screen, I knew I couldn't waste time worrying about Hayley right now. There was a target on my back and I really needed to do something about it.

Chapter 71

STACEY JAMES

AUSTIN GRAND PRIX

Sunday 24ᵗʰ October

She was starting in *pole* position. The rumble of the engine sounded beneath her and vibrated through her body as she adjusted her grip on the steering wheel, the gloves feeling clunky as always.

Her qualifying race had been fantastic and Eden had been thrilled. His pep talk this morning had been all about how she could wipe the floor with the lot of them. She smiled at the thought.

"All good? Can you hear me?" said Kyle in her ear.

"Loud and clear," she said, and could barely contain the excitement humming through her.

"Good luck," he said and she smiled. It had nothing to do with luck.

She shifted one foot and then the other. She was ready for this. Ready to win. Ready to *own* this.

Ottokar was in third place, and it was Dima who was in second. She'd have to be careful, stick to her racing line, and drive smoothly. He was a worthy competitor and she couldn't afford a single slip up.

She took a deep breath and relaxed her shoulders. If she tensed up, things would go wrong. She needed to stay loose and focused.

The countdown began in front of her, and she readied herself. This was it. All five lights went out and she pressed down on the accelerator. The car sped away from the start line and adrenaline coursed through her system.

This. Was. It.

She could see the back of Dima's car in her wing mirror. He was close, and staying close.

The first turn came up fast and she leaned into it. The start was always the hardest, the cars close together, no opportunity to gain any ground yet, and so she needed to be careful. She couldn't afford to clip another car, to spin out or crash.

She gave Dima enough space to take the corner on the inside line and she kept wide. It was a necessary manoeuvre, but one that would pay off as it would position her for the inside line on turn two and that's when the advantage would start to build.

She was already increasing the gap between them.

"Great start, Stace," said Kyle. "Car's performing as it should. Need to ease up for turns three, four and five. More acceleration through turn six."

"Got it."

Kyle's soothing tones talked her through all the turns, accelerations, decelerations, and driver standings as she completed lap after lap. He regularly updated her on her own timings, noting when she was fastest, what was slowing her down and how the car was performing. His chatter was almost constant, as if he was right there with her.

It helped to keep her focused, never letting her attention waver for even half a second. And it was paying off. All race she'd been increasing the distance between herself and the other drivers. She had a healthy lead that would take some effort to close.

"I think you need to watch your back," said Kyle.

Stacey glanced in both of her mirrors as she braked on the long stretch to take turn 12. She could see Dima, and he was coming up fast.

"What's going on?" she asked.

"Looks like he's chancing his luck. The guy is pushing himself and his car."

Stacey frowned.

"How close is he?"

"If he keeps up this reckless driving, he'll be catching up in a lap and a half."

Shit.

"Just keep doing what you're doing," said Kyle. "Stay steady. He won't be able to keep it up. No way he can out drive you."

"Thanks Kyle," she said. But that didn't stop her glancing in her mirrors again. Dima was definitely closer, and it looked like he was taking the corners too quickly. If he wasn't careful, he was going to come off the track.

Stacey did as she was told. No silly stunts this time. No need, considering she was out front. But that didn't stop Dima from gaining ground.

It was the last lap and Dima was so close behind her. Every time she completed a turn, a glance in the wing mirror told her he was right behind.

"Don't let him get in your head," said Kyle. "You've got less than a minute and a half to stay ahead. Easy peasy."

She smiled.

"Easy peasy," she said. But that didn't stop her from glancing in her side mirror again. He was so close. And it was making her nervous. All she had to do was keep steady, stay smooth, stay focused.

She took turns seven, eight and nine in quick succession, Dima keeping pace close behind her. She had less than a minute left of the lap, that was it. Less than a minute.

"Steady now," said Kyle. "Let's increase that speed for turn ten but be prepared for a harder break on turn 11."

"Will do," she said.

She could feel the burn in her muscles from working so hard. Each race was a physical and mental strain. And it always surprised her just how much of a toll it took on her body. She'd feel bruised tomorrow, that's for sure. But then with the amount of G-force pressure she felt during the race, it wasn't surprising. Every acceleration, every turn, every time she braked, they all pushed down with an unbearable weight.

She leaned into turn 19. This was it. The final stretch. And Dima was still right behind.

"Don't push too hard," warned Kyle.

She leaned into turn 20, the final turn of the track. The final turn of the entire race. As she came out of the turn, she accelerated as hard as she could. She needed to hold onto this win.

The finish line was just ahead, and she was confident she'd done enough to win. There was no way Dima could have taken those last two corners faster than her. No way he'd be able to gain that precious ground.

But the view in her mirror didn't lie. And Dima was almost parallel. It was going to be tight, within a fraction of a second.

She passed over the line. The chequered flag waved and she had no idea whether she'd won or not.

"Kyle?"

There was no reply.

"Kyle!" She shouted, panic edging her voice. She tried to keep herself calm but she could feel herself spiralling.

"They're just reviewing footage. It was too close to call."

She slowed the pace as she waited for the verdict.

"I'm sorry, Stace. Volkov claimed it. 0.004 seconds."

"Ugh!" She hit the steering wheel in frustration.

That damn Russian bastard.

Although she couldn't help but smile.

Well played, Dima.

Chapter 72

JASON HUNTER

SOMEWHERE IN LONDON

Sunday 24ᵗʰ October

"What is this place?"

Cameron turned to look at me and I had to blink a couple of times to make sure that what I was seeing was real. Gone were the outrageously red clothes. She was dressed in ripped jeans and a grey hoodie, with a baseball cap pulled low on her head covering most of her red hair. The rest was tucked into the neck of her hoodie.

"It's a safe house," she said.

We were standing in the bare kitchen of a first-floor apartment in a neglected, run down apartment block.

"What do you need a safe house for?" I asked. "Or do I not want to know?"

She shrugged. "It's a precaution Mickey put in place. Untraceable, anonymous, and certainly not bugged."

"Is the club bugged?"

"I'd say no, but you can never be too careful. Mickey's a great example of that."

I nodded, understanding what she meant. I didn't want to be here any longer than I needed to be, so I pulled the memory stick out from my coat pocket and placed it on the counter next to us.

Cameron's eyes went wide.

"Tell me that's not what I think it is."

I didn't reply.

"Jason," she hissed, scooping it off the counter as if it would leave burn marks behind. "What are you playing at?"

"I had a visitor. Who kindly left me a present." I put my hands in my pockets and nodded towards her fist.

"A visitor? Who?"

"It doesn't matter." And it didn't, at least not right now.

Cameron opened her fist and looked down at the small black stick nestled in her palm. She looked nervous.

"What are you going to do with it?" she asked and glanced up at me.

"I don't know. I was hoping you could help."

"How?" Her nervousness was immediately replaced with suspicion, and I honestly couldn't blame her.

"I actually don't know," I admitted, and it was the truth. How exactly was Cameron going to get me out of the shithole I now found myself in? What could she do that Mickey couldn't?

"What do you want?" she asked.

"I want this target on my back to go away," I said. "And I have no idea how to do that."

"Just get rid of it."

"I can't. They think I have it, and things have started getting messy. If I just get rid of it, they won't leave me alone."

"Can your police friend not help?"

I shook my head. "It's too risky. The police came to my office with a bogus search warrant the other day."

"Shit," said Cameron, and she looked worried.

My phone vibrated in my pocket. I pulled it out and saw a withheld number.

"Don't—" said Cameron, but I'd already answered the call and was pressing the phone to my ear.

"You were warned," said the familiar mechanical voice.

Suddenly glass exploded behind me. I dove for Cameron and dragged her to the floor as furniture shattered. I could feel the bullets whizzing past us as I pressed her into the ground, shielding her body with mine.

Cameron screamed and I clamped a hand over her mouth. She stared at me, eyes wide and terrified. We lay like that, motionless, as the apartment was destroyed around us.

And just as suddenly as it started, it stopped.

My phone was still in my hand. It vibrated with an incoming text from an unknown number. With a shaking hand, I opened the text to read an address. It was somewhere in Bromley by Bow. An area I'd never heard of. It had an E3 postcode so I guessed it was still within central London.

My phone vibrated again. This time, it was a photo and my stomach dropped. It was a slightly blurry image of Adrianna's face. There was a gag tied around her mouth and her makeup was smeared.

Jesus Christ.

What had they done to her? More importantly; what were they going to do with her?

My phone vibrated again. Another text.

You have 30 minutes.

"I need to go," I said, peering around the breakfast bar that separated the kitchen from the living room at the smashed window that faced the apartment block across the street.

"What?" asked Cameron, her voice shaky, her mascara smudged.

"I need to leave. Now." I got to my feet, conscious of the open window exposing us.

"You can't just leave me here." The indignation rose in her voice and she seemed to regain control of herself. "What the fuck was that?"

"A message."

"A message?!" she shrieked.

"Ssh."

"Jason, what the absolute fuck is going on?!"

I showed her the screen of my phone and watched her face as she read the texts. She looked at me, disbelieving.

"I'll come with you."

I shook my head. "It's not safe."

"Oh, because being here is?" she asked sarcastically, waving a hand around the room. "Some safehouse," she grumbled as she dusted herself down and then surveyed the damage. "Shit."

I grabbed hold of her arms and gently turned her to face me. "Go to the club," I said. "Make sure people see you. I'll text you as soon as I'm safe, okay?"

She nodded. "At least call someone for back up."

"I will," I said. "Are you going to be alright?"

She nodded. I gave her arms a quick squeeze and then headed for the door.

"You can't give it to them, Jason," she said.

I turned to look at her. She was right. But Adrianna was in danger. And everything so far told me they wouldn't keep her alive for the sake of it.

"I know," I said. But I couldn't let Adrianna die.

Chapter 73

JASON HUNTER

SOMEWHERE IN LONDON

Sunday 24th October

I ran down the stairs of the apartment block to my car that was parked half a block away. I assumed I'd been followed here, but I'd been extra careful, and had regularly checked for a tail, just to make sure. I'd looped back around on myself a couple of times, too. And while a few things recently indicated I might be losing my touch – the gunman getting into my house being one of them – I couldn't believe that someone had followed me all the way from my place and I'd failed to notice them.

I climbed into my old, beaten-up BMW and jammed the key into the ignition.

If I hadn't been followed, then it was likely I was being tracked. And they could be doing that in a whole bunch of different ways. Whoever was behind this clearly had sway with the Met Police, so tracing my phone wasn't completely out of the question. There wasn't much I could do about a tracking bug in my car; it would take a full sweep to find it and get rid of it. Something I didn't have time for right now. Besides, tracking my location would only work in my favour now.

I copied the Bromley by Bow address into the Maps app on my phone and clipped it into the phone holder on my dashboard. I was already pulling away from the curve and driving down the deserted street, reaching around for my seatbelt to clip it in and silence the annoying pinging sound.

The app said it would take me 27 minutes to get to the address, which meant I'd be too late, although I was pretty confident I could shave a few minutes off en-route.

I drove down the quiet residential street. Eerily quiet considering there had just been gunfire. Where were the cops? Where were the bystanders in the street? But I didn't have time to think about it.

The traffic got steadily heavier as I joined the main roads, slowing my progress to a frustrating pace.

A text notification appeared at the top of my screen. I pressed it, desperately trying to keep one eye on the road as I went.

20 minutes.

The bastard was clock watching. Whoever he was, he was going to thoroughly enjoy himself if I was even 30 seconds late.

Enough of this shit.

I pressed my foot down on the accelerator and overtook the car in front, earning myself some glaring horns from oncoming traffic in the process.

I needed to be quick, but I also couldn't afford to draw attention to myself. The last thing I needed was to be picked up by the police.

I took a deep breath and pushed on through the overcrowded streets of London, pressing the accelerator when I could, overtaking when it wasn't too reckless and squeezing through as much traffic as possible.

I arrived with 6 minutes to spare.

Climbing out of my car, I looked around, glancing down at the map on my phone to check I was in the right place. The little notification saying I'd arrived at my destination did nothing to convince me.

In front of me was a derelict warehouse. The yard out front was empty except for an abandoned Renault Kangoo van that was missing at least one wheel and had enough rust over half of its body to know that it would never move again.

The giant wooden doors to the warehouse were covered in a peeling, pale blue paint with a thick chain threaded through the handles, secured with a chunky padlock that gleamed under the moonlight.

One side of the building had three huge windows made up of smaller panes of glass, many of which were either cracked, broken or missing.

I needed to get inside and it looked like the main entrance was off limits. I unlocked my phone and took another look at the picture of Adrianna, ignoring the look on her face and taking note of the clothes I could see – it would be easier to find her that way. It was hard to tell but it looked like she was in a pink sweater, the kind she'd wear to the gym. The colour was dull and grubby, making it hard to see any other details. I pocketed my phone.

Edging around the window-side of the building, it was clear there was no way in. Just more doors that were boarded up. I ran back to the front and then down the other side. More boarded up doors and broken windows. Except these single pane windows were about two feet above my head.

I could just about grip hold of the bottom of the window frame, but I was going to need a boost to get me through the window.

I scanned the area around me, looking for something I could use as a leg up. There must be something in this dump of a place. There was rubbish and debris everywhere, scattered through bushes and abandoned on the roadside.

I spotted a couple of planks of wood from an old pallet not too far away. Dragging them across to the warehouse, I leaned them up against the wall underneath one of the smashed windows, angled enough that they weren't too steep. I cautiously climbed the makeshift ramp, getting as high up the wood as I dared. I grabbed hold of the window frame and jumped, hooking my elbow over the inside of the frame and hoisting myself up until my head and shoulders were all of the way through.

Looking down, I realised I hadn't thought this through. It was a hell of a drop and I was going to go over head first. The minutes were ticking by quickly, and I didn't have time to get hurt.

Getting my second hand on the window frame, I was able to push the top half of my body through the window, but my arms nearly buckled under me as a searing pain sliced through my stomach.

I toppled forward, the strength leaving my arms and I tried to tuck my head in as I crashed to the floor. The wind was knocked from me and I couldn't breathe. I pulled myself up into a sitting position, wincing at the pain in my stomach. I glanced down to see a tear in my t-shirt and blood seeping through.

I touched the area around it gently and winced again. A quick check confirmed there were no obvious chunks of glass sticking out of me and I clamped a hand over the wound. I looked up at the window. There was nothing there that I could have cut myself on, no shard of glass still clinging to the window frame. Either way, something had cut me pretty nasty.

I scrambled to my feet, grimacing with each movement, and looked around. I didn't dare look at my watch to see how late I was. I didn't want to face the consequences. All I could hope for was that being on the premises was enough to keep Adrianna alive.

And then I chastised myself. They wanted the memory stick. Of course she was going to be alive.

Chapter 74

STACEY JAMES

JASON'S HOME

Sunday 24th October

She unlocked the door and crossed the threshold.

"Hey," she called out as she stepped into the dark hallway.

Closing the door behind her, she made her way through the living room and into the kitchen.

"Anyone home?"

All the lights were out.

"Jason?"

She pulled out her phone and sent him a text. She'd wanted to surprise him by getting home early but it was no good if he wasn't even here.

While she waited for him to get back to her, she decided she'd open a bottle of wine and maybe run herself a bath. If he got home sometime soon, he could always join her. She smiled at the thought.

Pulling a bottle of wine from the rack under the kitchen counter, she opened the cutlery drawer to find the bottle opener. And stopped short.

Nestled between the knives and forks was a phone. It wasn't Jason's. This was old, a cheap throw-away phone.

A burner phone.

She didn't know where the thought came from or why Jason would even have one.

Picking it up, she turned it on. Maybe it wasn't Jason's. Maybe it belonged to Adrianna. Although that wasn't an explanation.

It pinged to life and a text lit up the screen. She opened it.

I'm already here.

She read the message again, trying to work out what it could mean and why. She flicked back to the conversation and read the last few. They'd all happened on Tuesday, five days ago.

She scrolled back further through the text exchange but it was impossible to tell who Jason had been texting. Assuming it was Jason's phone.

There was a sent message on the 5th.

Thursday arrival. One man team.

The text before that was the 22nd of September.

And that was when she noticed a pattern. The texts were sent ahead of race weekends. They didn't say much, all similar stuff.

Thursday arrival. One man team.

Thursday arrival. Two man team.

Thursday arrival. Four man team.

They were updates on her security detail.

She copied the anonymous number into the keypad and pressed call. On the second ring, the call connected but there was no greeting.

"Where is he?" she asked.

"Stacey?" Cooper sounded genuinely surprised.

"I take it that you know where he is?" She couldn't help but feel annoyed. She knew Jason had been contacting Cooper before every race so she wasn't sure why the annoyance swept through her. It wasn't a surprise. Perhaps just the fact that she'd found the evidence.

"How—"

"Just answer me."

"I have eyes on him," he said.

"What does that mean?"

"It means I know where he is and I'm watching his back."

"You need to tell me what the hell is going on right now," demanded Stacey,

Cooper let out a sigh. He knew she wouldn't let up until he spilled the beans.

"I've got a situation, alright? It's dangerous and Adrianna may be at risk."

"Adrianna?" said Stacey.

"I can't talk," he said, lowering his voice to just above a whisper. "Actually, I'm glad you called. There's something I need you to do."

Chapter 75

JASON HUNTER

THE WAREHOUSE

Sunday 24th October

The warehouse was as derelict on the inside as it looked on the outside. Graffiti covered the walls. Puddles of water stagnated in the corners. The place smelled damp and musty. Moonlight filtered through the missing sheets of corrugated iron.

The place was deserted.

There was a scuffling sound and I tried not to think about what might be scurrying along the floor nearby. I shivered.

I couldn't see Adrianna. In fact, I couldn't see anyone. And I couldn't see any evidence that anyone had been here recently either. But the shiny new padlock that I'd spotted on the front door said otherwise.

Still clutching my stomach to stem the bleeding, I moved further into the warehouse. There was a door at the other end, darkness yawning from the entryway. I crossed to it, digging my phone from my pocket as I went and switching the torch on. There were several notifications on my screen from Stacey, including a missed call, but I ignored them. She was in Austin, with Sam.

I shone the torch through the doorway, illuminating a flight of stone steps. The beam was just about strong enough to light the stairway but I couldn't see anything through the doorway at the top.

There was another scuffling sound, and this time a moan.

My heartbeat quickened.

Adrianna.

I climbed the stone steps as fast as I dared, wincing every now and again at the pain in my stomach. Whatever had cut me had gone in deep. But I didn't have time to think about that right now, I just had to push forward and get both me and Adrianna out of here.

At the top of the steps, I could see into a large room. It was only a fraction of the size of the main warehouse, with large empty windows along one side. A broken desk was pushed up against one wall, and debris lay scattered across the floor, broken bits of wood, rubble, old bits of cardboard boxes and god knows what else.

In the middle of the room, tied to a chair, was Adrianna. I rushed forward and her eyes went wide as she recognised me. Her hands were tied behind her back, and each of her ankles were strapped to a chair leg. A gag had been roughly tied across her face and was digging into the corners of her mouth.

"Hgmmm," she said as I cradled her face in my hands, checking to see if she was alright.

"I'm gonna get you out of here," I whispered.

"Are you now?"

I froze, my hands hanging limp in the air. I knew that voice.

Spinning on the heels of my feet, I turned to face Alik Gromov as he stepped out of the shadows.

"You do love to play the hero, don't you?"

"What?"

My mind was trying to catch up. So Gromov was behind the texts. But did that mean he was behind everything else too? Or was he simply a puppet for a higher power? Had he colluded with the Mayor of London to turn my clients against me? Had he manipulated the Met Police into planting drugs in my office? But that didn't make sense; Gromov had been the one to sort that issue out for me. Why would he do that?

Then I remembered the conversation that came next.

There's no monetary cost, as such. But I'll call in a favour when I need to.

I suddenly had a sneaking suspicion about what that favour was going to be.

"What do you want, Alik?" I snapped, my anger getting the better of me.

"Wrong question."

I frowned, in no mood to play games. He'd kidnapped Adrianna, done god knows what to her and lured me here.

"You already know the answer to that question," he said, waving a hand in the air. "Try asking another."

"I don't know what you think you're playing at, but I'm going to untie her, and we're going to leave."

"Ah," he said, smiling slightly and leaning heavily on his cane. "I can't let you do that."

Two large men dressed in black suits appeared from the darkness of the stairwell, blocking our escape path.

"You have something of mine, and I'm not letting you, or your ex-wife, leave until I have it."

"I don't have it," I said,

"Of course you do. You had it at Cameron's apartment. I know you wouldn't have been stupid enough to leave it there, and it's not like you're going to let it out of your sight."

I tried to think of something to say but I was struggling to understand how he knew so much.

"Yes, I know who she is," he said, waving a hand with an air of impatience. "Do you think I wouldn't? When my—" he paused for a moment as if thinking of the right word, "—contractor didn't retrieve the memory stick from Mickey's apartment, I assumed he'd already given it to her for safe keeping. I didn't think the useless bastard would double cross me. That's a new low, even for him."

So the gunman had taken the memory stick for himself, thinking it was valuable, and then got a hell lot more than he'd bargained for. I guess he'd chosen to disappear once he'd dropped it to me, not wanting anything to do with it. I didn't blame him.

"I'm telling you, I don't have it," I said, holding my hands up in the air.

Gromov gave a soft chuckle before nodding his head in my direction. The two goons lurched forward, grabbing me with rough hands. The pain in my stomach flared and my vision swam. I tried not to cry out, but I had no idea if the scream was in my head or not.

I could see Adrianna fighting against her restraints in the corner of my eye, but I needed to keep Gromov's attention on me.

One of the goons started rummaging around in my coat pockets, starting with the one on the inside. I realised in that moment that I'd been incredibly stupid. The goon pulled the memory stick from my inside pocket and handed it to Gromov with a smirk.

Smiling, Gromov took hold of it and held it up so we could all see it more clearly in the moonlight.

"Such a lot of trouble for something so small," he said almost wistfully.

I was desperately trying to think of a way out. The pain in my stomach was burning a fire within me, and it was hard to think past it. I couldn't focus.

"Kill them," said Gromov with an air of finality. He turned and walked towards the doorway.

"Risky move," I said.

He paused and turned to look at me, and then frowned.

"How?" he asked.

"Well, you don't know exactly what's on that stick yet. You might still need me."

"Jason," he sighed. "That is a pathetic attempt to save your life. You and I both know you didn't take this to the police, and I've already demonstrated how much control I have there. It would be fruitless. And if you've made a copy, I'll be able to tell the moment I see the files. And if that is the case, I'll go through every member of your family to get it." He shrugged. "Children can be great motivator."

I felt sick.

"The same can be said for a bullet in the right place." A crouched figure appeared in the doorway and edged into the room, carrying an L115A3 sniper rifle that was expertly trained on Gromov's left thigh.

I'd never been so relieved so see Cooper.

"How—" I started.

"Later," he cut in.

"I'd think carefully about your next move," he said, still focused on Gromov. "We can always put a bullet in you and test my theory. How does that sound?"

"Bill Cooper." Gromov clapped his hands together. "What a delightful reunion. I remember you bleeding out on my office floor last time we met. In fact, I've been doing a bit of digging on you since then. What an interesting employment record. Shame you didn't put yourself forward for my contract."

"I'm picky about who I work for." He shrugged.

Gromov laughed again.

"You've got until I count to three to unhand my friend there." He inclined his head in my direction, his eyes never once leaving Gromov's face. "Or I'll start shooting. One."

The men holding me tensed, their eyes flicking to Gromov even as their hands loosened slightly on my arms.

"Two."

I didn't wait for Cooper to get to three, instead I yanked my arms free and ran to Adrianna. It only took a couple of seconds to untie her hands and ankles. She stumbled to her feet and I tried to support her but another wave of pain coursed through me as I took her weight.

"Over here," said Bill, gesturing behind him. He'd inched his way further into the room, almost backing Gromov into a corner.

We did as he said, the stone steps materialising out of the darkness in front of us. I eyed the two goons, trying to judge their next move. I couldn't tell if they were being cautious or waiting for something. Instinct told me that Gromov had a way out of this. He always did. He wouldn't have brought me up here, into this room, if he didn't have a contingency plan.

I could feel Adrianna clinging to my arm, her nails digging into my skin.

I frantically scanned the shadows, desperately searching for another way out, but it was too dark to see anything. With where Gromov was standing, I could take a good guess at there being an exit in the far-left corner, but we'd never make it across the room. And as my eyes strained against the dark, I made out a shape against the wall, directly behind Gromov. About waist heigh and cylindrical. Was it an old water cooler from when this place was an office?

Cooper took a half step back and I understood the signal. It was time to leave. I edged toward the open door.

And that's when I heard it. When we all heard it. The sound of the chain being pulled from the door. It echoed throughout the empty warehouse. Looking past the two bodyguards, I saw the unmistakable shape of the warehouse doors opening, and heard the thudding of boots and half shouted commands as people entered.

Adrianna let out a soft whimper.

"You should have trusted me," said Gromov with a half-smile.

The two goons leapt into action, both pulling a semiautomatic handgun from inside their jackets.

Cooper didn't hesitate.

"*Cyka blyat*," screamed Gromov as a bullet embedded itself in his upper thigh. He crumpled into a heap on the ground, his cane dropping from his hand. And then Cooper swung the barrel of his rifle to point at the two goons.

One of them rushed to help Gromov to his feet, while the other stepped in front, his gun trained on us. Leaning heavily on his bodyguard, Gromov was panting.

"This isn't over," he said through gritted teeth.

The three of them slowly backed into the corner, but Cooper didn't move. The boots on the warehouse floor were getting closer now, and there was more shouting.

"Shoot him," I muttered.

Cooper didn't move. He didn't even acknowledge that I'd spoken. Instead, he steadily watched Gromov and his two bodyguards leave.

That's when the second goon, the one still aiming his gun at us, suddenly changed target. He swung his gun around and fired a single shot into the gloom.

The room exploded into a fiery white light and I was thrown backward into the stairwell. Adrianna's grip on my arm loosened as I felt my body tumble down the stone stairs.

Chapter 76

JASON HUNTER

THE WAREHOUSE

Sunday 24th October

There was a loud ringing in my ears. I tried to open my eyes but my head was pounding and the pressure was excruciating.

I rolled over onto my side and threw up the contents of my stomach. The smell of vomit mingled with burning as I continued to retch.

Forcing myself onto my hands and knees, I realised I was feeling hot. Unbearably hot. Using the wall next to me, I managed to drag myself to my feet, the pain in my stomach slicing through me. I looked up the stairs to see bright orange flames licking at the doorway and it all came rushing back; Cooper shooting Gromov, Gromov being dragged into the shadows to whatever escape route he'd already planned out, and his bodyguard turning to shoot at... at something obviously explosive.

I frantically looked around for Adrianna. She was lying on the floor a few feet away, motionless. Rushing over, I swept her hair out of her face and patted her on the cheek.

"Adrianna," I said. "Adrianna," I tried again, this time louder. She didn't respond and I patted her harder. I tried thinking back to the first aid training we'd had in the office, the countless number of CPR sessions I'd sat through over the years.

I lay her down on her back and pressed my ear to her mouth. I couldn't tell if she was breathing or not. Placing one hand in the middle of her chest and the second on top, I began chest compressions. Pumping down and then up to the sound of the Bee Gees in my head. After a few pumps, Adrianna spluttered to life, gasping, and relief flooded through me. I sat back, giving her space to lift herself up onto her elbow. Her face was covered in dirt as she leaned over and coughed.

"You okay?" I half shouted over the ringing in my ears.

She nodded, still bent over and coughing.

"I'll be right back," I said, ignoring the terrified look in her eyes.

Lumbering to my feet again, I began to climb the stairs, stopping to cough every few steps as billows of black smoke poured through the doorway.

Cooper had been standing right in front of us, so I had no doubt that he'd taken the worst of the hit. But he'd clearly not tumbled down the stairs like me and Adrianna. Which meant he was still up there, and most likely going to burn to death if I didn't do something about it.

Each cough strained out of me, sending lashes of pain through my still-bleeding stomach. I was doubled over, barely able to move, leaning against the stone wall for support and summoning the energy to continue the climb.

I needed to get to the top. I couldn't just let Cooper die.

You'll die trying to save him.

I ignored the small voice in the back of my mind and concentrated on moving one foot in front of the other, climbing one step at a time.

I reached the top, the smoke even thicker as it filled my lungs. The pain in my stomach wouldn't let me crouch, so I slid to the floor and crawled forwards on my hands and knees.

When another coughing fit brought about another wave of excruciating pain, I pulled on the sleeve on my coat and clamped it over my nose and mouth.

I looked around for Cooper but couldn't see him.

Pulling my hand from my mouth for a brief moment, I yelled his name, my voice trailing off into another hacking cough.

The flames were licking up the walls, casting the whole room in an eerie orange glow. Black smoke billowed to the ceiling, making the air thick and hazy. I could only see a few feet in front of me as I called out for Cooper again. A low groan answered and I crawled towards the sound.

Cooper was sprawled on the floor, his arm twisted at a grotesque angle. He must have been thrown back by the force of the explosion, but instead of tumbling down the stairs with Adrianna and I, it looked like he'd hit the stairwell and been flung across the room.

I glanced a look down at his leg and saw that his foot was also bent at an unnatural angle. I winced.

Grabbing hold of his good arm, I sat on the floor and shuffled along, dragging his body with me. We only moved a couple of inches and I was panting from the exertion.

I tried again and managed a few more inches. We were still too far from the stairs. I needed to change tact.

Looping a hand under his armpit, I dragged him across the floor. This time he moved more easily. We made steady progress toward the doorway, and when we finally reached it, my whole body was shaking.

Carrying Cooper down the stairs was out of the question. But I couldn't just drag him down. It would cause irreparable damage to his body. Not to mention I could kill him if I happened to clip his head.

Gritting my teeth, I pulled off my coat, jumper and t-shirt, and then pulled my jumper back on over my bare skin. Ignoring the rip to the midsection of my t-shirt and the surrounding blood, I began to tear it into strips. Tying my coat around Cooper's head like a makeshift helmet, I used the strips of t-shirt to strap Cooper's ankle. Then, with the bits I had left, I tied his broken arm to his body as gently as I could.

Preparing myself for the pain, I hoisted Cooper's head and shoulders up until they were nestled in the crook of my arm and began to slowly drag his body over the stairs. He groaned but I ignored him. As I pulled more of his body forward, my anticipation for what came next grew. The moment his backside slid over that first step, there'd be no stopping him, pain or no pain.

I took a slow, steadying breath, coughed from the smoke and then finally pulled his body over the threshold. He thudded onto the second step and the weight of him pushed me forward quicker than I would have liked. I winced, but held fast.

We went down the second step, and this time his body jostled me in such a way that I let out a cry of pain.

I coughed again. The smoke was choking. I didn't have much time.

I edged down, one step at a time, trying to ignore the pounding in my head and the nausea that flooded me.

In what felt like an eternity, I reached the bottom, Cooper's body just three steps away from the floor. But my legs gave way and I crashed to the floor.

Two hands caught me and a long swish of blonde hair flickered on the edge of my vision before darkness overwhelmed me.

Chapter 77

STACEY JAMES

THE WAREHOUSE

Sunday 24th October

"Come on," she said. "Don't give up now."

She held onto Jason where she caught him, just inches from hitting the floor. But the weight of him and Bill was a lot to take. And she wasn't sure how she was going to be able to lower one without hurting the other.

Suddenly the weight lifted, and she looked up to see Adrianna taking Bill's weight.

Stacey gave her a small nod and managed to lower Jason to the floor.

"Go! Go!" Adrianna shouted as she struggled with Bill.

Stacey managed to pull Jason into a sitting position, his head lolling to one side. She tried not to think about the smoke inhalation and damage it was doing. She knew there were ambulances on their way, so she just needed to get him out into the fresh air where his chances of survival would be so much better.

Pulling one arm across her shoulders, she levered his body forward until she was bearing most of his weight.

God, he was heavy.

She was suddenly grateful for all of the long hours she'd spent at the gym.

Her thighs burned with the effort as she straightened up, staggering under his weight. She paused, steadied herself, and then pushed forward again. With each step the air became cleaner and it was easier to breathe.

She stumbled out through the warehouse doors and collapsed onto the floor, rolling to the side before Jason landed on top of her.

Police rushed forward but she didn't have time to check if he was okay. She turned back to the warehouse, ignoring shouts of her name as she ran back to Adrianna.

She had managed to lay him out on the floor and had hooked a hand under each knee, waiting for her return. Stacey didn't hesitate in grabbing him under the armpits and hoisting him up. They stumbled to the doorway, letting themselves slump to the floor as soon as they were outside.

Chapter 78

JASON HUNTER

THE ROYAL LONDON HOSPITAL

Tuesday 26th October

It was dark and I was cold. A steady, rhythmic beeping filled the silence. And then I heard the shuffling of feet, the murmuring of voices. I tried to swallow but I couldn't. There was something in my throat, pressing against the back of my tongue.

I slowly opened my eyes to a white tiled ceiling. The beeping was louder now, more insistent, like it was trying to tell me something. I glanced to my left where a lamp sat on the bedside table, casting the room in a soft glow.

Looking to my right, I found the source of the beeping. A machine stood by the bed, cables leaking out across the floor, up the side of the bed and underneath the covers.

I tried to swallow again but the pressure in my throat persisted. Reaching up a hand, I felt a tube attached to my face that went into my mouth. My mind flitted back to what had happened. I couldn't remember much, but I remembered fire. I pushed up on an elbow in an attempt to sit up but the pain in my stomach caused me to flop back down on the bed with a groan. Lifting the bed covers, I looked down at the hospital gown I was wearing. Tenderly, I touched my stomach and felt the outline of a gauze bandage taped to my skin.

The door to my room opened and Stacey walked in. Her face lit up when she saw me and she rushed to my bedside.

"You're awake," she breathed. She reached for a button above the bed and pressed it, before gently placing a kiss on my cheek, unshed tears shining in her eyes.

I tried to speak but the tube in my throat made it impossible, a garbled noise escaping me instead.

"Don't talk," she said, taking my hand. "You've been through a lot. They had to rush you into surgery and treat you for smoke inhalation. The tube is to protect your throat, reduce the swelling and lung inflammation."

I nodded and gently squeezed her hand, telling her I understood.

A tear rolled down her cheek.

"I didn't think you'd wake up," she whispered.

I lifted a hand and wiped the moisture from her cheek. The events of the warehouse were coming back to me in bits and pieces but it was mostly just a hazy recollection of fire and pain.

Chapter 79

JASON HUNTER

THE ROYAL LONDON HOSPITAL

Thursday 28th October

I was propped up in bed, the tube in my throat had been removed and I was watching Bradley Walsh on the muted TV. He was standing next to a nervous-looking woman in her mid-fifties. The next question came up on the screen: Who discovered penicillin?

A very apt question considering my current situation. Bradley read the question aloud to the contestant and when the answers appeared, I deliberated for half a second.

"Alexander Flemming," I guessed, my voice raspy from lack of use and the damage to the inside of my throat.

"You talking to yourself?" said Stacey, standing in the doorway, a takeaway cup in each hand.

I smiled at the sight of her and nodded toward the TV. "In a way."

She came in and placed both of the cups on my bedside table. "A tea," she said.

"Thanks." I lifted the remote and turned the TV off. "You managed to persuade the doctors yet?"

She smiled and shook her head. "Another couple of days at least."

I sighed. It was frustrating but I knew it was for the best. The damage to the lining of my throat might be irreparable, meaning I'd forever sound like I smoked fifty cigarettes a day. With any luck it would improve, but there was a high chance I'd be left with other side effects such as reduced lung capacity.

Stacey had paid for me to be treated privately, which meant they weren't discharging me early, no matter how much I protested.

"You've been through a lot," she said, trying to placate me. She knew how frustrated I was feeling, how utterly bored I was becoming. There was only so much daytime TV I could stomach.

I reached for the tea. She picked it up and handed it to me before I could stretch the stitches in my stomach. Apparently I'd lost a lot of blood from that one and was lucky I hadn't severed anything. The assumption was that I'd pierced myself with a shard of glass as I climbed through the window, but the laceration was so deep, it was a miracle it hadn't lodged inside. I shivered at the thought.

Accepting the takeaway cup with a small smile, I tentatively took a sip. And that was when I realised Stacey hadn't sat down. The chair by the side of my bed was her usual spot when she visited, which was daily. She looked worried, her eyebrows knitting together.

"What is it?" I asked.

Slowly, she reached into the handbag slung over her shoulder and pulled out a single piece of card inside a plastic wallet. I held out the takeaway cup which she took with one hand as she handed me the clear plastic wallet with the other.

Inside was a postcard. On the front were the words *Greetings from Austin* in an easily recognisable vintage style. The word *Austin* was written in big chunky letters and filled with scenes from around the city. I turned it over to see the hastily scrawled message:

Great job today. See you soon.

Love L x

I fought the urge to crumple the postcard in my fist, rage sweeping through me.

"Has Hayley seen this?" I croaked.

Stacey shook her head. "I wanted to show you first."

"Call her. Now," I rasped, my voice protesting the effort. I ripped back the covers and swung my legs over. The machines hooked up to my bedside began beeping wildly.

"I will. Jason—"

A nurse came rushing into the room.

"Mr Hunter. You are not to be out of bed," she said firmly. I waved her away as I stood. Pain coursed through my body and Stacey caught hold of me as I swayed.

"Mr Hunter!" said the nurse, with more indignation than concern. She was clearly unused to being ignored by her patients.

"I'm calling her now, okay?" said Stacey, allowing the nurse to take over and pulling her phone from her pocket.

Another wave of pain enveloped me as the nurse helped me back into bed. She quieted the machines, muttered something about pain medication, and then left the room.

After a short conversation, Stacey hung up the phone and turned back to me, propped up in the bed.

"She's on her way," she said.

I nodded, my eyes on the postcard. It had fallen to the floor in the commotion and lay there, untouched.

"Where was it?" I asked.

Stacey glanced over at the postcard. "Under the door at your place."

"Shit," I whispered and glanced at her face. She looked worried, but I didn't know if that worry was because of me or the homicidal stalker that had just promised to revisit.

"I'm fine," I grumbled.

"Well, that's the understatement of the year."

"Have you—"

"Checked the cameras? Yes. I've spoken to Sam too. Nothing."

I nodded, processing this. Trying to work out what Liam was up to.

"He broke into your place last time, didn't he? So I'm guessing he knew the address."

I nodded again. I didn't like how vulnerable it made me feel, especially with Max and Lily staying so often. Some fancy new cameras weren't going to change that.

We lapsed into silence and I realised just how exhausted I was. The tension and anxiety that had been balled up inside me surfaced again, only made worse by Liam's postcard.

"Any news on Cooper?" I asked.

Stacey shook her head. "Nada."

I rolled my eyes. He'd been unconscious for a few days, but as soon as he was well enough to speak, he'd discharged himself in the middle of a busy day shift and no-one had seen or heard from him since. I knew Hayley was frantically trying to track him down; it didn't look good to have him slip through her fingers twice.

"Has Hayley got an update on Gromov?"

"Speak of the devil and she shall appear," said Hayley from the doorway.

Stacey spun around to face her. "That was quick."

"I was already on my way when you called," she shrugged. "How're you doing?" she asked me as she came in and sat down in Stacey's usual chair.

"I've been better," I grumbled. I could feel the raspiness of my throat getting worse every time I spoke. I reached out for the tea again and this time it was Hayley who passed me the cup.

"As for Gromov," she said. "No. I don't have an update. His residency has been evacuated. His staff and everything in the place has gone. The forensics team is still working on the substance he ignited to cause the fire. Whatever it was, it was definitely placed there deliberately. My guess is to clean up after himself once he was done. I doubt he was banking on you and Adrianna getting out alive."

"How is Adrianna?"

"I checked in on her this morning," said Stacey. "She's fine. Worrying about you and keeping the kids close."

I nodded. I'd be doing the same if the roles were reversed.

"So what did you want to show me?" asked Hayley.

Stacey picked the plastic wallet up from the floor and handed it to Hayley. She took it and examined the front before turning it over to read the back. Her eyebrows shot up and she looked at Stacey, then me, and then Stacey again.

"Another one?" she asked.

Stacey nodded and moved so she could grip the end of my hospital bed.

"When did it arrive?"

"This morning," replied Stacey.

"Anyone see who delivered it?"

Stacey shook her head.

"I'll speak to the other houses on your street. There are enough camera doorbells these days that someone must have seen something."

"Is there not more you can do?" asked Stacey, and I heard the accusation in her voice.

"I'm doing everything I can," said Hayley.

"Are you?" demanded Stacey, angry now. "The stalker who nearly killed me is back, the Russian mobster who tried to kill Jason, Bill, and

Adrianna is on the run with millions of pounds of laundered money, and—"

"Who said he had the missing money?" asked Hayley.

Stacey faltered. "He took the memory stick from you," she said, turning to face me. "Adrianna said she saw them take it."

I nodded. "He did take it," I said. "Except it wasn't the right memory stick."

She turned to look at Hayley, who was grinning.

"Jason paid me a visit before going to see Cameron. The real memory stick is currently with my tech team who are piecing together the mother of all cases against some of the most powerful men in London. The one Gromov has is a dud. It looks real. It's pretty convincing when you look at the data, but it also contains a tracker. And no cryptokeys."

"So how come you can't find him?"

"The location pinged once, pretty soon after the warehouse incident but by the time we were able to get there, he was long gone. My guess is he was checking it wasn't a fake. And considering Jason here is still in one piece, I'd say he's convinced. So it's just a waiting game. He'll want to get somewhere safe before extracting what he needs."

Stacey looked at us both, dumbfounded.

"You called his bluff?" she said to me.

I nodded. "Of course I did."

"I still don't know how you got there before me," said Hayley, looking at Stacey with an arched eyebrow.

"I—," she started, clearly unsure how to explain herself. "I found your burner phone," she said to me. "And knew you'd been using it to message Bill. I called him and he gave me your location."

"How did Cooper—" Hayley started.

"That one I actually don't know," I said. "I was under the impression that he was in Austin, watching Stacey." I shrugged. Only Cooper would be able to answer that one.

"Whatever you do next time," said Hayley. "Don't go running into a burning building on your own."

Stacey rolled her eyes.

Hayley stood up. "Glad to see you're on the mend," she said, placing a hand on my shoulder.

"Thanks," I replied, my voice still raspy.

"I'll get this to the lab team," she said, holding up the postcard. "See if they can get anything from it. But don't hold your breath. There's one hell of a backlog at the moment, and it won't be a priority."

"Thanks Hayley," said Stacey.

Hayley gave a quick nod and then left.

Chapter 80

JASON HUNTER

THE ROYAL LONDON HOSPITAL

Friday 29th October

My eyes flew open but the room was dark. I glanced around, trying to see what had woken me. My eyes flicked from the door to the chair by my bedside, to the sofa on the other side of the room and the TV. But everything was silent, except for the constant low humming sound that came from outside my room.

Moonlight filtered through the window between the cracks in the curtains, filling the room with a surreal glow.

I propped myself up and looked around. Something had woken me, I was sure of it. Unless it was Liam's postcard giving me the creeps in my sleep. But the room was definitely empty.

Now that I was awake, though, I really needed to pee.

Sitting up properly, I swung my legs over the side of the bed, wincing slightly from the movement. I was still sore, and my body ached all over. With a hand on either side of me, I went to push myself off the bed, but before I could move, something was digging into my neck, choking me.

My hands flew up to my throat, grappling for whatever it was that was cutting off my airway. I could feel a thin wire digging into my neck and I desperately tried to get a fingernail underneath it as I gasped for breath. I could feel the panic rising, began clawing more desperately at the ligature digging in, and felt the scratches it left in the skin of my neck.

That was when I heard the voice in my ear.

"You should know better than to double-cross me, Mr Hunter."

The voice made my blood run cold.

Alik Gromov was here, in my hospital room, choking the life out of me.

I tried to speak, but I couldn't force the words out. I kicked my legs out in front of me as I attempted to throw myself backwards and into my attacker. But with nothing to kick against, they just flailed helplessly in the air. My body was still so weak, still recovering from the trauma of the warehouse.

"Was Mickey's dead body not enough of a message? Don't. Take. What's. Mine," he snarled in my ear.

There was a renewed tug on the wire and it dug further into my throat, making my vision swim.

I tried to speak, but the sound that came out was just a garble.

"He took my money and thought he could use it against me. Thought it would protect him. And just when I believed we'd come to a truce, Jason -" another tug on the wire "- you double-cross me. Where is it?"

With my right hand, I frantically tried to feel about in the bed for my emergency call button. I knew it was here somewhere, I'd used it to request more pain relief just a few hours ago. But my fingers were getting tangled in the sheets and my body was starting to become sluggish.

The longer I went without air, the harder it became to move. It felt like I was moving through treacle, pushing against a fog. My vision swam in and out of focus as I tried to push against my attacker once again. But I was too weak, the strength leaving my body fast.

"Where is it?" he said again, this time loosening the wire just enough for me to gulp down air. "Where are my cryptokeys?"

"I don't have it," I croaked, managing to get a single finger under the ligature.

"Don't play games with me, Jason. I have millions tied up in those assets. And so do my contacts. Your head on a platter just won't cut it," he said through gritted teeth as he yanked again on the ligature.

I spluttered, and felt my body jerk backwards. A crashing wave of fatigue washed over me as I realised how weak I was. My body was beginning to shut down, movement becoming impossible.

This was it.

This was the end.

My mind flashed to Lily and Max, to Stacey, to Adrianna and Hayley. To Sam.

The blinding overhead lights came on and a huge body came barrelling towards us. Distracted, Gromov's hold on the wire loosened. Air rushed into my lungs and I immediately used the distraction to my advantage, lunging forwards and pulling him across the bed.

Taken by surprise on two fronts, Gromov found himself in on my bed, Sam's huge bulk pressing down on him. I was in a heap on the floor, pain coursing through me. I touched the bandage across my stomach and it was clear I'd torn at least one of the stitches as bright red blood oozed out the side.

"I don't think I've ever been so pleased to see you," I said to Sam, and winced as I tried to push myself up into a better sitting position.

Chapter 81

JASON HUNTER

JASON HUNTER

Friday 29ᵗʰ October

Technically still the middle of the night, Hayley did not look pleased to see me.

"Where is he?" she snapped.

I winced, my head pounding from being starved of oxygen.

"Sorry," she added, noticing my wince, but also not caring enough to mean it.

"Down there," said Sam. "Second door on the right."

She gave him a nod before marching down the corridor in the direction he'd pointed.

The hospital security had handcuffed him to the bed in another room and locked the door, standing guard outside waiting for Hayley to arrive.

"What the actual fuck is going on?!" said Stacey, bursting in a moment later.

I winced again, the drumming in my head getting louder.

"Sorry," she said, coming to sit by my bed. "You okay?"

I nodded. "I'll live," I whispered, my throat raw.

Stacey James

Casino de Monte-Carlo

Sunday 29ᵗʰ May

She stepped out of the black Bentley onto the red carpet as the paparazzi crowded forward for a photo. The flash of the cameras was blinding but she did her best to look past them.

Her gown was a deep midnight blue and sparkled under the bright spotlights. She'd hired a professional to do her hair, which now hung over one shoulder in an elaborate fishtail braid. She raised a hand and smiled and the cameras went wild. The throng of people pushed harder, held at bay by thick velvet rope.

The car door clicked shut behind her and for the first time in a long time, she walked a red carpet event on her own. It was as surreal as it was exhilarating.

Of course she wasn't completely on her own. Sam and her team of protection officers followed at a distance.

The evening's event was to celebrate the closing of the Grand Prix in Monaco for another year, and while Jason had wanted to be there to take part in the festivities, he'd been held up with work. He was due to arrive in the morning, and she just hoped she was able to get at least a few hours of sleep between now and then. But the last time she'd partied in Monaco, she hadn't made it to bed until 2am. But the last time she'd partied in Monaco she hadn't been a World Champion, and a small part of her wondered if she'd make it to bed at all.

The thought made her smile as she walked along the red carpet to the main entrance, her head held high and the cameras still flashing. Halfway down, she stopped and turned one way and then the other, posing for the photos.

Since winning the Championship title last season, the paparazzi couldn't get enough of her. It was one thing to be disrupting the leaderboard as a woman, but something else to come out on top. And she was soaking up every glorious second of it.

When she'd had enough of smiling and waving, when the cool prickle of the evening air skimmed across her skin, she made her way inside.

Despite having visited many times over the years, the casino still took her breath away. The grand 19th-century hallway was vast, with huge diamond chandeliers and soft lighting. It looked like something from a fairytale castle. Everywhere she looked there was opulence and grandeur. It almost didn't look real. And through the archway were the slot machines, the gambling tables, and all manners of entertainment.

She saw Aldric St Pierre across the lobby and gave him a small wave. He smiled and excused himself from the group surrounding him to stride over.

"No Jason tonight?" he asked.

"He's flying in tomorrow."

"Shame. He'll miss all the fun."

"I know," she said and smiled. "But, you know," she shrugged, "work."

St Pierre chuckled. "Can't argue with that." He held out his arm. "In that case, I would very much like to be your escort for this evening," he said.

She placed her hand in the crook of his elbow and they walked into the main area where waiters stood, carrying trays laden with flutes of champagne.

"Excellent race today," said St Pierre.

"Thank you," she replied, picking up a flute and taking a sip. "How's retirement treating you?"

He shrugged. "I'm restless. It might take a while."

She smiled; she knew what he meant, but she also knew his enthusiasm for the racing lifestyle had somewhat ebbed over the last couple of years. He no longer wanted the rigorous routines, the constant training, the disruption to life. The travelling itself took a toll. Now that he'd found Elijah, life was starting to look a little different. She wondered if the same would happen to her. Would she choose to settle down with Jason and retire from Formula One for the privilege?

The night passed by in a blur of conversation, laughter, and cheers when someone won big at the roulette table. The casino was alive with the chatter of its patrons and live music had started up in one of the event halls.

"I'm just going to go to the bathroom," she said to Sam, shouting over the noise.

He gave her a single nod.

Her team escorted her to a long corridor where heavy wooden doors divided the men's room from the women's. She gave a small wave over her shoulder and stumbled slightly as she pushed the door open. She'd clearly had enough to drink. And to be honest, she was ready to go back to her hotel room, kick off the Swarovski crystal heels that were killing her feet, and sink into the thick duvet on her bed.

Entering one of the cubicles, she placed her clutch next to the sink and hitched up her dress. Once she was done, she fixed her dress back into place, washed her hands and touched up her makeup in the mirror. Satisfied she was presentable, she unlocked the cubicle and stepped out into the main bathroom area where there were full length gilded mirrors and round plush sofas in the middle of the room.

Expecting it to be empty, she was surprised to see a man standing by the door, blocking her way out. He was dressed in a tailored tuxedo and was casually leaning against the wall. His face lit up when he saw her and she stopped in her tracks. She knew that face.

"Hello Stacey," said Liam. "It's been far too long."

ABOUT THE AUTHOR

I'm a book-loving, writing enthusiast. I love to travel, drink tea and pet every animal I meet. When I'm not elbow-deep in the writing world, you can usually find me helping other authors through my editing services.

I live in Hampshire, UK with my husband and young son.

Instagram: @writernatashaorme
Website: https://writer.natashaorme.com/

ACKNOWLEDGEMENTS

As always, there's a whole bunch of people who helped me write this book. Particular thanks go to Simon at Blackstone Consultancy who took the time to answer my questions and inspire my storyline.

Thank you to my wonderful editor, Becky, at Opal Grove Editing who was able to whip my story into shape and help me with a rather tight turnaround. To Malcolm who is always a whizz when it comes to cover design. Thanks also to my team of beat readers who gave some much-valued feedback.

Special thanks to my Dad who took on the role of proofreader and was my final checkpoint to make sure everything made sense.

I'd also like to thank the unwavering support I have from my friends and family, particularly the Eastleigh Book Club who have encouraged me and volunteered their time in helping me. Thanks to my mum who is always my biggest cheerleader.

Finally, I'd like to thank my husband Lee for supporting me when I was writing in the evenings, on the weekends, and on holiday, for cooking dinner and looking after SJ so I could write just one more page.

Printed in Great Britain
by Amazon

42683309R00199